SPY MASTER

DEADLY STORM

FATAL VOYAGE

JAN BURCHETT & SARA VOGLER

Orion
Children's Books

Orion Children's Books
First published in Great Britain in 2017
by Hodder and Stoughton

3 5 7 9 10 8 6 4 2

Text © Jan Burchett and Sara Vogler 2017

A CIP catalogue record for this book
is available from the British Library.

ISBN 978 1 4440 1074 9

Typeset by Input Data Services Ltd, Bridgwater, Somerset

Printed and bound in Great Britain by Clays Ltd, Elcograf S.p.A.

The paper and board used in this book are from well-managed forests
and other responsible sources.

Orion Children's Books
An imprint of
Hachette Children's Group
Part of Hodder & Stoughton
Carmelite House
50 Victoria Embankment
London EC4Y 0DZ

An Hachette UK Company
www.hachette.co.uk

www.hachettechildrens.co.uk
www.burchettandvogler.co.uk

Contents

DEADLY STORM

*For Jackie Kirk. Thank you for
your interest and support,
love from Jan and Sara*

1

'This weather is the work of the devil,' Mark Helston shouted. 'The Court should never have set off.'

At once his eyes widened with fear. King Henry rode past, huge and magnificent on his chestnut stallion. He towered over us as we squelched along, almost blinded by the driving rain.

'Do you think he heard me, Jack?' groaned Mark. 'After all, it was his idea to travel today despite all the warnings.'

'You'll be in the Tower as soon as we get back to Greenwich Palace!' I replied. 'The very thought of one of His Majesty's scribes questioning the judgement of our esteemed monarch!'

Mark gave me a frightened glance. He was never sure when I was joking.

'Though that won't be for three days at least,' I told him. 'He might have forgotten it by then.'

Mark pulled his cloak up over his ears and tried to become invisible.

'Don't worry,' I yelled into his hood. 'He couldn't have heard you above the wind and rain.'

'Thank God for that,' Mark yelled back.

'Anyway,' I carried on, 'you were only speaking the truth. Even Lady Anne Boleyn complained about us setting off from Knole House in this weather.'

'Well there's one good thing,' said Mark. 'February storm, June will be warm. That's what my mum always says.' There was a flash of lightning and a deafening crash of thunder above our heads. 'I wish it was June now,' he added, looking terrified.

I wiped my wet face and tried to see ahead. 'Did you say it was just a few miles to the river crossing? It seems like we've been travelling for hours.'

Mark nodded. 'I studied it on a map. We cross the River Darent at the Old Welsh Bridge – it's called that because all the stones came from Wales. Of course that was hundreds of years ago but they're an unusual colour for this area.'

I didn't like to tell him that all I wanted to do was get across the bridge, not examine what it was made of!

'Make way!' came an imperious voice and Oswyn Drage jiggled past on a donkey. He scarcely gave us a glance.

'There goes the magnificent Weasel-face,' I laughed. 'The poor boy, having to scribe with two lowly minions – especially a foundling like me.'

2

'Oswyn does come from a well-connected family,' said Mark.

'That doesn't matter,' I said vehemently. 'Master Cromwell thinks we're good enough to work for him, so Oswyn can go and boil his head.'

To tell the truth I'd been very lucky that Thomas Cromwell, one of the King's most important ministers, had given me a job when I'd been sent from my old home at St Godric's Abbey by my godfather, Brother Matthew, to work in the royal kitchens. Instead I'd managed to persuade the great man that he couldn't do without me.

Ahead I saw the King summon Master Cromwell to his side. They drew apart from the procession and were deep in conversation as courtiers, guards and servants with cartloads of luggage trudged past. Nicholas Mountford, one of the yeomen guard, quickly joined them. I knew the King had to be protected but I couldn't imagine any villain bothering to turn out in this weather! His loyal gentleman guard would have been more useful holding a tarpaulin over him.

Mister Mountford would often tease me about how we'd first met – when he'd had to chase me all over Whitehall Palace thinking I was a vagabond. But today he just gave Mark and me a weary nod, the rain dripping off his hat.

A shower of hailstones crashed down. Close by, a carter muttered about evil spirits and tried to calm his pony between the shafts of a wagon. The sky was almost as dark as night, though it could only have been the middle of the afternoon.

A strong gust of wind whipped around us, turning a pile of leaves into a whirlwind and spooking a nearby horse.

We watched the rider control his mount. 'It's lucky Mister Aycliffe is such a fine horseman,' murmured Mark. 'He'll be glad to be back at Court and doing some safe lawyers' work, I'll be bound.'

I didn't answer. Although Mark was a good friend, I couldn't tell him that Robert Aycliffe carried out other, secret work which was far from safe. Or that I only knew this because I too had been recruited as one of Master Cromwell's spies for the King. Apart from His Majesty, those outside the network knew Mister Aycliffe simply as a young lawyer in training, and Jack Briars as a lowly Court Scribe.

A shout went up at the front of the column. The river had been sighted. That news filled me with hope. I'd been wondering if we'd ever see the Darent. But soon I could see more of it than I wanted to!

The river raced along in a grey mass, sending waves of water gushing over the land.

The front of the line was turning towards a narrow bridge. This must be the one Mark had told me about. We'd been going slowly before, now we barely moved as the long column plodded across, one after the other. The river coursed along underneath it, so high that there was hardly a gap between the water and the arches.

'I do hope Master Cromwell persuades His Majesty to find shelter,' said Mark, too worried to notice the Welsh stone. 'I think we shall all catch chills if we don't get warm soon. I remember an old man in our village who fell in a pond and died from his soaking.'

'Are you sure he didn't die of drowning?' I asked Mark, trying not to laugh at his worried face.

'Don't jest, Jack,' said Mark. 'This weather can be deadly. I fear for the King's health.'

I pushed back my dripping cloak hood to glance over my shoulder. Our sovereign didn't seem to pay heed to the rain and wind. He was still at the rear of the procession, discussing some matter with my master.

We were nearly at the bridge now, wading through mud. The carthorses were straining, the carters shouting and everyone was hunched against the rain. Most of the party had reached the opposite bank.

I watched Robert Aycliffe leading his horse across. He had a tight hand on its bridle. With the storm raging overhead and the river pounding below, the stallion was skittering nervously from side to side.

'Jack!' A piercing voice cut through the noise. Cat Thimblebee was perched, straight-backed, on a pile of chests on one of the carts ahead. She looked more like a princess than a seamstress. Well as princessy as she could in plain servant's garb with her curly red hair hanging in dripping rat-tails. She'd arranged her cloak across the staves of the wagon over her head in a makeshift roof. She gave me a stately wave.

5

'You may accompany me if you wish,' she called down. 'I am sure Ben won't mind.'

Ben the carter nodded and beckoned. 'One on the cart and the other on Polly,' he called.

Mark started trembling with fright, as he always did when Cat appeared. I had to admit he had good reason. Cat could be as fiery as her hair. You just needed to know how to handle her. And when I found out, I would tell him!

But for all that, Cat and I were becoming friends. The nearest thing I'd had to a friend at the abbey had been Brother Matthew, but he'd been more of a father to me. I felt as if I was making up for lost time. Mark, and now Cat.

'It'll be fun to ride,' I said, pulling Mark along towards Cat's cart. 'It'll save our legs, and you know the old saying,' I added, inventing madly. 'Your legs you should not wear, for you haven't any spare.'

For once Mark didn't take any heed of a wise old saying.

'I'm not going on that pony,' he insisted, 'and if I get on the cart I'll be right next to . . .' He gulped. '. . . Her.'

I gave up. 'Hold my cloak for me then,' I said, handing it over. 'I'll take it back once I'm settled.'

I ran to the front and swung up onto Polly. I was no rider – Cat would agree with that after the lessons she'd given me. But I'd told Master Cromwell that I could ride when he'd made me a spy so I'd had to plead with her to teach me. I decided that nothing could happen to me while my trusty steed was in the shafts.

'Look, no hands!' I shouted, waving my arms to demonstrate to Cat how my horsemanship was improving. Polly began to toil up the slope of the bridge. 'I'll show you how to do it if you want!'

Cat could probably have done it with her eyes closed. She didn't bother to answer but stuck her tongue out at me instead.

At that moment I heard a clatter of hooves and frightened whinnying. The horses ahead were hurrying across the bridge, as if it had become red hot.

Polly seemed to catch their fear. Ben spoke to her to calm her down but she was tossing her head and I could see that her eyes were wild and frightened. She tried to retreat from the bridge, pushing the cart backwards down the slope.

'She doesn't like it,' I heard Ben shout. 'I'm going to unhitch her from the shafts and lead her across to show her it's all right. We can drag the cart by hand.'

Gulping down his nervousness, Mark helped him to wedge chocks under the wheels, unhitch Polly and lower the shafts to the ground. Freeing the pony only increased her panic. I felt her tremble underneath me.

'Jump off, lad!' Ben shouted to me.

It was too late. Polly reared up, snorting with fear. Taken completely by surprise, I made a grab for her mane but felt myself sliding off. The next minute I landed hard on my bum on the bridge. Polly galloped off across the river, with Ben racing to catch her.

I heard an irritating laugh and saw Cat's grinning face above my head. 'Well, so much for your horsemanship!' she said, jumping from the cart and pulling me to my feet. 'I reckon you need a few more lessons – even to ride a nag.'

I was about to make some retort when we heard a distant, rumbling roar.

'What's that?' gasped Cat.

'The river!' Mark shouted from the bank, pointing in terror. A huge wave was boiling down from upstream. It moved relentlessly, sweeping all before it. Bushes and trees and rocks tumbled over and over in the foam as it surged towards the bridge.

'Run!' I shouted. But before we could move, a noise like the end of the world filled my ears and the wave crashed over us.

W e were plunged into the raging torrent and
swept along, the river relentlessly taking us
and everything else in its path. The current sucked me
down and bowled me over. I tried to clutch hold of Cat's
flailing arms but it was impossible. She disappeared
under the white foam. I broke the surface and gulped
in deep breaths. They were so cold they hurt my chest.
Branches and stones were swirling around, tearing at
my skin.

There was no sign of Cat.

'Help!' I heard a spluttering cry and a hand clamped
my arm in an iron grip. I was torn between relief and
terror. Cat was alive – but she was pulling me under
the water in her desperate efforts to save herself. I
kicked upwards to try to keep us both afloat but the
strength of the river was overwhelming. I felt Cat's
fingers tighten and then slip from my arm. I thrashed

around, trying to get hold of her. For a short moment she struggled to reach me, then she went limp, tossed in the swirling water as if she was a rag doll, her hair streaming around her like blood.

I snatched at the hair and pulled hard, bringing her face up into the air. But she didn't move.

Something smashed against my back and pain shot through me. I felt Cat's lifeless body slamming into my chest.

I hooked an arm round her as I tried to see what had happened. We were caught on a tree trunk. It must have been carried there by the current and had got wedged on the bank. But not for long. I could feel the river sucking fiercely at it.

'Jack!'

Above the roar of the water, I heard Mark's voice.

'Catch this!' he yelled.

A rope snaked through the air. With my free hand I caught it and twisted it around my wrist. At that moment the tree trunk lost its battle with the river and was torn away downstream. The rope tightened. I thought my arm would be ripped off but I held on, grasping Cat as hard as I could and praying that it wasn't too late for her. Gradually we were pulled to the bank. Hands dragged us to safety.

I staggered over to Cat. She was lying very still. Mark was feeling for a pulse. The yeoman Nicholas Mountford stood beside him, shaking his head.

'There's a faint heartbeat but she's not breathing,' said Mark. 'I fear she will die.'

I had a memory of being very young and seeing a child pulled out of the millpond back at Acton Village. Everyone had thought it was a hopeless case but the blacksmith had come forward and blown air into the boy's mouth and saved his life.

'She won't die if I can help it,' I muttered. Cat's face was still, her skin white with blue edging her lips. I lifted her chin and had a sudden picture of the blacksmith pinching the boy's nose. I did this and then blew hard into her mouth. Nothing happened so I blew again and again. Cat lay motionless, eyes half closed, seeing nothing. This couldn't be the end for her.

'Come back!' I cried and breathed into her mouth once more. My efforts seemed hopeless but I couldn't give up on her. I forced another, desperate breath into her. And I felt her move! Cat gave a choking cough. I quickly turned her onto her side. A gush of river water poured out, followed by most of her breakfast. But she was breathing again – in between puking.

'You did it,' cried Mark. 'It's a miracle!'

Cat lay in the mud, shivering violently with cold. I ignored the icy wet clothes that were clinging to my skin and dragged myself to my feet. Mark and I helped her to sit up. She leaned against us weakly.

'Well done,' said Nicholas Mountford. His voice was almost lost in the lashing rain. 'That was a brave rescue, Jack. Though nothing about you surprises me.'

He fetched his horse and swung himself into the saddle. 'Put Cat up here with me,' he ordered. He held out a hand and between us we got Cat seated in front of him. For a moment she stared wildly at him as if she didn't know where she was. Then she feebly grasped the pommel, her head lolling. Mountford wrapped his arms around her.

'Cat's as white as a ghost,' Mark said in my ear.

'At least she's survived,' I answered, shivering as well. I didn't even want to admit to myself how frightened I'd been. 'Thank you, Mark. We wouldn't have got out of that river without you.'

He looked pleased. Then a thought stabbed me, as sharp as the lightning that still streaked across the sky.

'The King!' I gasped. 'Is he safe?'

'He is, God be praised,' Mountford called down, calming his horse at a new crash of thunder. We followed him, splashing along the bank.

'And Master Cromwell?' I feared for my master as much as for the King!

'He is also unharmed,' said Mountford. Two figures came into view. King Henry and Thomas Cromwell, side by side on their horses.

'Good thing this didn't go in the river!' Mark put my cloak round me. He'd been holding it for me since I got on to Polly. I smiled at him for his kindness and stumbled after him to join the others. As we got near, I spotted Oswyn on his donkey, sheltering behind Cromwell. *Just my luck*, I thought. *Everyone else gets*

12

across and we're stuck with Weasel-face! I noticed that he hadn't made any move to pull me out of the river. Oswyn didn't like me and would have been more likely to push me under.

His Majesty stared fixedly at the opposite bank. At least, he stared at the sheet of rain that pounded on to the raging water. It shielded the land beyond like a thick curtain.

'I pray my Anne is safe!' he exclaimed. 'I should have been with her. I will never forgive myself if . . .'

'Lady Anne was at the head of the procession,' Master Cromwell reminded him calmly. 'She will be safe, my Liege, I am sure of it. There are many yeomen with her.'

That should reassure our monarch, I thought. After all, the King's yeomen guard were all men of good family, tall, strong and brave. But King Henry still looked worried.

'And I'm certain that Robert Aycliffe will not leave her side if there is any danger.' Cromwell paused and I saw the King nod. He had understood. Lady Anne had one of Cromwell's best spies close by.

My master gathered up his reins. 'Now to find shelter from this fiendish storm.' He spoke briskly, taking charge.

'Shelter?' bellowed the King. 'How can you speak of shelter when my lady could be in peril? There must be another bridge. We shall find it or die in the attempt!'

This was a dangerous moment. When the King

13

ordered, we obeyed. I watched my master's face, praying that he could make him see sense. If not, I was sure we'd all perish from cold or flood. Cat groaned weakly and almost fell from Mountford's saddle. Master Cromwell saw the yeoman steady her.

'Your concern for Lady Anne is most natural, Sire,' he said, his tone even. 'But the next bridge is thirty miles hence. I beg you to imagine how she would feel to hear that you set out boldly to the rescue and – did not manage to reach her.' He'd chosen his words carefully. No one spoke of the King's possible death for fear of it being thought treason, yet he'd painted a picture as clear as any artist might.

His Majesty slumped and I saw a brief wave of relief pass over Cromwell's face.

'We will find shelter,' said the King. 'And the moment the storm has passed, we will set out for that bridge.'

'Where should we head?' asked Mister Mountford.

'There is an abbey in this area,' said Cromwell. 'The Franbury monks will take us in.' He turned his back on the swelling river. 'I believe it is south-west of here.'

Mountford led the way. The horses were spooked by the moaning wind and only the skill of the riders stopped them bolting. Oswyn's donkey seemed not to care one way or the other, plodding along in their wake. I struggled on, Mark by my side.

'Please God we reach the abbey soon,' he said, glancing anxiously at me every time I stumbled in the puddles. 'I fear you won't survive much longer. I heard of a boy who . . .'

'I'll be all right.' I cut him short. I couldn't face hearing one of Mark's tales of woe. It was sure to be about some poor lad whose eyeballs froze or who shivered so hard his head fell off.

Soon we'd left the flood behind, although the road was almost a river itself.

'This is no ordinary storm,' growled the King, his words barely audible over the crashing thunder. 'It smacks of witchcraft. I can hear fell voices in the air.'

'We'll be inside before long, my Liege,' Cromwell tried to assure him, although he didn't sound convinced of it himself.

The wind shrieked like screaming phantoms. We could barely see the ground in front of us. And no cloak was able to withstand the stabbing shafts of rain.

As if a giant had flung them from the sky, we were assaulted by a fresh barrage of hailstones, stinging our frozen faces and hands. Cromwell cursed as one struck his cheek, leaving a thin trail of blood.

A tree fell, thundering into our path. Mountford's horse reared in panic. He fought with it, his arm clamped round Cat. I could see she was conscious, her eyes wide open with fear.

'We'd better find your monastery soon, Thomas,' shouted the King, 'before this storm is the death of us.'

3

We stared at each other. The King was right. If a falling tree didn't crush us, we'd die of cold. I couldn't feel my hands, and my feet felt like blocks of ice.

'What's that?' Cat's voice came to us through chattering teeth.

'Has the girl seen something?' demanded His Majesty. He brought his horse up beside Mountford. We huddled round.

'A light,' said Cat, feebly trying to raise her finger to point. 'Over there.' She slumped, shaking her head. 'Must have imagined it.'

We strained our eyes through the rain. Nothing. Then a flicker. Then it was gone again, blocked by the trees thrashing in the wind.

'It's all we have,' said Cromwell. 'We should make for it.'

'Aye,' said the King grimly. 'I pray it's not some evil spirit leading us to our doom.'

Above us, the arch of trees creaked and groaned as the horses picked their way over the branches scattered on the path.

'It's a castle!' cried Mark.

We left the trees and halted. Ahead rose an ancient tower with a light burning in one of the windows.

King Henry made to urge his horse forward.

'Wait, Sire!' said Cromwell.

The King's eyes narrowed. 'I sense food and fire in that wonderful vision ahead and I warrant they won't deny either to their monarch! This had better be important, Thomas.'

'If it please Your Majesty,' said my master, 'I would counsel you not to appear as our King.'

'Why, pray?'

'Because you have only one guard with you and, tall and strong as your gallant Mountford is, you could be in grave danger if your true identity were revealed. We don't know anything about the house we are heading for.'

King Henry gave a cold laugh. 'Then are we to disguise ourselves? Vagabonds perhaps? Wandering minstrels? You have lost your wits, Thomas.'

'Nothing so dramatic, I assure you, my Liege.' Master Cromwell hid his impatience well. 'I suggest you change clothes with Mountford. That should present no problem as he is almost as tall as you.'

'What are you saying, man?' demanded His Majesty. 'That he will be King and I a mere yeoman?'

I saw Nicholas Mountford's horror at this suggestion.

'No, Sire. We will present ourselves at the castle as part of the King's party who have been separated from His Majesty. Mister Mountford will be a courtier. With his heritage and noble bearing he will easily pass for one. With your gracious permission he will be wearing your clothes.'

Mister Mountford looked anything but noble at the thought of promotion to a higher status than his King.

From King Henry's angry face, I could see my master wasn't winning the argument. Yet I knew how easily danger could come to our monarch even in a well-guarded palace, let alone a remote castle. An idea came to me, but I wasn't sure if my life would be worth living if I dared speak. Then I decided that if we stayed rooted there for much longer I'd freeze to death anyway. I was caught between an adder and a pot of poison, as old Brother Jerome back at the abbey used to say.

'Your Majesty,' I said. 'This will give you the opportunity to show us what an accomplished actor you are. And when we leave, you will reveal your true identity, and your hosts will be astounded! I cannot forget the masque at Greenwich where no one knew who the grand figure of Neptune really was until you declared it!' The whole Court had known of course, but we'd all acted shocked, to the delight of the King.

There was a moment of silence and I saw horror on Mark's face at my audacity. Oswyn's wore a different expression. He was ever hopeful that my days at Court were numbered – and now he must have thought his luck was in.

'A happy notion, Jack Briars!' declared His Majesty, to my enormous relief and Oswyn's disappointment. 'I wonder you did not think of it, Thomas. Excess of water has softened your brain.'

Master Cromwell bowed his head humbly but I was sure I'd seen a fleeting smile on his lips. He didn't mind how it was achieved, as long as the King was safe.

A flash of lightning showed up an outbuilding close to the castle tower. The horses – and donkey – followed Cromwell towards it.

The faint sounds of chomping told us we'd reached the castle stables. The riders dismounted outside and tethered their horses to rings on the wall. Mark and I pulled open the stable door. Well, it was mostly Mark – my muscles seemed to have been washed away in the river! We hurried in after His Majesty. Cat staggered along behind, supported by Nicholas Mountford. With the door shut, it was nearly pitch dark.

I knocked my head against something hanging on the wall. I reached up to see what it was.

'I've found a lantern,' I said. 'Or rather the lantern found me.'

'Hand it over, lad,' said Mountford. 'I have a tinderbox.'

I walked carefully towards his voice and did as he said. It took him several attempts to strike the flint by touch alone but finally with the help of another flash of lightning he had the tinder smouldering and the lantern working. The humble stable was like a palace to me.

Cat sank into a pile of hay. I knew no one should make themselves comfortable before the King though he didn't seem to notice when Mark and I collapsed beside her. I would happily have stayed where we were. It was dry and the hay would make a warm bed. But not for a king, of course.

His Majesty was removing the ring bearing the royal seal from his finger. 'I refuse to be parted with this,' he said. He pulled out a fine chain that hung under his shirt. There was a small portrait hanging on it. I couldn't see who it was but I had no doubt it was Lady Anne. The King unfastened the chain and slid the ring on to it. Soon it was hidden under his shirt.

'Now I am ready to exchange clothes!' he said. He stood motionless while Cromwell unbuttoned his doublet and lifted it off his broad shoulders. 'Remember, Mountford, that you are a noble courtier,' said His Majesty. 'If you forget, the inhabitants of this place may smell a rat.'

I thought it more likely that His Majesty would be the one to forget his new station, so different from his own. But I wasn't going to mention it. I didn't have a death wish!

King Henry wistfully fingered the rich, embroidered doublet as Mountford began to put it on. 'And have a care with your monarch's apparel. The gold thread in those sleeves came from the Orient.'

I saw fear flicker over Mountford's face. He was so strong he could probably fight three enemies at once without turning a hair, but this new task clearly terrified him!

The King was now dressed as one of his own yeomen guard. 'For my part, my name will be . . . Adam, after the first man. And my surname is Brown.'

'Though we shall call you Adam, my Liege,' said Cromwell, with a small bow, 'I know you will hear the unspoken "Your Majesty" in our words. You need have no fear for we shall all be vigilant on your behalf. Your safety is paramount, as ever.' His gaze fell on us all, yet I felt his words had a special meaning for me. It hit me like a hammer on an anvil that I was to have a heavy responsibility. Of all the men of Cromwell's secret service, I was the only one present.

The wind and rain lashed at us as we ran from the stable to the huge wooden doors of the castle. Mark and I supported Cat, whose legs seemed to have no strength in them. The tower rose above us. In the fading light it was barely visible against the stormy sky.

Mountford thumped upon the wicket door in the ancient double gates. Long moments passed.

'Did we dream the light?' asked Cromwell. 'The place cannot be deserted. There are horses in the stables.'

21

Mountford knocked again.

'I wish we could be back in that nice warm hay,' murmured Cat.

'Who goes there on such a foul night?' came an angry shout from inside.

'Thomas Cromwell, minister to the King,' replied my master. 'And Nicholas Mountford, courtier to His Majesty. We and our companions seek shelter.'

'A bold claim,' grunted the man. 'Let me look at you.'

Bolts were slid back. A shuttered grille in the huge arched entrance opened a crack. Two eyes, no doubt belonging to the porter, peered at us suspiciously – as well they might. It wasn't every day that one of the King's most important ministers knocked at a castle door and demanded entry. Then he must have caught sight of our livery. The eyes lost their suspicion and widened in surprise.

He swung open the wicket door and bowed low to let us pass. Master Cromwell walked in, calmly taking the role of the most senior member of the King's Court. However, Nicholas Mountford hesitated. If it hadn't been so serious I'd have laughed at the consternation on his face. Instead I poked him in the back, propelling him forwards. The King followed, walking far too regally for his new station. I saw him bristle when the porter didn't throw himself to the flagstones before him. His Majesty was used to drums and trumpets and everyone kneeling as soon as he appeared.

We stood in a huge vaulted hall, lit only by the porter's candle and a fire at the other end.

'I am sorry that I hesitated to let you in,' the man gabbled, plucking nervously at his grey, straggly beard. 'I was fearful . . . it is such a wild night . . . if I'd known who you were . . .'

'I understand,' said Cromwell. 'Floods have separated us from the King and his party. We beg shelter of your master.'

'My master, Sir Reginald, is lately dead,' said the man sorrowfully. 'My mistress is Sir Reginald's widow, the Lady Margaret Norbrook. Please, come this way and warm yourselves at the fire while I fetch her.'

None of us needed telling twice. We automatically stood back to let the King take the place nearest the flames, then remembered ourselves and made way for Thomas Cromwell and Nicholas Mountford, who looked very embarrassed to be given precedence. I would have loved that moment of glory! The porter stared curiously at us for a moment as we jostled about like sheep at market.

As soon as he'd lit the torches in their brackets, he headed up a wide staircase that wound round the high walls. We fell away and allowed His Majesty to feel the full heat of the fire.

None of us spoke. We were all too busy thawing out! Cat still looked very pale.

'Master Cromwell?'

A tall, slender woman walked down the stairs

23

towards us, two servants at her side. Her face was pale above her black mourning clothes. It didn't take much guesswork to realise that this was Lady Margaret. She gazed at each of us with a grave smile. She seemed to linger on the King's face.

Had she recognised him?

4

At last her gaze moved on.

'I beg your pardon, gentlemen,' she said. 'My porter, Barnabas, told me that you are the King's men. But I have never been to Court so I do not know which of you is which. It was my husband's choice to remain here at Norbrook Castle and I abided by his wish.'

I'd wager everyone felt the same relief to hear that she'd never been near Court and had no idea that her King was standing in front of her.

Master Cromwell stepped forward. 'I am Thomas Cromwell,' he told her. 'This is Nicholas Mountford, courtier to the King, and Adam Brown of His Majesty's yeoman guard.'

He didn't introduce the rest of us and I was tempted to pipe up with 'and three scribes and a half-drowned seamstress at your service'. But I held my tongue.

'We are sorry to intrude upon you in this way when

you are so recently widowed,' continued Cromwell. 'We were travelling with the King when this foul weather fell. The River Darent has flooded and the bridge was washed away, separating us from our party. We beg shelter until we can travel again. We took the liberty of tethering our horses outside your stable.'

'You are most welcome,' replied Lady Margaret. 'Sir Reginald, God rest his soul, would have been greatly honoured by your presence. I am sorry to say it was the plague that took him from me.'

'The plague!' gasped the King. Instinctively Mountford drew near to him.

'Have no fear,' she went on. 'I broke the news too harshly. It was more than forty days ago and no one else has succumbed since.'

The King didn't appear to be reassured.

'Then no one is at risk,' said Cromwell firmly. 'It is well known that forty days is enough.'

I watched His Majesty's face. It showed outrage at Cromwell's commanding tone but he said nothing.

Cromwell was still talking to Lady Margaret. 'It must have been a bad time, my lady.'

Her eyes welled with tears. 'Only three of us fell ill,' she said, 'unlike the abbey where many perished. Here it was just my husband and our scribe, Joseph, who died. I had it too but God in his wisdom thought to spare me . . . But I am rambling on with my own concerns while you all stand there, wet and cold.' She signalled to one of her serving men. 'Tell William to see to our visitors' horses straight away. And inform Mister Erskine that we have guests and that rooms must be prepared with fires and dry clothing. Mister Erskine is my steward,' she explained to Cromwell. 'The staff will tend to your servants.'

The other man led Mark, Cat and me through a small door in the corner to a much newer part of the castle. We walked down a passageway, past several small rooms and into the warmth of a busy kitchen. Oswyn followed at a distance. A cheerful man with a snowy beard was directing servants to clear away their supper and sweep the floor. They looked up and grinned as we were ushered towards the crackling fire, where we huddled gratefully.

We heard a whisper of voices. I could make out the words 'King' and 'royal'. Oswyn pulled himself up to his full height.

A woman, dressed in a thick kirtle with a clean pinafore over the skirts, came along with a pile of clothes for us. 'Get your wet things off,' she said shortly, a deep frown creasing her forehead. 'Lady Margaret commands me to make sure they are put to dry. You boys can change in the dairy. The girl in the stillroom next to it.' She waved a hand towards two doors beside her.

'Come, Ruth,' called a man who was stacking pots. 'We should welcome these poor souls, not turn our noses up at them. Besides, they work for His Majesty.'

'That's of no import,' the woman hissed at him,

loudly enough for us to hear. 'I'm my lady's tiring woman and should concern myself with her clothes and no one else's.'

We thanked her politely. Well Oswyn didn't. He just took the best of the clothes and set off for the dairy, Mark and I trailing behind. We were soon back, dressed in green Norbrook livery.

Cat returned from the stillroom, wearing a voluminous skirt and a baggy bodice.

'Don't you dare laugh,' she said.

It seemed that Cat had recovered her usual bossiness. It was amazing what a warm fire and the smell of good food could do.

Mark put his hand over his mouth, fearful that he might disobey her.

Cat caught sight of herself in a shiny pan and began to chuckle. 'All right, you can laugh. I'm like a child in her mother's clothing!'

Ruth picked up our clothes between finger and thumb and began to hang them on a wooden rack in front of the fire. Cat hurried to help her but she didn't seem very grateful.

A serving man put his head round the door. 'Is Oswyn Drage here?' he asked. 'Master Cromwell requests that you eat with him in the Great Hall.'

Oswyn followed him out. I could see he was doing his best to hide his surprise and act as if this sort of thing happened every day. As a result he looked like a half-witted herring.

I was surprised myself that Cromwell was showing the arrogant Weasel-face such favour but I was too tired to care. It was warm and friendly in the kitchen.

'Sit yourselves down,' said the man with the snowy beard. He put dishes of steaming broth on the table. 'I'm Mister Brandiscombe, the cook here at the castle. We've not long finished our supper and there's plenty to spare. We don't have many visitors here at Norbrook and never ones who've seen the King. Tell us about him.'

I could feel Cat's eyes on me. What would these fellows make of it if I said they only had to pop up to the Great Hall to get a peek at their sovereign? I had to tread carefully.

If I described him too well, they'd recognise Adam Brown at once.

5

'We don't get near enough to the King to know much,' I said. 'But he's a fine horseman.' I stuffed my mouth full of the delicious bread so that I didn't have to say any more.

'And he's very . . . royal!' said Cat helpfully.

After a while Oswyn swaggered in, accompanied by a man in plain but well made clothes.

'Good evening.' The man smiled as he spoke to Cat, Mark and me. 'I am Mister Erskine, steward to Lady Norbrook.'

We replied with our names. I could imagine the other two were feeling as surprised as I was at his welcoming tone after the tiring woman's coldness.

'Master Cromwell has offered me your services while you shelter here. And I am in great need of scribes after the sad death of young Joe, so your arrival is opportune. I'll be putting you to work straight after breakfast.'

'I'm happy to help too,' Cat chipped in. 'I'm the best seamstress in the palace.'

That was true. But then, she was the only seamstress. The others in the sewing room were men.

Mister Erskine smiled. 'We're a small household and with our visitors we'll need every hand. I'm sure Ruth will find plenty for you to do.'

He left and Mister Brandiscombe brought out a platter of almond tarts.

'Lady Margaret made these with her own hands,' he said proudly. 'She puts me to shame with her baking – apple tansies, gingerbread and all sorts.'

'This is delicious,' I said, taking a huge bite.

'They taste so sweet,' said Cat.

'That'll be the honey,' said the cook. 'It's particularly flavoursome this side of the River Darent.'

'And it's so good for you,' said a skinny little boy with spiky hair. 'The mistress always gives it to us when we're ill.'

'I reckon that's what saved her when the plague struck,' added Mister Brandiscombe.

The mention of plague brought silence for a moment. It was broken only by Oswyn who, although he'd eaten with the royal party, began to munch loudly on his fifth tart. With full bellies and the warmth of the fire, it wasn't long before we were struggling to stay awake.

'You'll be wanting your beds, I'll warrant,' chuckled the cook, seeing our heads nodding. 'You can share with Bessy, young lady.'

A stooped old woman rose from the fire. 'I'll be glad to have her, Mister Brandiscombe,' she said, taking Cat's hand. 'I've no liking for sleeping in a room on my own. And I'll tell you why . . .'

Cat looked aghast. 'Are there ghosts here?'

'It's nothing like that,' said Bessy. 'But something dire happened. Something most foul. Something that would have you wishing it *was* just phantoms.'

The servants' heads popped up in interest. I suddenly found myself wide awake, ears flapping.

'You know that's utter nonsense, Mother,' snapped Ruth. 'Keep your silly story to yourself – for that's all it is.'

'It's the truth, I tell you,' insisted Bessy. She drew herself up. 'I have a duty to speak – for the sake of the household, and even more for the sake of our guests. Why should they not be aware of the dangers here?'

'Hold your peace, Mother!' exclaimed Ruth, looking thoroughly frightened now. 'I forbid you to say another word!'

Old Bessy pursed her lips. 'Very well. I can see I won't be believed so I'll not bother anyone with my tale. Though I'll warrant each of you will be begging me to speak in the end.' She led Cat off. 'My bed is in the stillroom,' she told her as they went. 'I can't manage the stairs.'

I felt cheated.

'You're a lucky boy, Charlie,' called Mister

Brandiscombe. 'The three scribes will be sleeping in with you.'

The skinny boy threw down the logs he was stacking and bounced over to Mark and me.

'Come this way,' he said with a grin, taking the candle that the cook was holding out.

'Fancy you knowing the King,' Charlie said over his shoulder as we followed him across the Great Hall and up the stairs. 'I'm going to meet him one day too. I'm going to be spit boy in his palace when I'm a man and he'll tell everyone that no one turns a hog as well as me.' He chattered on until we arrived at the top of the tower. 'I hope you're staying a long time. I've been on my own up here since Joe died when the plague came. Did you know, it started at the abbey and killed most of the monks? Then it stretched its deadly fingers to the castle.' Charlie waggled his own fingers dramatically, half enjoying his tale. 'Here we are,' he said, opening the door to a bedchamber.

Mark and I stood and stared at the sight before us. It wasn't a big room, but it had a proper bed and a thick mattress on the floor.

'What are you gawping at?' demanded Oswyn as he strode up the stairs and barged into the chamber. 'Never stayed in a castle before?'

'We're going to sleep on mattresses!' exclaimed Mark.

'Of course,' said Charlie. 'Every servant does here.

Sir Reginald insisted on it, God rest his soul. He said we'd work all the better if we were well rested.'

There'd be no sleeping on office floors as we did in the Royal palaces.

'The bed's mine,' said Weasel-face, sitting down on it. 'I have been chosen as taster to the King . . . King's party,' he corrected himself. 'Therefore I need a good night's sleep. I shall be dreaming of her ladyship's own gingerbread cakes that I've just sampled. I managed three whole ones. They're not for the lower servants, of course.'

Oswyn seemed to be taking his job too seriously. He was supposed to be taking a mere mouthful of each dish before the King, to make sure it wasn't full of poison – not snaffle the lot!

'I think you'll find the bed is Charlie's, Oswyn,' I corrected him.

'That's right, Oz,' said Charlie cheekily. 'You'll share with me.'

I swallowed down a laugh. Oswyn was always so keen to tell us that he came from a good family and here he was, being ordered about by a kitchen scullion!

'You two boys can have that mattress,' Charlie went on before Oswyn could protest, 'if you don't mind being on the floor.'

It was no hardship at all to lie down on a mattress. Outside, the wind battered the old stone of the tower and found its way in through a small gap in the window, but I was warm under a thick blanket. I thought about the old woman who'd wanted to tell us something and how her daughter had shut her up. It took me an age to get to sleep. It might have been the mattress, too soft for a boy used to the floor. But more likely it was the old woman's words. Each time sleep began to cloud my brain, they came back to me.

'Something most foul. Something that would have you wishing it was just phantoms.'

6

The sound of rain hammering on the window woke me the next morning. Storm clouds were scudding across the sky. It was well past dawn but very little light had managed to creep in to our bedchamber. Charlie's side of the bed was empty but the next minute he poked his head round the door.

'Morning!' he called. 'You lot were sleeping like the dead! And there's food in the kitchen. Oz, you're to go to the Great Hall to do that fancy job of yours.'

I'd never seen Oswyn dress so fast. He only had time for one quick sneering glance before he was out of the door.

We followed Charlie down the tower steps. Voices came to us from the Great Hall but he led us along a wide gallery, brightly lit by torches, to another winding stairway. We found ourselves coming into the kitchen near the stillroom. I was hungry, but more than that, I wanted to hear what Bessy had told Cat. Was there a mystery here at Norbrook Castle? I hoped Cat would have something to tell me. Bessy's story sounded intriguing. She'd spoken of danger. That might simply be the exaggeration of a very old lady but I couldn't be certain. One thing I was sure of though. My interest wasn't purely curiosity. I had to make sure that nothing endangered the King – even in this remote castle where no one knew who he was.

The warm kitchen was full of servants. Mister Brandiscombe sat at the head of the table, carving some beef on a platter. The table heaved with trenchers of bread and stone flagons. One man was laying the fire under the spit and Charlie raced to help him.

Servants were coming in and out carrying trays of food to the Great Hall. No doubt they were all going to be tasted by Oswyn.

'Come and sit down at the table, boys,' called the cook cheerfully. 'There's plenty for all.'

I spotted Cat next to Bessy on one of the long benches. The old lady was gazing into the air, aimlessly twisting a handkerchief in her hands.

'Well?' I whispered as I squeezed in between Cat and Barnabas the porter.

'Well what?' she whispered back, tucking into a slice of beef.

'What did the old lady tell you when you were alone?'

'Well, I found out she's much friendlier than her daughter.'

'But what about the mystery?' I hissed.

She grinned annoyingly. 'Bessy probably told me all the mysteries in the world but as I was asleep in the wink of an eye I didn't hear any of them. She reminds me of my grandmother. A dear old soul but apt to ramble.'

I pulled off a huge hunk of bread. Part of me couldn't help wishing she'd found out something grim and gruesome to think about while we were marooned here. Norbrook Castle was very different from the busy royal palaces I was now used to – more like the boring, silent abbey where I'd been raised – so any mystery would be welcome.

'Pour yourself some more ale, lad,' said Barnabas, nudging my arm.

I took the flagon, wondering if I could ask him about Bessy's strange words.

The door to the kitchen courtyard was suddenly flung open. A short, stocky man with long matted hair and ragged clothes stumbled in out of the rain. A gasp went round the table as he lurched towards us.

He reminded me of the wild ram that had chased me once, fierce and mad. Although the ram hadn't stunk of drink.

The cook got to his feet, clutching his carving knife. 'You were told never to come to this house again, Fulke,' he said fiercely.

'I'm not here to talk to you.' The man's voice slurred. 'It's her ladyship I want and I'm not going until I see her. I've been wronged, I have.'

'You lost your job here fair and square,' said Ruth. 'You were lucky Sir Reginald didn't have your hand struck off for your thieving.'

'Well his lordship's dead and good riddance.' He swiped at the table, sending tankards and trenchers flying.

Bessy flinched and I saw Cat put her arms round her.

Barnabas and Mister Brandiscombe grabbed Fulke and began to force him back to the door. 'Get your hands off me!' he growled, peering blearily at them.

'He's so drunk he can't see straight,' whispered a man at the end of the table.

Fulke threw his two captors aside as if shrugging off a coat.

'It's not sapped his strength though, William,' whispered another.

'If you don't get her ladyship now, you'll regret it,' bellowed Fulke, fists clenched.

'We're not going to put our mistress in danger!' declared Barnabas.

'I won't hurt your precious mistress,' snarled Fulke. 'If I did she wouldn't be able to pay me what she owes. You'll be the ones in danger if you don't fetch her now.'

The cook whispered something to Charlie. Charlie dodged round Fulke and ran off.

The drunkard stood swaying and muttering under his breath until Lady Margaret appeared in the doorway,

Charlie peeping round her skirts. Mister Erskine, the steward, followed her in, looking nervous.

'You wanted to see me,' she said in a calm voice.

Fulke thrust his head forward as if trying to bring her into focus. 'I've come for my money. I want what I'm owed.'

'You're owed nothing,' said Lady Margaret. 'You were given more than you were entitled to.'

'It wasn't enough for my needs.'

'That's because you've spent it all in the tavern, you scoundrel,' put in Mister Erskine. 'You practically live there.'

'I have been more than fair with your pay,' said Lady Margaret. 'If you come here again I will consider it my duty to tell the constable of all your villainous ways.'

'Why wait, my lady?' said Barnabas. 'Don't forget we've got one of the King's yeomen guard in the Great Hall!'

The others nodded.

'You don't expect me to believe that, do you?' snarled Fulke. 'What would the likes of him be doing out here in the middle of nowhere?'

'It is true,' said Lady Margaret. 'Some members of the Court were stranded here by the foul weather, one of the royal yeomen among them.'

'He's huge,' said Charlie.

'Shall we fetch him?' asked the cook.

I had a sudden fear that they would do just that, and bring His Majesty into danger!

40

I jumped up and seized my livery jacket, drying by the fire. 'See this,' I called. 'This is mine. I am a servant at the palace.' Fulke leaned forwards, his breath nearly intoxicating me on the spot. 'Mister Brown the yeoman is three times my size.'

'I'm not scared of him,' growled Fulke.

'The boy's right,' called Barnabas. 'The guard is at least two yards high. And there's a courtier near as big with him.'

Fulke stood swaying on his feet, staring belligerently at us all. Then he seemed to shrink, like a pricked pig's bladder.

'Now be gone!' said Mister Erskine.

'Give him some food to take,' said Lady Margaret. 'In Christian charity it's the least we can do.'

Ruth bundled some bread into a cloth and thrust it into Fulke's hands. He snatched it and staggered back across the kitchen. When he reached the door, he turned.

'Christian charity!' he spat. 'You know I'm owed more than that.'

Everyone was silent as Fulke's splashing footsteps faded away. Cat still sat close to Bessy, comforting her. Mark looked terrified.

Mister Erskine came round and offered Lady Margaret his arm. 'Let me escort you back to your guests, my lady,' he said, glancing through the window as if he feared Fulke would return. 'I'm sorry you were troubled with this.'

'You did right to call me,' said Lady Margaret firmly. 'These things are my responsibility since my lord was taken by the plague.'

Bessy suddenly pushed Cat aside and slammed her fist down on the table. 'It was no plague that killed my master,' she declared.

'What are you saying, Bessy?' gasped Lady Margaret, turning at the door.

'Hush, Mother!' hissed Ruth. 'I've told you before, no one wants to listen to your wild tales. And my lady's had enough upset this morning.'

I caught Cat's gaze. Was the old woman about to tell us the mystery at last? I hoped her daughter wasn't going to shut her up. Lady Margaret came to my rescue. She looked pale but determined.

'Let Bessy speak,' she insisted. 'Perhaps we can allay her fears.'

'But my lady,' Ruth sounded scared. 'You don't want to be listening to my mother's rambles.'

'I'll not be silenced.' Bessy stared at us all. Her eyes were clear and sharp now. 'I had care of my master since he was a baby and I knew him like my own. My beloved boy did not die of the plague. He was murdered!'

7

A gasp of horror ran through the kitchen. Lady Margaret sank down onto a bench.

'Murdered?'

'This is mad talk.'

'Aye, she's mazed!'

Bessy put her bony old hands on the table and pushed herself to her feet. 'This is no fancy,' she said slowly and clearly, cutting though the murmur of voices. 'I am not mazed. After Sir Reginald died, I went in to see him one last time.'

'You should not have done that, Mother!' cried Ruth.

'You could have been struck down with the plague yourself!' added Lady Margaret, her voice hoarse with shock.

Bessy gave a sad laugh. 'I had no fear of the pestilence. I'd been with enough souls who'd died of that to know I wouldn't catch it. Besides, what if I had? I had nothing to live for once my boy had gone.' A tear spilled down her wrinkled cheek. 'It's not as if my kin care about me. My own daughter thinks I'm mad.'

'Well it's no surprise when you say such things,' retorted Ruth hotly.

'You may not have had the pestilence but I warrant you have brain fever now,' said Barnabas.

'I know what I saw,' insisted Bessy, looking round at us all. 'There were hives on Sir Reginald's skin—'

'Buboes – from the plague,' put in Charlie. 'As big as eggs, I bet.'

'Not like any plague buboes I'd ever seen,' continued the old woman. 'Forgive me, Lady Margaret, you wouldn't have recognised that they weren't raised and the skin around them hadn't blackened. I expect you were too ill yourself to notice. But it was no plague that did that. It was poison.'

'Poison?' breathed Lady Margaret. Her hands were shaking.

'Aye, and I know the exact one . . .' began Bessy.

'Oh Bessy, what are you saying?' interrupted the cook. He grinned at her. 'It was my cooking they had. It was put outside the sickroom door at every meal. And no one else was allowed to come near the house. Are you saying my food was bad?'

'Who would have wanted to poison our master?' asked Mister Erskine before Bessy could answer.

'I can think of someone,' said Barnabas sourly. 'And he's just been here.'

44

'It couldn't have been Fulke!' protested Mister Erskine. 'Sir Reginald dismissed him long before he was taken ill. Has anyone seen him at the castle since?'

The servants all shook their heads.

'Then it must be someone who lives here,' said Charlie. There was a mixture of horror and excitement in his tone.

'Impossible!' Lady Margaret shook her head weakly. She looked ready to faint.

'See what your words have done to our mistress, Mother!' hissed Ruth.

'I'm not saying . . .' quavered Bessy. She seemed very frail all of a sudden. 'I'm not accusing . . .' Her mouth opened and closed but no words came out.

'Mad as a March hare!' muttered Barnabas.

I had to admit that the old lady did seem deranged. She was plucking at her cap with her bony fingers. Cat got up and tried to take her arm but she swatted her away as if she was a fly.

'Calm yourself, Bessy,' said Mister Erskine. 'The girl means no harm.'

'Look, Mother, the rain has stopped,' Ruth said to the old woman. She took an old blanket and put it round her shoulders. 'Why don't you go outside? You know a walk always calms you down.'

Bessy stumbled away from the table, tearing at her cap and breaking the strings. She threw it down as if it disgusted her.

'I'll go with you,' said Cat. Bessy didn't answer.

45

She tottered towards the door. The wind caught it, slamming it behind her.

'Leave her be,' said Ruth firmly. 'She's lost her wits before and they come back all the quicker if she's left alone.'

'I don't mind,' insisted Cat. 'Only she looked so sad.'

'You've not been here a day and you know my mother better than I do,' snapped Ruth. She flounced off into the stillroom.

'Ruth's right,' said Mister Brandiscombe. 'Bessy's like to strike out when this mood takes her.'

'See here,' said Charlie, proudly displaying a bruise on his arm. 'Bessy did it the other day. She claimed I was the devil!'

'You can be the very devil at times,' laughed the cook.

'A moment please,' said Lady Margaret. She stood and faced us all, her expression grave. 'Bessy has been a loyal servant here for many years. I would have you all be kind to her in her confusion – for that is what I believe it is.'

There were mutterings of agreement around the room.

'And Charlie,' Lady Margaret went on. 'Remember how kind Bessy has been to you since you came to the castle.'

Charlie looked shamefaced. 'I meant no harm,' he muttered. 'She couldn't have been better to me if she'd been my own grandma.'

Lady Margaret smiled at him and then turned to make her way out. The steward moved to help his mistress.

'I am well, Mister Erskine,' she said, but I noticed she walked slowly through the door as if Bessy's news had sapped all her strength.

'What a morning!' said Mister Brandiscombe. 'Everyone back to the table. Some of you had only had a mouthful before that scoundrel Fulke arrived.'

I was happy to comply. But while I munched, something scratched at the back of my brain. Supposing the servants were wrong. What if Bessy hadn't been rambling? What if there was a killer at Norbrook Castle? The King could be in danger. Usually he would have Master Cromwell's secret network to seek out those who would do him harm. Here there was no one but me. I had to speak to Bessy and get the whole story.

Cat got there before me.

'I'm going after the old lady,' she announced. 'I can't leave her in that state.'

'I told you to leave her be,' snapped Ruth, storming back from the stillroom.

'Let her go,' said Mr Brandiscombe, kindly. 'What's the harm?'

'I'll help you, Cat,' I offered. 'If that's all right with you, Mister Erskine?'

The steward nodded. 'Bring the poor old soul back to the fire.'

Cat closed the door behind us and lifted her borrowed skirt up out of the mud. 'You've got that

47

calculating expression on your face. The one like Mister Cromwell's. It's not the old woman's well-being you're concerned with. You just want to know if there really has been a murder.'

Cat's words stung me although I knew I was right in my duty. 'I have to think of His Majesty,' I protested as I followed her down a narrow path, past the kitchen garden. 'If there's been a murder at the castle, the killer could still be around. Don't forget, I am the only one of Cromwell's spies here.'

'Mister Mountford is with the King all the time,' she countered. 'He won't let anything happen to him.'

'His Majesty couldn't have a better yeoman,' I said, 'but Mister Mountford isn't trained to look for hidden dangers. And anyway, I do want to make sure Bessy's all right.'

'I'm glad of it, Jack,' said Cat, her tone softening. 'You know, it makes me so cross to hear everyone say Bessy's mad. She's a bit fanciful, like old folk can be, but not mazed. I'd stake my life on it.' The path joined another that ran along a high hedge. 'Now where do we go? I can't see any sign of her.'

'Let's try that archway cut into the hedge over there,' I said, leading the way. 'Looks like there's an orchard beyond.'

We hunted along the rows of bare fruit trees. Bessy wasn't to be seen. 'But is the old woman right about Sir Reginald's death?' I asked. 'Or was she seeing poison when it was the plague?'

'Her eyesight's poor,' said Cat, 'so she might not have recognised the buboes.'

'And she might have been crying,' I added.

'That's right,' said Cat. 'I remember when my mother was peeling onions with her eyes watering like mad and my youngest brother came scampering in squealing and she flapped her apron at him something rotten thinking he was the neighbour's pig escaped!'

'When we find her, could you see if she remembers any more?' I asked. 'I've got to get to the bottom of this.'

Cat's eyes suddenly sparkled. 'You mean *we've* got to,' she said cheekily. 'As usual, you can't do without my help! Anyway, I'd already thought of talking to her . . .'

She broke off as we heard squelching footsteps. Charlie suddenly popped up between us. 'I've come to help find Bessy,' he said. 'I could see you didn't know where you were going. She never comes to the orchard.'

'Thanks, Charlie,' said Cat. 'Where should we look?'

'Well,' said Charlie, obviously feeling important. 'She likes walking round the carp pond. And she sometimes wanders in the herb garden. You check there while I go to the pond.' He pointed out the direction and scampered off.

We walked back towards the arch in the hedge.

'I knew she wouldn't be in the orchard,' said Cat loftily. 'You see, you do need my help.'

I was about to make a rude retort when there came a cry that chilled my blood.

8

Cat and I stared at each other for a heartbeat.

'Bessy!' gasped Cat. 'But where is she?'

'The cry came from over there!' We bounded through the archway and along the hedge. The way opened up into a large herb garden. Feet slipping in the mud, we raced between the rows of low bushes, frantically looking for the old woman. We had reached the far end when at last we came upon Bessy. She was slumped against a low wall, her head on her chest. I tried to shield Cat from the sight of blood on the stone.

'God save us,' whispered Cat. 'She's fallen. Is she all right?'

I knelt down. Bessy's eyes were open but would not see anything in this world again. Despite this I felt her bony wrist, hoping to find the pulse of life there. But there was nothing. 'She's dead.' I said sadly.

'No,' whispered Cat, her eyes welling. 'Poor Bessy.

She must have tripped. If we'd caught up with her sooner, it wouldn't have happened.'

'What if it wasn't a fall?' I asked in a low voice. 'Strange that it came so soon after Bessy talked about murder.'

I jumped to my feet and looked up and down. We'd heard no sound of footsteps running away and hadn't seen any assailant. I checked for telltale footprints but the ground was so muddy, it was impossible to work out which were fresh.

Cat wiped her face on her sleeve and looked at me wildly. 'You're not saying . . . she couldn't have been . . . you think someone killed Bessy?'

'I can't be sure . . .' I began.

'You think that when she talked about Sir Reginald's death, someone wanted to shut her mouth?'

'I know it seems unlikely . . .'

'Don't forget she was very upset,' insisted Cat. 'She didn't know where she was going. She could have fallen. Or her heart failed her.'

'That's true. But it would be a big coincidence.'

'I wouldn't like to be in your head, Jack,' said Cat. 'You see murder everywhere.'

'It's my job,' I replied, grimly. 'And if I'm right, her murderer could be nearby . . .'

We both jumped as a wail filled the air.

'Bessy!' It was Charlie, horror all over his face. 'What's happened?'

Cat pulled herself together and put her arms around

him. 'It's sad news, Charlie,' she said. 'Bessy's had an accident. I'm so sorry but she's dead.'

The poor boy sobbed as if his heart would break.

Mister Brandiscombe came running. 'I heard Charlie from the kitchen,' he said. 'What's happened?' Then he saw Bessy and staggered back in shock. 'By the saints!' he exclaimed. 'The poor soul must have slipped and cracked her skull. It would have been quick, thank the Lord.' He bent down and stroked her cheek. 'Go and tell everyone, Charlie, then run to the stables and tell William to ride to the abbey. He's to ask one of the monks to come.' He looked up at the sky. Dark, angry clouds were gathering and the wind was strengthening again. 'With luck the weather won't stop William and she'll have a prayer for the dead said over her.'

Charlie hesitated. 'I don't think anyone will come from the abbey.'

'We have to trust they'll do their Christian duty, no matter what has gone before,' said Mister Brandiscombe firmly. 'Off you go, lad.'

Charlie hurried off, wiping his nose on his sleeve.

The cook gently picked Bessy up and we made our solemn way towards the kitchen.

I was just going over his words in my mind when Lady Margaret appeared, leaning on Nicholas Mountford's arm. The yeoman couldn't help glancing anxiously behind to make sure that the King was with them. Their grave faces showed the news had reached them.

Lady Margaret gazed at Bessy's small limp form, head lolling like a grotesque puppet.

'Bessy was a loyal and faithful servant, Mister Mountford,' she said in a choked voice. 'The castle will not be the same without her.' She turned to the cook. 'Take her body to Sir Reginald's chamber. She knew him all his life. It is the only honour I can do her now, to lay her upon his own bed. I will lead the way.'

The sad procession set off for the castle.

'You two get back to your duties,' Mister Brandiscombe whispered to Cat and me. 'There's nothing more that can be done now.'

He was wrong. My work was only just beginning. Bessy had cried murder and then she herself had died within the hour. There was something about this that stank to high heaven.

I had to see Master Cromwell.

9

I tracked my master down to the steward's room. It lay just off the Great Hall and I finally found it after stumbling into a small armoury close to the main entrance of the castle. I was relieved to find Cromwell alone. He was studying some documents with the Norbrook seal on them.

'What is it, Jack?' he said, looking up. 'I have a good deal to do here. I little thought that my skills in law would be needed while we were away from London. However, in return for her ladyship's hospitality I have agreed to deal with Sir Reginald's will for her. Therefore be brief.'

Shut away in the office, he hadn't heard of Bessy's death. I told him how her body had been found.

'A sad affair but how does it concern us?' he asked. He appeared completely callous. But I knew he had learned to keep emotion out of his work. It was something that I still failed at, whatever Cat thought.

'I don't think it was an accident, sir,' I said bluntly.

'Strong words, Jack,' said my master. He put down his quill and pressed his fingers together, staring at me with his hooded eyes. 'Can you back them up?'

I quickly told him about the old lady's claims that her master was poisoned. 'Bessy spoke out about her suspicions – and she was dead not an hour afterwards,' I finished.

'Have you any evidence of a crime?' asked Cromwell.

'No,' I admitted. 'We didn't see anyone else in the garden before we heard her cry out. But there's more to this, I'm sure. As old Brother Jerome used to say, I can feel it in my water.'

'Then we have only your *water* to go on,' said my master dryly. 'Yet my experience tells me I would be a fool to ignore your instincts.' He got up and walked over to the window. The rain had returned, battering against the glass. 'Is it possible that you're mistaken? It is not uncommon for the elderly to lose their footing and fall.'

I nodded in agreement. Was I seeing a mystery where there was none? But I couldn't leave it. 'If a murder is committed anywhere near the King it has to be investigated by the coroner.'

'Indeed,' agreed Cromwell. 'That is the usual practice.'

'But we cannot fetch the coroner while the river is flooded,' I said, 'and even if we could bring him here, all the castle would then know that the King is with us.'

'You have the difficulties in a nutshell,' replied my master. 'One of Lady Margaret's serving men has ridden out even as we speak, to see if the river can be crossed, but I doubt he will bring good news. So what do you suggest?'

'That I investigate the death, sir,' I said.

The door opened and Mister Erskine came in.

'Jack has just been telling me about the old woman,' my master said smoothly. 'A sad business.' He went back to his table and picked up his quill. 'Go to your scribing duties,' he told me.

I hoped that he was saying this for the steward's benefit. Or was he telling me to leave well alone?

'I'll show you where Oswyn and Mark are,' said Mister Erskine. I followed him out into the Great Hall.

'And Jack?' Cromwell called after me.

'Yes, sir?'

'Deal with that other business when you have a moment.'

'Yes, sir!'

'But no flights of fancy.'

I knew he was reminding me that it might still be an accident but no words could dampen the rush of excitement I felt now I'd got permission to investigate the strange death. Though I suspected that his refusal wouldn't have stopped me.

'It may have been an ill wind last night that separated

you from the King's party,' Mister Erskine told me, 'but it has proved useful to me. Lady Margaret has yet to write letters breaking the sad news of her husband's death. Although with this weather, who knows when those letters can be sent?'

He was leading me across the hall to the staircase when Ruth burst out of the kitchen passageway. She ran up to the steward and grasped his sleeve.

'My mother!' she cried. 'Where is she?'

'There, there, Ruth,' said Mister Erskine, nervously patting her hand. 'Bessy's at peace.'

'If only I hadn't been so cruel to her,' Ruth wailed, tearing at her clothes, face creased with grief. 'I must see her.'

'I'll take you at once,' said the steward. 'She's in the master's room.' He turned to me. 'You go ahead. It's the chamber on the first floor of the old tower.'

I nodded and went up the stairs. In the hall below Ruth was quiet now, her head bowed. Barnabas the porter had left his place at the entrance doors and was helping Mister Erskine to support her as they made their slow way across the flagstones. I confess I was surprised at her behaviour. From what I'd seen, Ruth hadn't seemed very fond of her mother. Was this a genuine show of sorrow? I couldn't be sure.

I found the chamber easily enough. Mark was seated at a table, trimming a quill, a half finished document in front of him. Oswyn sat at the end, hogging the fire of course.

'Where have you been, Jack?' he demanded. 'Mark and I have been working for a full hour.'

I ignored his question and took a seat beside a pile of documents. Oswyn slammed a paper in front of me.

'You're to copy this letter to all these people.'

A long list of names was slapped down beside it.

Mark was looking anxiously at me. I grinned at him and without a word to Oswyn selected a quill from a pot between us.

'You'd better make up a good excuse for your skiving,' Weasel-face went on. 'We're not at one of His Majesty's palaces now, pulling the wool over Mister Scrope's eyes. Not only am I the royal taster but I'm also taking charge of you scribes.'

Mark had gone pale with terror at the thought of the spiteful Oswyn being his master, even for a few days.

'So our new Chief Scribe will of course know everything that's going on,' I said airily.

'Of course.'

'Then you will have heard the terrible news this morning,' I went on.

'What terrible news?' snapped Oswyn before he could stop himself.

'About poor Bessy,' I said.

'Who's Bessy?' he demanded rudely.

'She's the old servant who was found dead here in the herb garden only an hour ago,' I told him. Mark gasped in horror and crossed himself. I was sorry he'd learnt about the tragedy in this way.

'Oh, her,' said Oswyn, flustered. 'Of course.' It was obviously the first he'd heard of the tragedy.

'Then you'll know that I was one of the people who found her,' I said. 'That's why I wasn't here. We've all been very busy since.'

Oswyn looked defiant. 'Surely they've got enough staff at the castle to deal with somebody dying! I warrant they didn't need their guests getting in the way.'

'I expect you're right,' I agreed, 'so you'd better go and tell His Majesty. He was there too, getting in the way, no doubt. Or shall I go for you, *sir*?'

Oswyn blanched. Lips pursed in a thin line, he bent his head over his work. And we heard no more from our Chief Scribe.

It seemed a long morning. I was soon sick and tired of the words 'sad news' and 'regret to inform' and 'tragic demise'. And I had more important things to be doing. Bessy had cried murder and had then died herself.

At last Charlie stuck his head round the door. I pushed back my chair, thinking it must be time for lunch. Breakfast had been plentiful but my belly seemed to have forgotten all about it.

'Oi, Oz,' he called. 'They're all waiting in the Great Hall and they're saying they can't start without you. I don't know why.'

Weasel-face rose from his chair like an emperor. 'It's Mister Drage to you,' he said, looking down his nose at Charlie.

'If you say so, Oz,' said Charlie, giving us a wink as he scampered off.

Oswyn had just reached the door when there was another knock and Cat appeared. Mark gulped and tried to hide under the desk.

'Is Jack Briars here?' she asked Oswyn, pushing past him. 'Oh there you are, Jack. There's a problem with your royal livery. You've got to come with me.'

I knew there was no problem with my livery, beyond the fact it was wet, muddy and ripped to shreds and I couldn't help with that. So what was Cat playing at?

'Bring his clothes here, girl,' snapped Oswyn. 'Or he won't get any work done.'

Cat looked him up and down as if he was a mere earwig. 'Who are you to tell me my job, Oswyn Drage? I've had orders. He's to come down to the kitchen at once!'

Oswyn seemed about to argue.

'Don't forget Yeoman Brown is waiting for you,' I told him.

The Royal Taster stalked off to do his lunchtime duty.

'I gave myself the orders,' said Cat with a grin as we headed down the tower steps. 'Follow me. I've discovered something really important.'

10

I pulled her to a halt. 'What is it?' I demanded.

'Not here,' she hissed. 'We have to be somewhere private and I know the very place.'

She put a finger to her lips and led me around the landing. I crept behind her. In the Great Hall below, the Royal party sat eating their luncheon. She took me to the wide gallery. The torches were still burning brightly, showing how dark the day was.

Cat pointed to the nearest door. 'There's Lady Margaret's chamber,' she said in a low voice, 'and next to it is Sir Reginald's where poor Bessy lies now. Then that one's Master Cromwell's and beyond it is Mister Mountford's and the last one is . . .' She lowered her voice even more. ' . . . The King's.'

'You've brought me here to tell me that?' I said incredulously.

'No, you dolt! I'm telling you so you keep your voice

down. Any of them could come to their rooms at any moment and we have no business here. Ruth is still in with her mother, I do know that.' She pushed me onto a window seat in a deep alcove. 'But for all that, it's quiet and I've got information for you.' She looked fearful, but there was a strange spark of excitement in her eyes. 'You might be right about Bessy's death.'

I gawped at her. Cat never admitted I was right about anything! Before I could speak, she went on.

'I went after Mr Brandiscombe to help him lay her on the bed in Sir Reginald's chamber, so she looked nice. When I was arranging her skirts – I didn't have long, because Ruth came in and sent us packing – anyway, when I was in there, I noticed a very odd thing.'

'What was it?'

'Poor old Bessy had mud all over the front of her clothes,' Cat told me, 'and her face. What d'you think of that?'

'Is that it?' I asked, disappointed. 'I saw that for myself when we found her.'

'You're being a dullard, Jack,' was the reply. 'Bessy fell *backwards* on to the stone wall. Why would her front be muddy?'

'If her death was just an accident, she could have tumbled forwards into the mud, got herself to her feet and then fallen back,' I reasoned.

'But if *I'm* right that's not what happened.' Cat was whispering now. I leaned forward to catch every word. 'I was placing her hands on her chest, and I noticed how lovely her nails were, well cut and cared for.'

'I'm sure they were as pretty as a queen's!' I interrupted, wishing she'd get to the point.

'Her palms were clean too.' Cat sat back triumphantly. 'There. Now you can congratulate me on my expert investigating.'

'What expert investigating?' I demanded. 'So Bessy kept her hands nice. I can't see how her washing habits help us to decide how she died.' I got up and turned to leave. 'I'm going back to work!'

Without warning Cat gave me a hefty push from behind. I stumbled forwards and found myself sprawling on the floor. I glanced up and down to make sure no one was coming to see what the clatter was.

'What did you do that for?' I demanded furiously as I staggered to my feet.

'Oh, sorry,' said Cat, cheekily. 'Did you bump your nose on the floorboards?' She inspected me closely. 'No, of course you didn't. Because you put out your hands to save yourself. Bessy didn't.'

I stared at her as the truth sank in.

'You're right,' I said. 'If Bessy had fallen forwards her instinct would have been to put out her hands.'

'Exactly,' said Cat. 'They should have been caked in mud like the front of her apron.'

'And falling forwards doesn't give you a wound on the back of your head,' I added. 'So Bessy made her announcement about Sir Reginald's murder to everyone in the kitchen, then she stumbled off into the castle grounds.'

'And someone followed her . . .' said Cat.

'. . . Hit her over the head . . .' I added.

'. . . And arranged her body to make it look like an accident.' Cat shuddered. 'It's horrible.' She paused. 'Well, aren't you going to tell me how well I've done, finding that out?'

I knew I had to congratulate the wretched girl. 'Very good,' I managed to say. I sat back down next to her and rubbed my sore knee. 'However, next time, could you do your demonstrations a bit more gently?'

'You were being rather slow on the uptake,' said Cat with an annoying shrug. 'I could see you needed a little . . . *nudge* to get to the truth.'

We both jumped as the sound of voices came to us. Footsteps were approaching the far end of the gallery. We heard Lady Margaret speaking.

'Bessy served my husband's family all her life,' she was saying. 'What a sad end for such loyalty.'

'You must not blame yourself, my lady.' That was the King.

'I can't help but do so,' replied Lady Margaret. 'The death weighs heavily on my heart. Thank you, gentlemen, for accompanying me. I will rest awhile in my bedchamber, as you suggest.'

They came into view. Lady Margaret walked at Cromwell's side, with His Majesty and Nicholas Mountford close behind.

Cat caught my eye and I could see her fear. What business could a seamstress and a scribe have here?

11

Cat jumped up from the window seat and into a deep curtsey at the sight of the King. Her nose almost touched the floor.

'Sorry to be in your way, Your Ma . . .' She suddenly realised her mistake. 'Your Madameness,' she said, twisting quickly to address Lady Margaret as she rose. 'Only I met this scribe and he pestered me about mending his livery. I tried to get away but he would follow me wherever I went. That's how I ended up here.'

I nodded and kept my mouth shut. I was going to emerge from this tale looking completely foolish but there was nothing I could do. At least she was getting us out of trouble.

'And I told him that there's a long rent in the sleeve and he must have caught it on a branch, clumsy oaf, and it will take me an age to repair it.'

I was sure that Master Cromwell was trying not to laugh.

'And the silly boy said . . .'

Thankfully any more insults from Cat were stopped short. A serving man came striding up, his mud-stained cloak streaming with water. He looked exhausted.

'What news?' asked Lady Margaret.

'The river is flooded like a sea,' the man replied wearily. 'There is no way to reach the next bridge. What paths remain are mostly blocked by fallen trees and in one place there has been a landslide.' He wiped his face. 'I spoke with an old man who remembered the river flooding many years ago. He said it took more than a week before the water subsided.'

'A week!' gasped the King. 'I shall die if we stay a week!'

Lady Margaret gasped at the outburst.

'Forgive my yeoman speaking out of turn, my lady,' said Master Cromwell. 'It is simply that he is a loyal servant and anxious to return to His Majesty's service. Yet we are most grateful for your hospitality, are we not, Mr Brown?'

'Yes indeed,' said Yeoman Adam Brown, trying to look humble. 'I am sure that the King would forgive my outburst . . . were he here,' he added. Although he sounded contrite I thought I detected an edge of steel in his tone.

'Go and dry yourself at the kitchen fire,' said Lady Margaret to the soaked serving man. She turned to

Master Cromwell. 'My home is yours for as long as you have to stay. Whilst I know that your duties to the King will take you from me as soon as is safe, yet I am glad of your presence. It has lifted my sorrowful spirits . . . and now with poor Bessy's death . . .'

'You have been kindness itself, my lady,' said Cromwell. 'And in such difficult times.' He glanced at King Henry who was shuffling from foot to foot beside him. I held my breath. The King's tempers were notorious and the frustration of being a mere yeoman must have been making him boil inside. 'Lady Margaret, may I beg a favour of you?'

'Of course, Master Cromwell. How could I refuse when you are so good as to use your expertise to help us get back on our feet?'

'I have seen that you have here a fine collection of weapons,' answered my master. 'I would be glad if Mister Mountford and Mister Brown could study them. They are expert swordsmen and I know they would relish the chance to handle such arms.'

How clever, I thought as I saw the King's eyes light up. *That'll keep His Majesty busy for a while.*

Lady Margaret smiled. 'They are yours whenever you wish.'

'This is most lucky!' King Henry slapped me on the shoulder. I nearly fell over with the force of it! 'You will remember that a little while ago the King made you a promise, young scribe.' All traces of his impatient mood had vanished.

'A promise, sir?' I nearly said Sire but managed to change it at the last minute.

'Indeed, and as we all know, King Henry is an honourable man who never breaks his word.'

Everyone nodded vigorously.

'This worthy young man was due a reward,' His Majesty told Lady Margaret, who wore a puzzled expression. 'He did the King a service and our noble sovereign has not forgotten it.' I felt a thrill of excitement run through me but kept it hidden – I hoped. The King had indeed offered me a reward after I had unmasked a traitor. 'You will remember that you are to have sword fighting lessons, Jack Briars,' he went on.

'Yes, sir,' I managed to say.

'Now, I believe Robert Aycliffe offered himself for the part of tutor but he is not here with us.' The King was enjoying his playacting.

'I would be happy to give Jack some instruction,' said Nicholas Mountford, drawing himself up and trying to look like his monarch's superior. 'It will be no hardship, Mr Brown. The boy is quick on his feet.'

'I'd be honoured,' I said and felt Cat dig me in the ribs. She was beaming from ear to ear.

'No,' said the King firmly. 'I will give the lesson myself ... I mean, with your permission, sir.' King Henry had obviously remembered that Mountford was supposed to be a courtier!

'I give my permission,' said Mountford awkwardly.

'I promised His Majesty that I would do this if Mister Aycliffe were too busy,' the King added quickly. 'Therefore I will see you when the tower clock strikes nine tomorrow morning, Jack, outside by the sundial in the kitchen courtyard – if the weather permits. I'm sure you can be excused from your scribing duties.'

He turned to Cromwell who nodded.

I felt my mouth drop open and my insides churn like a millwheel. The greatest monarch in the world was going to teach me, a mere foundling, how to use a sword.

'Close your mouth, Jack,' said Master Cromwell. 'You'll be catching moths!'

12

I returned to the scribes' room in a daze. Even my empty stomach couldn't dampen my delight. Was I really going to be given a sword fighting lesson by the King of England? I could scarcely believe my luck.

I pulled my thoughts back, but not to the letter in front of me. Bessy had been killed – I was sure of that, at least. The old lady must have been right. Sir Reginald had been poisoned. I considered all that I'd heard since we'd come to Norbrook Castle. The servant, Fulke, had been dismissed for theft. He was no friend to Sir Reginald. I had witnessed his ill feeling first hand and he only left minutes before Bessy went out. And there was Bessy's daughter. I had no reason to think that she'd had anything against her master but I'd seen her behaviour. She'd tried to stop her mother from speaking her accusations. She'd sent Bessy outside and could easily have slipped out after her.

I suddenly realised that Weasel-face was talking. 'Even when Briars is here he doesn't do a lot of work,' he said loudly to Mark. 'I haven't seen his quill move for an age. I wonder what Master Cromwell would think of that?'

'If you were busy staring at me, you'd have to tell him that you weren't doing much either, Oswyn,' I retorted, keeping my tone light. I could not afford to give him any fuel for his suspicions.

'You forget, I have a more important job now,' drawled Oswyn. 'Taster to the King. I shouldn't be surprised if I'm promoted from scribe to taster when we get back.'

It was on the tip of my tongue to tell him that I was to have a royal sword lesson tomorrow! That would wipe the silly smirk from his face. But then poor old Mark would hear me and I knew that the thought of it would scare the breeches from him. He'd probably tell me about a boy who tried to cut his toenails with a sword and chopped his feet off!

I bent dutifully over my copying. But my head was full of the suspects – and my coming encounter with King Henry.

❧

I was out in the courtyard long before my appointment with His Majesty the next morning. I prayed that the heavy grey clouds overhead wouldn't shed their load over Norbrook Castle.

Was the King really coming to teach me to use a sword? Well, he'd find me a fast learner. At last the clock on the tower struck nine but no one came. I began to wonder if I'd dreamed what had happened yesterday. I had to be patient. The King was allowed to be as late as he liked.

I was practising a bit of fancy footwork in front of a stone cherub holding a sundial when I heard my name being called. I stopped, feeling foolish. Oswyn Drage popped up from behind a hedge.

'So there you are,' he sneered. 'I've been searching for you. Trying to avoid work yet again?'

'I have good reason to be here,' I replied calmly.

'What's that?' said Weasel-face. 'Skipping round statues? Master Cromwell will be most interested to hear what you get up to!'

I had no time to reply as the King arrived, followed by Nicholas Mountford, who was carrying two swords. Oswyn's face broke into a triumphant smile. 'Even better,' he hissed, ducking behind the hedge. 'Let's see what "Mister Brown" has to say when he finds you loitering.'

His weaselly little eyes shone with delight as King Henry strode up. I just about remembered not to bow, but gave a slight nod instead as a secret homage.

'Good lad.' He greeted me in a booming voice. 'I see you're keen to start your lesson.'

Out of the corner of my eye, I saw Oswyn's head round the hedge – and his face fall in disbelief. The next minute I caught sight of his shifty figure scuttling away. Sadly I was too busy trembling inside to enjoy my moment of triumph.

'Now, Jack,' said the King, 'if we were making a display, we would be fencing with shorter swords.' He fixed me with a stare. 'However, I have the feeling that a boy like you would prefer to learn how to fight in combat.'

'Thank you, sir!' I answered. To Mister Mountford I was just a young scribe relishing a bit of excitement in his dull life. But His Majesty and I both knew that this could be a much needed skill.

The King raised his weapon above his head. 'A long sword is always held in both hands,' he explained. 'It is a grip that is strong yet allows for movement.' With that the blade whirled about in a blur of steel. I felt my jaw drop with admiration. His Majesty laughed. 'It will take more than one lesson for you to learn to do that!'

'Don't be scared,' said Mountford, handing me my sword. 'These are practice weapons – completely blunt. I found them in the armoury.'

'Let us begin. When you step forward, you must be light on your toes.' The King demonstrated, darting towards me at pace, the sword held out in front of him.

He made me copy this again and again. It felt very strange at first and more than once I slammed my foot down in a puddle and splattered him. I waited for the royal rage but it didn't come. I tried again, concentrating on my feet.

I was starting to see the sense in the King's instructions. After a while, I could move quickly back and forth without too much wobbling. We did a lot of leaping about, our swords swished in front of us like scythes but it didn't seem anything like a proper fight – unless looking like a dancing frog could kill someone.

I found myself wondering if we'd ever get round to real combat.

The King suddenly faced me. 'Attack!' he commanded.

I found my hands were shaking. If I accidentally wounded my monarch I could end up in the Tower!

'What are you waiting for?' he goaded me. 'You're giving your enemy time to slice your head off.'

I lunged at him with my sword. Except he wasn't there. He'd darted aside and now had the point of his blade at my ribs.

'It's not all clashing steel,' he said with a smile. 'Dodging the thrust is equally important. Again.'

This time he stayed put. Our swords clanged. In a second, he'd used my sword to slide his own down towards my neck. He could have beheaded me!

'Now you try,' he commanded.

I had a go. It wasn't easy. But the King was proving to be a patient teacher, taking each move slowly.

'Once more and the lesson is done for today,' he said at last.

I was disappointed that it was over so soon. Although my muscles weren't. I felt as if I'd been fighting a hundred men. I took a moment to think out my strategy. Two quick steps forward, a thrust and out of range. Then I'd go at him from the side. I thought about my riding lessons with Cat and decided that swords were easier to control than horses.

'Attack!' the King commanded again.

I was on him in a trice. With a clang that jarred my whole body, King Henry had knocked my sword from my hands and sent me sprawling backwards. I crashed into a bush, arms and legs flailing. I heard the King and Nicholas Mountford roar with laughter. Perhaps I needed to revise my opinion about horses versus swords. I seemed to end up on my bum either way.

But I was going to come out fighting. As I struggled to my feet, my fingers found a piece of rough wood. I jumped up, swinging it round my head.

'I'm not beaten yet!' I yelled.

'Well done, Jack Briars,' said His Majesty. He lowered his sword. 'You showed great resourcefulness.'

I lowered my stick.

'You've had a lesson in an ancient and noble art,' the King went on, 'but in a real fight your opponent may not play by the rules. Sometimes a swordsman has to improvise or use the element of surprise – and you've done exactly that. There are plenty of other tricks to remember. For instance, a tall man like me cannot so easily defend his legs. A low swipe with your blade could unbalance such an opponent.'

Nicholas Mountford took both weapons. 'Knowing Jack, he'll come up with some tricks of his own.'

'I don't doubt it,' said the King. 'But his lessons will continue. Remember, Jack, your monarch gave his promise. We'll be gone from this place soon. Robert Aycliffe will tutor you when we are back at Court.'

I stopped myself bowing in time. 'Thank you, sir,' I said.

His Majesty and his yeoman strode back to the castle. I watched them go. I'd just fought the greatest king on earth! I thought of my godfather and his hopes that I'd find kitchen work at King Henry's Court. He'd never believe what had happened here.

I realised I was still holding my wooden weapon. I'd chosen well – it was strong and stout. I was glad I'd stopped short of whacking His Majesty with it! I was puzzling over how it had come to be deep inside a bush when I noticed there was something on it.

The end was covered in a sticky mess that looked like crushed berries. But I knew it wasn't anything so innocent.

It was dried blood – and a single strand of grey hair.

13

I stared at the hideous sight. There was no doubt in my mind what I had in my hands. This stick had been used to kill poor Bessy.

I felt my gorge rise at the thought of the heavy club smashing into the old lady's skull. It was a cruel, calculated act. It must have stricken her unconscious or killed her outright for her not to put her hands out to break her fall.

After he'd arranged her to make it seem like an accident he'd thrown the murder weapon into this thick bush, believing that no one would find it.

He never expected a scribe to land in the middle of that very bush.

There was one more thing I needed to do, though it wasn't a job I was looking forward to. I hoped the body hadn't been washed ready for burial yet because I had to make absolutely sure my theory about the murder weapon was right. I remembered that where Bessy lay there was only mud and stone all around her. That meant that if I found splinters of wood in Bessy's hair, they could only have come from that bloodied stick.

I placed the wood back exactly where I'd found it and started for Sir Reginald's chamber. Then I stopped. Ruth could still be in there tending to her mother, and she wasn't likely to let me in, especially if she had anything to hide. But she might let Cat pay her last respects. Everyone had seen how fond she was of Bessy. I'd have to make sure my faithful assistant came with me.

Cat was outside the kitchen brushing mud off Cromwell's cloak.

'Did you enjoy your lesson?' she said in glee. 'I saw you out of the window. You had the King quaking in his boots.' She jumped around, poking me with her brush.

'Very funny,' I replied. 'But enough of that. I have an important task and I need your help.'

'That goes without saying!' she exclaimed.

'I've found the murder weapon!' I told her.

'What is it?' she demanded.

I described how I'd come upon the stick with the blood on it.

Cat was torn between hilarity at my fall into the bush and horror at what I'd discovered.

'Poor Bessy,' she gasped. 'What kind of person would do such a thing to so lovely an old lady?'

'That's what I intend to find out,' I said. 'But first I need proof before I go to Master Cromwell. I've reported my suspicions to him, but I didn't have any evidence then.'

'So what is this task that you need my help with?'

I told her.

Cat looked horrified. 'You can't go messing about with a body that's being laid out, Jack,' she said. 'It's disrespectful and I'm having no part of it.'

'But I need you,' I said. 'Ruth might be in there and she's . . .' I decided not to tell Cat my suspicions about Bessy's daughter yet. She'd be even less willing to agree to my plan. '. . . not very friendly. At least you got to know Bessy. It wouldn't seem strange that you want to see her. I bet I won't get in without you if she's around.'

'You probably won't,' agreed Cat. 'I happen to know that Ruth hasn't left the chamber. She said she alone was going to prepare her mother and then sit in vigil until the burial.'

'Then will you help?' I asked hopefully.

'I will not,' replied Cat firmly. 'I'm not one of Cromwell's spies so I don't have to have any part of it. Besides, I'm far too busy. That storm wreaked havoc with our clothes and I don't know when I'll get the mending finished – and I'm helping with all the laundry.'

She stalked off inside the castle and down the empty passageway.

'Then the murderer will go free,' I said, catching her up as she went into a small storeroom where our clothes were now waiting to be mended. I didn't add that the murderer might go free anyway as I had no idea yet who'd wielded the stick! 'He could be rubbing shoulders with the King at this very moment. He could even be sharpening a knife as we speak.'

Cat stopped, twisting the cloak in her hands.

'Oh, all right.' She turned on me crossly. 'Come on. Let's get it over with. I don't know why I ever agreed to help you with your investigations!'

I decided not to remind Cat that it was usually her who insisted on sticking her nose in!

'When we get there,' I said, 'go on about how close you became to Bessy before she died and could you have one last moment alone with her.'

'And that would be the truth,' said Cat. She looked at me sternly. 'You're becoming like him. You know – Master Cromwell.' She shook his cloak disdainfully. 'Not showing any emotion and using people for your purpose.' She folded up the cloak and put it on a shelf. 'Come on then. She set off up the winding staircase to Sir Reginald's room.

I had to admit there was some truth in what she'd said. It had sounded as if I'd merely been thinking about solving this crime and had forgotten the humans involved.

'It's important we find the murderer,' I said lamely. 'I'm sorry about Bessy too.'

'I know. And I haven't forgotten that you risked your own life in the river to save mine.' But Cat's face was still grim.

As we got to the gallery, the door of the room where Bessy lay clicked open. A man in a monk's habit came out. There was something in his furtive manner that made me pull Cat back out of sight.

'Anselm.' Ruth's voice came from inside the room. 'Take care my lady does not see you.'

The monk nodded, drew his cloak around him and hurried away to the far end of the gallery.

'What do you think of that?' said Cat in excitement. 'Charlie and Mister Brandiscombe talked about some problem with the abbey and it looks as if they were right. The man's creeping about like a criminal.'

'It's suspicious,' I agreed. 'We must try to find out more.'

I knocked on the door of Sir Reginald's room. There was a long pause. Then the door was thrust open.

'What do you want?' Ruth asked. She stood full square in the doorway, blocking our way.

'If you don't mind,' said Cat gently, 'I've come to see Bessy. She was so kind to me.'

Ruth looked suspiciously at her. 'Come to sob over someone you've only known a day?'

Cat's eyes filled with tears and I don't think she was acting. 'I didn't know her as you did, of course, but I was fond of her even so. You were her daughter. You must know how she touched the lives of others.'

The tiring woman hesitated. 'Maybe,' she said gruffly. She gave a brief nod in my direction. 'But he doesn't have to come in with you, does he? We don't want all and sundry gawping at her.'

'Jack's my good friend,' Cat answered, undaunted. 'He only wants to pay his respects.'

'One minute then and no more.' Ruth stepped back and pushed the door open to let us pass. The strong smell of herbs barely disguised the smell of the dead. Bessy lay with her hands arranged over her chest and pennies over her closed eyes. Cat stroked her arm and murmured a few words. We knelt either side of the bed and Cat closed her eyes and muttered a prayer. I hoped Ruth would close hers too, but she didn't.

Ruth stood very close, her beady gaze fixed on us. This so-called vigil of hers did not look like true devotion. It smacked more of an excuse to keep prying eyes away from the evidence. I had a shiver of disgust at the thought that Ruth could have killed Sir Reginald and then was willing to silence her own mother to protect her terrible secret. And where did Brother Anselm come into this?

'I hope you found comfort in the monk's prayers,' I ventured, throwing a line into the pond to see if the fish would bite.

'Monk?' snapped Ruth. 'There's been no monk here.'

'I thought . . .' I began.

'You thought wrong!' said Ruth, picking up a basin of water. 'You have to go now. I've got things to do.'

'Of course,' said Cat soothingly. 'We'll get out of your way.'

What was she up to? We couldn't leave yet! I hadn't checked the wound on the back of Bessy's head.

But Cat seemed to be making for the door. As she passed Ruth she tripped. The basin flew out of Ruth's hands, water splashing to the floor in a huge puddle.

Ruth cursed and fell to her knees, trying to mop it up with her apron.

'I'm so sorry,' said Cat, dashing to help and blocking me from view.

I seized my chance. I placed my hand on Bessy's cold cheek. If Ruth saw, I hoped she'd think I was saying a final farewell. I moved the old woman's head very gently to one side. Now I could see that something was caught in her hair. I pulled it slowly free.

It was a tiny splinter of wood.

14

Ruth jumped to her feet, the puddle mopped.

'Get you gone this instant!' she snarled.

We fled to the door.

Outside, I showed Cat the splinter. 'Here's the evidence we needed,' I said.

Cat looked sick. 'I hate to think of Bessy suffering like that. I hope it was quick. Do you think the killer lives here at the castle?'

In a very low voice I told her my suspicions about Ruth.

'Surely not!' gasped Cat. 'Bessy was her mother! I know Ruth didn't want us in there, but I'm sure that's because she was truly upset.'

'She's an unlikely murderer,' I agreed, 'but I've learned that I'd be a fool to ignore it as a possibility. And don't forget the monk. He didn't act like someone who was there to say a prayer for the dead.'

In the distance I heard Oswyn's whining voice calling my name.

'Let's go!' I hissed. 'Before Weasel-face finds out where I am and drags me off to work.' We crept along the gallery and down the winding stairs at the end.

'So what's next?' whispered Cat as we reached the door to the kitchen.

'I want to find out about Anselm,' I replied. 'I'm going to ask in the kitchen.'

Cat rubbed her hands together. 'I'll help,' she said eagerly.

'Haven't you got work to do?' I asked. 'I think I can manage on my own.'

'I'm not so sure about that.' Cat grinned mischievously. 'After all, you needed me and my basin spilling skills back there.'

She flung the kitchen door open before I could find something clever to say in retort. The kitchen was hot and full of chatter. Beyond the large table where servants were preparing pasties for lunch, I could see Charlie by the fire, struggling single-handedly to turn a pig over the flames. He was being watched by Mister Brandiscombe, William the groom and another servant, who all had huge grins on their faces.

As soon as Charlie saw us, he stopped his efforts, and broke into a big smile that nearly split his grimy face. 'Jem here is letting me have a practice for when I get that job at the palace!'

Jem began turning the pig. 'You'll be fine if the King

doesn't mind his meat burnt on one side and raw on the other!' he said.

I decided it was as well that Charlie didn't know the real identity of Yeoman Brown, otherwise he'd have probably started pestering for a job there and then.

'I'm not listening to you, Jem,' declared Charlie. 'Bessy always said I'd make a lovely spit boy.' He looked sad. 'I wish she was here now.'

'Has Bessy had her prayers for the dead yet?' I asked. 'Only I thought I saw a monk in the castle earlier.'

'I'll be blowed!' William's face flushed red with anger. 'That was Brother Anselm, I'll warrant. His conscience has got the better of him, no doubt.'

'A monk with a bad conscience?' I said. 'What can he have done?'

'When Bessy died I set off for Franbury Abbey to get one of the monks,' said William. 'And I'd barely left the castle when I came upon Brother Anselm a little way down the lane.'

'That was lucky,' Charlie piped up.

'Exactly,' William agreed, 'especially as he was Bessy's own nephew. But do you know what he said? He told me his rheumatism always played up in the bad weather and he had to get home. Not very Christian if you ask me.'

I thought about the monk I'd seen in the gallery. There had been no hint of a painful joint as he'd hurried away. Either a miracle had cured Brother Anselm of his rheumatism or he was hiding something. Why had he gone to see Ruth so secretly?

Cat gave me a look. I knew what that meant. The minute we were on our own she'd be telling me there was something suspicious about the monk, as if she was the only one who'd thought of it. I wasn't going to give her the chance. I headed out of the kitchen making for the steward's office. I was hoping I'd find Cromwell there.

Cat was close behind me, no doubt waiting for a chance to stick her oar in.

But we'd barely gone a few steps along the passageway when Mark came rushing round the corner.

'I have terrible news,' he said.

He didn't seem to have seen Cat and I hoped she'd have the sense to keep back so he wasn't scared off.

'What is it?' I asked.

'The flooding has worsened since yesterday,' said Mark in a dramatic voice.

'How do you know?' I asked.

'I climbed up to the battlements to check,' he told me. 'I did the same yesterday. But don't worry – I didn't go anywhere near the edge. I heard of a man who poked his head over a tower wall and got blown away by a whirlwind. Never seen again. Anyway it looks as if we're almost surrounded by water now. *And* there's more rain to come by all accounts.'

I wondered whether sword fighting alone would be

enough to keep the King in a good temper if we were going to have to stay here much longer.

'Do you think the house is cursed?' Mark went on. 'First Sir Reginald and his lady were so ill and then Sir Reginald died – and that scribe. Next came this dreadful weather and then poor Bessy's accident and no one there to save her. If only that other person had been passing nearer to her . . .'

'What other person?' I demanded, my breath catching in my throat.

'I have no idea who it was,' said Mark, surprised at my eagerness. 'Yesterday when I was coming down from the battlements I glanced down from one of the windows on the second floor and I just caught a glimpse of someone in a cloak – he had his hood up of course because the weather was so bad – and I remember I was surprised that anyone was out when there could be a downpour at any moment!'

'What colour was his cloak?' I asked. I needed every detail.

Mark looked even more surprised. 'It wouldn't have mattered what colour it was. He could still have caught a nasty chill out there. I didn't know Bessy was outside too. Even worse for an old person.' He caught my eye. 'I think it was grey, dark grey.'

'And where was he going?'

Mark shook his head. 'I don't know. He was walking away from the herb garden. Away from where Bessy fell . . .'

He suddenly turned as pale as chalk and clutched at my sleeve. 'I know who it might have been.'

'Tell me,' I urged him.

'It was Death,' he whispered. 'Death in his dark cloak, taking Bessy's soul away.'

'Death!' Cat came running forwards to join us.

Mark jumped in fright. 'Oh . . . it's you, Cat Thimblebee . . . I must be going.'

And he hurried off.

It came to me that Mark was more scared of Cat than he was of the Grim Reaper!

'Do you think he really saw Death?' asked Cat nervously.

'I doubt it,' I said. 'I reckon it was . . .'

'Wait!' Cat interrupted me. 'I know it wasn't Death. I know exactly who he saw. He saw Bessy's murderer!'

15

Cat looked very pleased with herself. Curse the girl! I'd worked that out for myself but she'd got in first.

'Don't you see, Jack?' she went on. 'It all fits. The murderer, dressed in a dark cloak, was getting away from the scene of the crime.'

I was about to say that the cloaked monk we'd seen earlier was a possible suspect when she burst out again.

'It could be Brother Anselm! In league with Ruth – his cousin. That's why he was here today. But we'll have to leave that investigation till later. I really must get back to my mending.'

Before I could say a word, she'd gone!

I hurried to the steward's room and knocked. As soon as I heard Master Cromwell calling me to enter I marched in. I was pleased to see that he was alone, a half-finished plate of food by his side. It was his habit to work through meals and he seemed to be as busy here as at Court.

He motioned me to wait. I stood watching him scrutinise some close written document or other. He glanced up, catching me in the middle of stifling a yawn.

'Sir,' I began, 'it's about Bessy's death.'

Cromwell raised an eyebrow. 'I didn't expect it to be about some laundry account. So tell me. What have you found out?'

'My hunch about Bessy's death was right,' I told him. 'She was murdered and I believe I have proof. There is a cold-hearted killer in our midst and we are trapped here by the floods. Therefore His Majesty could be in danger.'

'And this proof?'

I quickly told him what I'd discovered, describing the strange behaviour of Ruth and her cloaked visitor. When I'd finished Cromwell sat impassively for a moment, observing me through his heavy-lidded eyes. As always, it unnerved me.

'You've made a compelling case, Jack,' he said. 'We must investigate – and quickly.' He pressed his fingers into his forehead. 'But we know nothing of this murderer, save that he may have had a dark grey cloak and that he wanted Sir Reginald dead for some reason. It is too little to go on.'

A sudden, bold knock on the door made me jump.

Cromwell's face cleared and he calmly took up his pen. 'Enter.'

The door swung open and the King came in. For an instant, I wondered why he'd bothered to knock. Then I remembered. The King was in his role as a yeoman guard. As soon as he'd closed the door behind him we bowed deeply.

'I am so bored!' he declared, slamming his fist on the table. 'A long afternoon stretches out before me. I've come to seek a chess partner. Nicholas is no good. He is too nervous about beating me. I've given him the slip.' He looked at my master mischievously. 'Well, Thomas?'

'Nothing would please me more, Sire,' replied Cromwell, 'but I have something of grave importance to tell you first.'

'What is it, man?' said the King impatiently. 'The board awaits.'

'I fear I have bad news, my Liege,' said Cromwell in a low voice. 'You could be in danger here at Norbrook Castle. Jack has found proof that the old serving woman's death was no accident.'

'You're saying someone killed her?' exclaimed the King. He suddenly cast a look at the door to the Great Hall. 'Then we must apprehend the murderer at once,' he added in a whisper.

He makes it sound so simple, I thought to myself. I had a sudden image of him gathering everyone in the Great Hall and commanding the killer to step forward!

'We would dearly love to bring him to justice in a heartbeat,' said Cromwell. 'But we have no notion who he might be.'

'In that case we should leave immediately,' muttered the King, pacing the floor. 'You know more than most, Thomas, that the monarch must be kept from danger. Especially one with no son to succeed him.'

'I would give anything to get you away from here, Sire,' Cromwell assured him, 'but young Mark Helston reports that the flooding has worsened.'

'Then what is to be done?'

'Jack and I will investigate the matter,' said Cromwell. 'And we shall do it with all speed, while being mindful of Your Majesty's safety.'

A curious expression came over the King's face. He seemed almost gleeful. It was hard to keep up with his moods.

'Not just you two,' he said, his eyes bright. 'I will help. I cannot sit idly by, trapped here, with a killer on the loose. After all, with my acting skills, I will be an asset.'

God's teeth! It was bad enough Cat trying to take charge but now King Henry was doing exactly the same. I had the feeling I'd come to a sticky end if I had to obey both of them.

I saw a flash of panic in my master's eyes. I understood his concern. How could we let our monarch loose in the investigation? How could we stop him?

The King sat purposefully on the largest chair in the

room. 'What do we know about this murder?' he went on, slapping his hands on his knees.

I realised that Master Cromwell was waiting for me to speak. I began to tell his Majesty what I'd found out.

'Are you saying that Sir Reginald was poisoned and someone shut this Bessy up when she spoke about it?' interrupted the King. 'Sounds as if the boy has lost his wits, Thomas!'

'I agree it seems an impossible tale,' replied Cromwell. 'But Jack has linked a weapon to the old woman's wound.'

'Has he, by St George!' King Henry listened intently while Cromwell told him about the stout stick covered in blood and the splinter in Bessy's hair. 'So it's murder indeed – and I'll warrant that both murders were perpetrated by the same person!'

'I think you have it, Sire,' said Cromwell, as if this was news to him. 'It's possible too that Lady Margaret was an intended victim of the poison and was lucky to survive.'

And don't forget poor Joe the scribe, I wanted to add. Cat would be proud of me now, remembering the underdog.

'There's something else, Your Majesty,' I said. 'Mark Helston saw a cloaked figure out in the grounds, not long before Bessy's body was discovered.'

'Then doubtless young Helston saw the murderer,' murmured the King, rubbing his hands. Cromwell and I nodded as if this too was something we hadn't considered. 'My task is clear. I shall speak to Lady Margaret and ask her who might have wanted her husband dead. I shall tell her I am investigating on behalf of King Henry. And that would be the truth.' He leaned back in his seat, looking pleased with himself.

'I know you will break it to her gently, Sire,' said Cromwell. 'She has no inkling of any foul play.'

'And Your Majesty must tell Lady Margaret to speak to no one about the matter,' I burst out without thinking.

The King shot me a furious look for my impudence.

'If the murderer came to know that Yeoman Brown is investigating his crime,' I went on quickly, 'then Yeoman Brown could be the next victim.'

Before King Henry could speak, Cromwell came to my rescue. 'Perhaps the danger is too great for our esteemed monarch to undertake and we should reconsider your involvement . . .'

'Curse it, Thomas!' hissed the King, struggling to keep his voice down. 'If I don't act, I will soon be dead anyway – from boredom!'

'As Your Grace pleases,' murmured Cromwell, bowing politely.

His face was the picture of obedience but I could imagine that inside he wanted to lock his monarch safely up and throw away the key.

'I shall go back into the Great Hall and speak with our hostess. I saw her there not a moment ago. Do not fear. I shall report my findings to you as if I were one of your agents.' The King made for the door but then turned. 'This is a strange feeling, is it not?' he said in glee. 'I am trying to solve a dire crime but it is exciting all the same.'

He grinned and gave Cromwell a mock bow. 'I will be your best investigator.'

And he headed off.

As soon as he'd gone Cromwell turned to me. He looked grave. 'We have no choice but to go along with our Sovereign's wishes. I would that it were otherwise.'

'So I am to do nothing more, sir?' I asked, disappointed.

'That would seem to be the case, Jack,' replied my master. 'However, if you should happen to be lurking in some corner from which you can hear the King's conversation, then I would not be averse to hearing what was said. After all, His Majesty may miss the little details.'

'I understand,' I replied.

'Good.' Cromwell smiled. 'Then go and start lurking immediately!'

16

I went into the Great Hall. The King and Lady Margaret were heading towards the fire. I marched up the stairs. I wanted it to look as if I was going to the scribes' room. The moment I was out of their sight, I ran along the landing. I was just hurtling past the grand bedchambers when Nicholas Mountford came out of the King's room. He grasped my arm, bringing me to a halt.

'Have you seen His . . . Yeoman Brown?' he asked, worry pulsing in every word.

'He's safe,' I said. 'He was in with Master Cromwell when I saw him just now.'

Mountford mopped his brow. 'I've never had such a difficult few days, Jack,' he said. 'You have no idea how hard it is to make sure the King is safe and keep that job secret!'

Little did he know how well I understood!

'So I have some minutes of freedom.' He rubbed his hands eagerly. 'I shall go up to the battlements and enjoy the solitude.'

I continued with my hurtle, almost throwing myself down the winding stairway beyond. Then I followed the passage that led past the kitchen and workrooms and back to the Great Hall. Luckily the door was closed.

I opened the latch and put my eye to the gap. It was a good position. I could make out King Henry standing next to Lady Margaret's chair in front of the fire. Her ladyship's face was drained of blood.

'And poor Bessy didn't fall?' she was saying. 'She was done to death because she claimed that my husband had been poisoned? How did she die?'

'I will spare you the details,' said the King, taking a seat beside her. 'Can you think of anybody who might wish to kill you and Sir Reginald?'

'I cannot imagine anyone wishing us dead,' replied Lady Margaret weakly. 'Of course my husband dealt with all our business but he was known to be a fair man and never did harm to a soul. He would agonise for hours over difficult decisions which might hurt another. Indeed, I believe his illness was made worse because his conscience was tormenting him over something that was not of his making.'

'Do you know what was tormenting him?' asked the King eagerly.

'It was a distressing time,' said Lady Margaret. 'There was trouble with Franbury Abbey.'

The abbey. This was interesting. I remembered the monk talking to Ruth and Charlie's worry that a monk would not come to Bessy. I listened hard, hoping that I was about to solve another line of this baffling riddle.

'Tell me all about it at once,' ordered His Majesty, forgetting his role for a few moments. 'I mean . . . if you can bring yourself to.'

'I will try, Mister Brown,' said Lady Margaret, 'but I don't quite understand these matters. The Norbrook family owns the land and buildings of the nearby abbey and Reginald needed to take them back.' She pulled at her sleeve distractedly. 'My husband must have been very short of money to resort to that. Now it falls to me to do the dreadful deed.'

'When the monks heard of your husband's decision, what was their response?' asked the King.

'Father Crawley was very angry,' Lady Margaret went on in an unhappy voice. 'I understood why. Naturally he didn't want to lose his home – he and all his monks.'

I would have whooped in excitement if it hadn't risked giving me away. The monks certainly had a motive for murder.

'Have any from the abbey come to Norbrook Castle since Sir Reginald died?' was the King's next question. 'Someone who might have heard of Bessy's accusations?'

'Not that I know of,' said Lady Margaret. Then the horrible thought seemed to strike her too for she could hardly get her words out. 'You don't think . . . surely a monk would not do such things . . . Is it possible, Mister Brown?'

'There are those who would,' replied the King bitterly. 'There is much corruption in our abbeys nowadays.'

'But would a man of God go so far as to kill? Poison us and murder Bessy? Besides, no one from Franbury Abbey has brought anything to the castle that could contain poison.' She stopped, aghast. 'Except the beer!' she whispered.

'The beer, my lady?'

I strained to hear Lady Margaret's next words. 'Father Crawley sent a gift after they heard of my husband's decision. We thought it was to help persuade Reginald not to take the abbey back. It was a keg of their best beer, especially for the two of us.'

'Indeed?' said the King. 'And you both drank it?'

'We didn't intend to. My husband felt we could not accept such a thing. But the steward did not get his instruction to send it back. We found it had been served at our meals.'

'I warrant that was the moment you both fell ill!' exclaimed the King.

'It was,' said Lady Margaret in horror. 'You have it exactly, Mister Brown. I was soon fighting for my life and Sir Reginald was on his deathbed.'

'It sounds likely that this was your poison,' said the King. 'It had struck me as odd that so few in your household succumbed to the plague. But wait . . .' He pulled at his beard thoughtfully. 'The beer does not account for Joseph, your scribe. He also died, supposedly of the same disease.'

Her ladyship looked perplexed. Then she gave a brief smile. 'Ah, poor Joseph. Our young scribe was a wonderful lad, but full of mischief. He must also have taken some of the beer meant for his employers. It would not have been the first time.'

King Henry slapped his knee. 'Then I think we may have our killers, madam!' he said triumphantly.

An expression of relief came over Lady Margaret's face.

I was wondering how Cromwell was going to take the news that our new investigator thought he'd found the murderer, even though he had little proof, when His Majesty seemed to come to his senses.

'But I will not discount the other suspects yet,' he said importantly. 'Depend upon it, my lady, I will leave no stone unturned until I find the culprit.'

'I pray you won't alarm my servants,' she said. 'They've been through so much.'

'I will speak of this to no one else, my lady,' the King assured her. 'For we do not know how many are involved. You have my word . . .'

God's wounds! For one terrible moment I thought the King was going to keep his investigation secret from Cromwell and me. Surely a monarch would not break a promise.

'. . . My word as a yeoman guard,' His Majesty finished. It was a relief. Yeoman Brown would say nothing to us – but our King still could.

Lady Margaret got to her feet. 'I am so grateful, Mister Brown,' she said. 'But please forgive me if I leave you. This news . . .'

'I quite understand, dear lady. It must have been most distressing.' The King rose too. 'I hope I have your permission to make a thorough search of the castle.'

'Will that be necessary?' asked Lady Margaret wearily.

'I fear that it will. The finger points to evil-doers outside your home, but who knows what I may find here. We cannot rule anything out.'

Lady Margaret said nothing more but nodded and walked slowly away.

Suspects were piling up faster than the bodies! I thought about the latest addition to the list. There was a difficulty. How could anyone at the abbey have known about Bessy's accusation – unless they had an accomplice here at the house? Could that have been Ruth? Anselm had been close by according to William but had she had time to get to the abbey and fetch him? There were horses in the stable.

I felt a hand grasp my shoulder.

17

Heart thumping, I swung round, fists ready to do battle. Cat was grinning at me.

'I've been searching everywhere for you!' she whispered. 'Up and down stairs, in and out of rooms and there you are, skulking in a passageway while I've been busy.'

'I'm not skulking,' I insisted. 'I'm lurking.'

She looked at me as if I was mad. 'What nonsense. Anyway, I've got more information for you.'

'If it's about Franbury Abbey . . .'

'Nothing to do with that. It's about Fulke – you know, the drunkard who burst in on our breakfast yesterday.'

'What about him?' I asked.

'Well, I got this from Charlie, and he'd had it from Mister Brandiscombe who heard it right from Fulke's own mouth on the day he was dismissed from his service at the castle.'

'What did he hear?' I said, trying to be patient.

'He heard Fulke threaten Sir Reginald,' said Cat, pleased with herself. 'He heard every word.'

'And are you going to tell me what the words were?' I asked, struggling to keep my temper.

'All in good time.'

'If you don't tell me soon there'll be another murder at the castle!' I hissed.

'You'll be sorry for this day's work,' retorted Cat.

'What?'

'I'm telling you what Fulke said, you dolt,' she laughed. 'He said to Sir Reginald, "You'll be sorry for this day's work."'

'Yet nobody's seen him since,' I said thoughtfully. 'Until yesterday. And I don't know how he could be linked with the abbey. You see, Lady Margaret thinks the monks might have been behind the poisoning.'

'Perhaps they were all in league,' Cat suggested. 'Now, out of my way. We'll have to discuss it later. I must get on.' In a second she was gone.

I wondered if Cat was right. But I certainly wasn't going to unravel that bit of the mystery in a hurry. I'd report it all to Master Cromwell, along with what I'd heard of the King's investigation.

I pushed open the door, intending to march straight through to the steward's office.

'Jack! Come and join us.' His Majesty waved me to a stool. My master was already there. The King lowered his voice conspiratorially. 'There is much to tell.'

I sat down, enjoying the roaring fire. It was almost sunset and Barnabas was just finishing lighting the candles on the walls.

'His Majesty has been telling me that his investigation is progressing well,' said Cromwell in a low voice. 'He has found out some very important information.'

'It took careful questioning,' said King Henry. 'As a result I will be clearing up this matter very soon.' He leaned forward in his chair. Our monarch was enjoying his new role. I hoped he wasn't going to try to keep it up back at Court! 'I'm not supposed to be sharing any of this with you. However, I am not breaking a trust. I assured Lady Margaret of my silence only as Yeoman Brown.'

'Most clever, my Liege,' murmured Cromwell.

The King related his conversation with Lady Margaret. At one point my master looked at me questioningly. He wanted to know if the King's report was accurate. I gave a slight nod. Although His Majesty was painting a very vibrant picture of his role as an investigator, the essence of it was true.

'In short, Lady Margaret was most helpful . . .' The King glanced over my shoulder and his manner changed abruptly. 'Of course, the Brown family have lived near Bognor for centuries,' he said, in a booming voice. 'We're mentioned in the Domesday Book, you know.'

For a moment I thought he'd lost his wits. Then I heard a soft footfall behind me. I turned. A tall figure was coming down the stairs. It was our hostess.

'That's enough of a history lesson for you today, Jack,' said Cromwell loudly. 'You can thank Mister Brown and return to your duties.'

We all started at a frantic knocking on the gates. Barnabas opened the grille, spoke with someone briefly and hurried to open the wicket door. A man stumbled in. He looked exhausted, his clothes mud-stained and sodden with rain.

His hollow eyes fell upon Lady Margaret who stood motionless at the foot of the stairs. He staggered past Barnabas and across the Great Hall towards her. In a flash, the King was in front of her, his sword drawn.

18

As we stood facing the intruder, Lady Margaret calmly put a hand on the King's arm.

'Please do not worry, Mister Brown,' she said. 'This gentleman is no threat. He is Reginald's younger brother. I am pleased to see you, Edward. But you look as if you've had a hard journey.'

'You speak as if nothing has happened, Margaret,' said the newcomer gruffly. 'I've come directly from the coast. When my ship docked I was greeted with the terrible news that Reginald was dead. I made my way through this infernal weather, all the time praying that the report was false. My horse lost a shoe and threw me in the mud so I walked, desperate to be here. And now Barnabas has confirmed my worst fears.' His voice broke and he covered his face. 'The last words I spoke to my brother were in anger. If only we hadn't quarrelled.'

'Come and warm yourself by the fire, Edward,' said Lady Margaret. 'You've had a terrible shock. I am sorry that I had no way to pass you the news sooner.' She beckoned to Barnabas. 'Please fetch food and wine.' The porter scuttled off to the kitchen.

Nicholas Mountford hurried down the stairs. 'I saw this man arrive,' I heard him murmur to Cromwell.

'All is well,' my master assured him, but the yeoman took his place at the King's side.

Edward Norbrook tossed aside his sodden cloak and threw himself into a chair. Lady Margaret sat down opposite him. I stood very quietly in the background, hoping I'd been forgotten. There was silence for a while, broken only by Edward draining a goblet of wine and munching hungrily on some pork and bread. His doublet steamed in the heat of the fire.

'I'm sorry for intruding when you have guests, Margaret,' he said, suddenly seeming to notice that the three men were still there. 'But we need to talk of . . . family matters.'

'You can talk freely,' said Lady Margaret. 'These gentlemen have been helping me in all my affairs.'

'Then I'm very grateful to you, sirs,' said Edward, pouring himself some more wine. 'But I am back now and will take over the running of my estate.'

'*Your* estate, Edward?' asked Lady Margaret, looking puzzled.

'The castle, of course,' he replied. 'I am Reginald's heir.'

I caught Cromwell's eye. Edward Norbrook had not wasted many tears over his brother's death before claiming his inheritance.

'He left everything to me,' said Lady Margaret quietly.

'But that's impossible,' gasped Edward. 'The Norbrook Estate has always stayed in the family. You and Reginald had no children so it comes to his only brother.'

'I would have believed that too if I hadn't seen the will with my own eyes,' said Lady Margaret softly. 'Reginald was heartbroken after your quarrel. He must have changed it when you left so angrily.' She gestured towards Master Cromwell. 'It was only when I received help that it came to light.'

'You're lying!' shouted Edward, jumping to his feet. 'Reginald would never have changed his will!'

'How dare you speak thus!' The King moved quickly to protect Lady Margaret. Mister Mountford was by his side – but I knew who he was protecting!

Edward was a tall man but King Henry and the yeoman towered over him. He slumped back into his seat.

'Lady Margaret speaks the truth,' said Cromwell, his voice low and calm. 'I have seen the will.'

'And who are you?' spat Edward, jabbing a finger at him. 'Some crony of Margaret's hoping to share the spoils?'

I thought the King was going to hit him but Cromwell held up a hand.

'On the contrary, I am a lawyer and acting on Lady Margaret's behalf in this,' he said. 'My name is—'

'I don't care what your name is,' shouted Edward. He rose, snatched up his cloak and made for the door. 'This is my castle and I will have justice!'

The slam of the wicket door echoed round the walls. We all stood in stunned silence. The only sound was the rain pounding against the windows. I glanced at Master Cromwell. He gave a very slight nod towards the door. I was to follow Edward Norbrook.

I bowed and walked sedately up the staircase as if I was returning to work. As soon as I was out of sight I bounded like a hare towards the spiral stairs, hoping that Oswyn didn't choose that moment to drag me away to work. As I passed the window seat I tore off my jacket with its castle livery – I couldn't risk that being recognised – and threw it into the alcove.

I hurtled down the staircase. Everyone in the kitchen was busy preparing the evening meal. Taking the chance that I wouldn't be noticed in all the noise and bustle, I slipped out. I ran round the castle walls to the wicket door, fearing that my prey had got away. It was almost dark now but to my relief I spotted a figure on the path ahead, making for the trees. Edward did not slacken his pace. I hurried to keep him in sight, dodging from tree trunk to bush. The rain splattering on the

leaves was loud enough to drown out my footsteps –
and the chattering of my teeth.

The moon was up but dark clouds scudded across
the sky. The trees were thrashing about in the wind,
their bare branches reaching out like fingers. The
whole wood seemed to be alive with monsters. Edward
Norbrook himself cut an unearthly figure, his cloak
flying out behind him.

He left the trees and turned briskly into a narrow
winding lane. There was no shelter here from the cold,
stinging rain and it was too dark to see the puddles
before my feet sank into them. Some were so deep my
shoe was nearly sucked from my foot.

I tried to drag my frozen mind back to my
investigation. Edward Norbrook's apparent distress
over his brother's death didn't sit well with me. Had
his behaviour been nothing more than playacting, I
wondered? I remembered how quickly he'd brought
the talk round to his inheritance. It seemed important
to him. Having quarrelled, could Edward have killed
his brother in order to get it? It was possible that he
hadn't come from his ship at all, but had been in hiding
somewhere nearby. And did he have an accomplice at
the castle who had told him of Bessy's words? Could it
have been Ruth? I thought about my suspects. Edward
Norbrook, the monks, Ruth and Fulke, the disgraced
servant. Were they all involved in some dreadful
conspiracy?

Edward came to a high wall. I followed along at a

distance. Instead of deep puddles, there was long wet grass here to trip me and soak me to the knee. But the wall gave some shelter from the driving rain.

I flattened myself against it as Edward stopped and turned to look behind him. I had to trust to the darkness. It was hard to control my shivering, with my sodden clothes and my back against freezing cold stone.

I waited for him to move on, but instead I heard the sound of a bell ringing out. Then silence. It rang again. Finally bolts slid across and a door creaked slowly open. I got a brief glimpse of a monk's habit. There were low urgent voices and Edward Norbrook was taken inside.

As soon as I heard the door close again, I made my way to where he had stood – at a gatehouse in the wall. Fixed above was a large wooden crucifix and beyond, against the dark stormy sky, rose the unmistakeable outline of an abbey chapel.

My master had said that there was only one such place in the area.

Edward Norbrook had come to Franbury Abbey!

19

My puzzled mind tried to grasp what this meant. The man who'd thought he was going to inherit Norbrook Castle had come to see the very monks that Lady Margaret believed had poisoned her husband. Surely this wasn't a coincidence! I could only find out more by getting inside. After my twelve years of abbey life, I knew that a traveller would always be welcomed, but not a traveller who wanted to sneak around and investigate.

The wall was old and crumbling. I stifled a gasp as I saw grotesque figures standing on top of it. Was the place protected by supernatural creatures? Then the clouds cleared for a moment and I realised they were just gargoyles glaring down at me. When Cromwell had warned me about flights of fancy, I was sure he'd never imagined I'd be conjuring up monsters in the forest and goblins on walls. These were not the actions of a cool-thinking spy.

I blew on my hands to warm them and began to climb the rain-slicked stone. Battling the howling wind, I pulled myself onto the top and crouched low, thanking the Lord and all the saints that the bad weather meant there was little moonlight to expose me.

I jumped down. A narrow path led over to the main buildings of the abbey. I could just make out two figures going through a door, a welcoming light spilling through.

'Jack!'

The voice had come from above. I looked up to see one of the gargoyles flapping its arms at me. Even as my deranged brain thought I was being spoken to by an ugly statue, I recognised Charlie.

'What are you doing here?' I hissed.

'I've come to help.' He landed next to me. 'They said in the kitchen that Edward Norbrook had burst in and threatened our mistress. And then I saw you slipping out and I knew you were after him.'

God's oath! I should have known that sharp-eyed Charlie would spot me leaving. If he ever got to Court he wouldn't be spit boy – he'd be taking my job!

'You're right, Charlie,' I said. 'I want to find out what Edward's up to. Everyone's been very kind to us at the castle and I'm determined none of you will come to harm. But you should go back. You'll be missed.'

There was a chance that the abbey was full of murderous monks, and I wasn't going to put Charlie in danger.

His eyes glittered with pleasure. 'I've covered my tracks,' he told me triumphantly. 'I told Mister Brandiscombe that I had a terrible bellyache and he sent me to bed.'

I admired the boy's thinking. Certainly Oswyn wouldn't care that Charlie wasn't there when he went up to the bedchamber. He'd just think he was being ill in the jakes. I hoped Oswyn wouldn't notice I wasn't there either. Hopefully he'd think I was ill too and in the jakes, puking my supper up.

Mark's anxious face popped into my head. With luck he'd also think I was stricken with the bellyache otherwise he'd be all for sending out search parties.

'It was very brave of you to come, Charlie,' I said. 'But you have to go home now.'

His face fell in dismay.

'But I want to track Edward down,' he declared. 'If it comes to a fight I'm ready for him!' He clenched his fists threateningly.

'That's not going to happen!' I made my voice stern, although I wanted to laugh at the thought of the little kitchen scullion locked in combat with Edward Norbrook! 'We can't run the risk of you being recognised,' I went on desperately. 'By the monks or by Mister Norbrook.'

'I won't let them see me,' said Charlie.

'It's too dangerous,' I said. 'Just go home! And tell no one where we've been. Otherwise we'll both lose our jobs.'

For a moment he looked mutinous. Then to my relief he hung his head and slowly climbed the wall. I could imagine just how he felt, deprived of his adventure. Yet I knew I'd done the right thing.

But now I'd lost my prey. I edged along a wooden building, making for where I'd seen the two figures enter the abbey. A faint whickering told me I was passing the abbey stables. I yearned to go in and bury myself in the warm, dry straw.

I reached the abbey door and eased it open a crack. A low murmur of conversation reached me as I peered into the room inside.

It was a small chamber, lit only by two stubby candles. Several travellers sat talking at a nearby table, huddled together for warmth. I knew I must be in the outer parlour. Travellers would be fed here and then shown to a bed for the night in the strangers' lodgings. The parlour was one of the few places in an abbey where talking was allowed and I could hear a low murmur of voices. At first I could see no one else in the room. But then I picked out the shape of a man seated on a stool in a shadowy corner. The man seemed agitated and unable to sit still.

'Edward!' A monk had entered through an arched door on the other side of the chamber and went over to him. It was only when Edward knelt and kissed the monk's hand that I realised that this must be Father Crawley, the abbot whose anger Lady Margaret had reported to the King. His plain grey habit was nothing like the clothes worn by the abbot of my childhood. Father Busbrig was always garbed in a very ostentatious silk robe and a fur-lined cloak when there was the slightest hint of a chill in the air. Father Busbrig wouldn't have bothered talking to travellers unless he thought they'd be generous to the abbey coffers, and then he'd hustle them off to a private bedchamber and roaring fire.

But I refused to be fooled by my eyes. Humble dress did not make a godly man.

The abbot sat down with Edward. I needed to get closer without Edward seeing me, in case he recognised me from the castle. I would have to play the traveller after all. I slipped through the door and quietly took a place on a bench on the other side of the table. The cold water dripped off my shirt and made a puddle on the earth floor!

A wizened old man in a grey habit came over with a jug of ale and filled a tankard for me. He looked thin and ill and had a rough blanket round his shoulders. I guessed he was a plague survivor. He motioned to me to take food from a platter but there wasn't much on offer. Trying not to shiver too violently, I took a piece of dry bread. The taste reminded me that I'd had no supper and my belly felt like a huge empty cavern.

I edged along the bench, keeping my face shielded and acting for all the world as if I was interested in the biblical carvings on the wall.

Edward suddenly jumped to his feet and I caught his next words.

'You don't understand! I, too, thought the inheritance would be mine but it's not.'

The abbot seemed horrified. He rose quickly and indicated to Edward to follow him.

'Come with me,' he murmured. 'We'll go where we can talk freely.'

I was about to get up and follow when a wrinkled hand caught mine. 'You've barely touched your food.'

I turned to see the old monk, his mouth open in a toothless grin – and cursed inwardly as I heard the arched door close on Edward and the abbot.

'I feared you were a ghost when you came in,' croaked the old man, as he eased himself onto my bench. 'I said to myself, Simon, that boy is too pale to be flesh and blood. What's your name, lad, and what brings you out on such a dire night?'

'I'm Ja . . . James,' I said. It didn't seem sensible to give my real name. 'I've come seeking a bed. I've heard there's a castle nearby and I've been making my way to it to find work but the rain was too bad for me to carry on. If you'll kindly point the way to the strangers' lodgings . . .' I rose.

Brother Simon's expression darkened. 'It'll be Norbrook Castle you're talking about!' he spat. 'Its lord and master – Sir Reginald – was going to turn us out to beg. He didn't even have the nerve to come and tell us in person. Instead he sent a letter to tell us he wanted his land back and there was to be no argument and we were no longer welcome at the castle!'

'How terrible!' I said. My search for Edward would have to wait. I might find out something important from Brother Simon. 'Has he changed his mind now?'

The monk shook his head. 'Not he! But God has punished him, for the plague took his life and now he must surely be in Hell.' His thin voice rose as he spoke, and several heads turned our way. Another monk came in through the arched door and hurried over to our table.

'Are you quite well, Brother Simon?' he asked gently, laying his hand on the old monk's shoulder. It was Bessy's nephew, Anselm.

'It's a wonder that I am well!' exclaimed Brother Simon. 'When the name of that devil Reginald Norbrook passed my lips, I marvel it did not stick in my throat and choke me.'

'Hush, now!' urged Brother Anselm. 'This is ungodly talk and we should not speak ill of the dead.'

I pretended to be interested in my bread while sneaking a look at the man. Was that a fleeting moment of fear I saw in his eyes? He was trying to sound like a good monk who wouldn't say bad things about others. But I had seen him sneaking out of the castle. Was he shutting Brother Simon up before he could tell me too much?

20

Brother Simon began to struggle to rise from the table.

Anselm offered his arm. 'I'll take you to your bed,' he said.

His apparent kindness could well be a ruse to get this talkative old man away from a nosy boy. I gnawed at my crust as he led Brother Simon to the arched door. I would be hurrying through there myself as soon as they were gone to look for Edward but their progress was as slow as two snails trying to lose a slithering race.

At last they were out of sight. I got up and made a big show of yawning as if I was now seeking my bed. Checking that the passage was empty, I slipped through the door. The abbot had taken Edward Norbrook somewhere they could talk. My abbey upbringing had been grim but it was proving very useful now. I decided to find the Chapter House. Talking was allowed there and strangers were not, so it was the perfect place for a private conversation. I crept along cold, dark passageways, past the refectory, the richly carved doors of the abbey chapel and several empty dormitories, their occupants no doubt in the graveyard, dead from the plague. The silence was so deep that every one of my footsteps seemed to shout out 'intruder!'.

At last I saw a faint light from under a closed door. I hurried up to it and pressed my ear to the wood.

'But Edward, I must counsel you against this dangerous path.' That was the abbot speaking.

'Have no fear, Father,' Edward replied. 'My plan cannot fail. And it will benefit us both.'

Whatever Edward was planning, I was sure it didn't bode well for Norbrook Castle. But I heard no more. Footsteps came to the door and the latch lifted. I leapt back and flattened myself against the wall so that I was hidden behind the opening door. Edward Norbrook and the abbot came out and set off down the passage. The candle in the abbot's hand flickered as he scurried along to match Edward's frantic pace.

I crept after them, keeping to the deep shadows.

'So you won't heed my advice?' Father Crawley sounded worried.

'No,' Edward answered tersely. 'I am determined on this course of action, Father, and I can call on expert help. We both stand to lose our homes if I do not win back my inheritance.'

'Well, if you will not reconsider, then the very least I can do is light you on your way.' The abbot took a lantern from the wall and snuffed out his candle.

So now I'd learnt that the abbot knew of Edward's plans and didn't like them. But all I'd heard of those plans were mere hints. I had to keep up with the man and find out more.

The cloisters lay ahead of us. The rain had stopped but it had driven through the open arches round the square and water was dripping off the edges of the vaulted roof. The lantern lit up large puddles on the flagstone path ahead of the two men as they hurried along. But behind, I was plunged into darkness. Edward thrust open a creaking door. I waited a moment before I risked going after them. I eased the door open, praying it wouldn't give me away and slipped through.

I used the wall to guide my way. The men must be far ahead as there was no helpful lantern light. The passage turned. A sharp voice spoke.

'I thought we were being followed!' Edward Norbrook lunged at me. I turned and fled back into the cloisters.

I had to get out of sight. I leapt onto the plinth of one of the columns. Reaching up, I hooked my fingers round a cross-shaped hole in the stone and pulled myself onto the roof above. There was a break in the cloud and a brief patch of moonlight showed a shuttered window close by. I began to prise it open.

'Where is he?' Edward's voice reached me from below.

'Do you think it was a thief?' asked the abbot.

'Why would a thief be following me?' growled Edward. 'When I left the castle I let my anger get the better of me. I told Margaret that I would return. I warrant she's sent a spy and if I get hold of him I'll . . .'

'Peace, Edward,' came the abbot's calm tones. 'This will not help your cause.'

I felt the shutter give way and swing open.

'What was that?' whispered Edward. 'It came from above. Give me the lantern.'

I slipped through the narrow gap, dangled by my arms for a moment and let myself drop. I could just make out that I was in a large chamber with mounds of sacking on the floor. As I tried to thread my way towards the door, I caught my foot and toppled forward onto one of the mounds. To my horror it let out a groan.

'Help!' it cried, sitting up. 'I'm being attacked.'

I tried to make my escape but all round, men were waking up and shouting.

I didn't know whether I was in one of the monks' dormitories or in the strangers' lodgings but whichever it was, I had to get out. Kicking away grasping hands, I threw myself out of the door and dashed down the passageway, heading I didn't know where.

I slipped into a little room, hoping I'd find another means of escape. A thin beam of moonlight had managed to get through the cracked glass of a high window. It showed a pestle and mortar, a shrivelled sprig of lavender and a row of glass jars on a workbench.

I was in the physic room where the apothecary would make his medicines – and possibly even a poison. An apron lay in the dirt on the floor. I didn't think the apothecary would be wearing it again. The room seemed abandoned and I reckoned he'd died in the plague.

I climbed onto the bench. The window was no use to me. There was no way of opening it. If I stayed any longer I'd be trapped.

I darted back out of the room. All was quiet, but as I reached a corner I could hear running footsteps. Edward Norbrook was still after me.

The doors of the chapel lay ahead. They were slightly open and the footsteps were coming closer. I took a gamble that the chapel was empty. It was too early for the Matins service, even if this community had it at two in the morning. I didn't think it was even midnight yet.

I hastily crossed myself and crept round the stone floor looking for a hiding place. The chapel was small and plain. Smelly tallow candles lit the altar but that was the only light. It was still enough to show me I was not alone. A solitary figure was kneeling in silent prayer in front of the statue of the Madonna. I knew I shouldn't intrude on anyone's private devotions but I was sure the Lord would understand that I was seeking sanctuary.

I crouched behind a pillar. The monk began to speak. 'Mary, Mother of Forgiveness, forgive me,' he mumbled, twisting his hands as if in agony. I recognised the voice. It was Brother Anselm and he was about to make a confession!

I listened hard. The monk wasn't using any of the prayers that were familiar to me. Perhaps he was too distressed to bring them to mind.

'I have done a terrible thing. I did not want to do my Christian duty yesterday. First I did not want to go out in the rain to visit the sick of the village. I only went reluctantly and not with the glory of God in my heart. But my second sin is worse.'

I held my breath. Was Brother Anselm about to confess to Bessy's murder?

21

I scarcely caught the monk's next words over the pulsing of blood in my ears.

'I spoke falsely,' he whispered. 'I was returning from visiting the sick of the village when I was asked to go to Norbrook Castle to pray over a poor soul who had just died. Because the hand of friendship in that place is no longer extended to us, I pretended I had rheumatism and could not walk far. I did this even though I knew it was my own dear aunt who lay there.' He wrung his hands in anguish. 'It is no excuse but I relented and went to her in the end.' He looked up at the statue of the Virgin Mother as he continued. 'Have pity upon me and take away the awful stain of my transgressions.'

So that was the sin that had weighed so heavily on Brother Anselm's conscience! He'd had no part in Bessy's death.

One of the chapel doors suddenly swung open,

banging loudly against the stone wall. Brother Anselm immediately fell silent, hands clasped tightly in prayer. Edward Norbrook entered and began to search. I cowered even further down behind my column, feverishly trying to think of some excuse if I was discovered.

'Anselm,' Edward declared, coming upon the kneeling monk. 'I am so sorry. I have disturbed you.'

Brother Anselm rose to greet him. 'I had finished,' he said. 'But I did not know you were here, Edward. Is it your brother's sad death that brings you to us?'

Edward hesitated. 'In a manner of speaking. I wish I had time to stay, but I have . . . pressing business.'

'You're travelling so late and on such a night?'

'I have no choice,' replied Edward awkwardly. He was obviously keeping his schemes from Anselm. 'I must take my leave of you. Father Crawley has offered me one of the horses.'

'Then I will unlock the gate for you,' said Anselm, 'and I will give you my blessing as we go.'

The two men left. I didn't dare move until I heard the chapel door close. I knew where the stables were. I determined to get there first. When Edward rode away, I would be galloping after him. Brave words, I decided, coming from a boy who still had trouble staying in the saddle. However, my lack of horsemanship couldn't get in the way of my mission.

I ran along the dark cloisters and out through the gardens. Following the boundary wall past the gatehouse, I came to the stables. A horse was tethered at the door, saddled and ready. I could see a bobbing lantern making for the gatehouse. I didn't have enough time to tack up another mount – even if I could remember how to! My ride was going to be bareback, and I had to be ready to go the moment Edward Norbrook left.

I hurried towards the stable door, but the cursed animal took fright as I approached and backed away, blocking the entrance. It stamped its hooves in panic. I knew better than to risk sliding under its belly to get inside.

I heard the gate creak open. Now the lantern was coming to the stables.

There was nowhere to hide, not a bush, tree or helpful statue. My only possible escape was over the high wall. I ran at it and tried to claw my way up. But this side was smoother than the other. I fell heavily to the ground.

A piece of cloth suddenly flopped down in front of my nose. 'Grab hold!'

I looked up. Charlie was perched on the wall.

'I thought you'd . . .' I began.

'Don't argue!'

I didn't. Feet slipping, I pulled myself up, using the cloth as a rope. I realised it was Charlie's breeches.

We crouched behind two gargoyles.

Below us, Edward swung himself into the saddle. He whipped the horse round, gave a wave to Anselm and was gone in a thunder of hooves.

I'd lost my prey.

'Thanks, Charlie,' I said when Anselm had locked the gate and walked back into the abbey. 'But you really should have gone when I told you.'

'I know,' said Charlie, cheerfully pulling on his breeches. 'But aren't you glad I didn't? Did you find out what Mister Norbrook's up to?'

'No,' I said. 'Let's go home.'

We plodded through the rainy night back to the castle. It seemed twice the distance for my weary, frozen feet.

I hadn't quite told Charlie the truth. I now knew that Edward was scheming to get his inheritance and that the abbot wasn't happy about the plan. Had they dreamed up the poisoned beer together and then silenced Bessy, and now Father Crawley was regretting his part in the sordid business?

I was sure that Brother Anselm was innocent but that didn't absolve Ruth, his cousin. And who was the cloaked figure, seen soon after Bessy's death?

There was one thing I was very certain of. This mystery was as tangled as a nest of vipers.

∽

It seemed hours before the castle loomed up ahead of us. In fact it hardly loomed at all. It was so dark we nearly missed it! An image of a warm, dry bed seemed to beckon, but I knew that getting to it wouldn't be easy.

'Everything will be locked up now,' said Charlie, running up to the wicket door. 'I'll wake Barnabas.'

'You mustn't do that,' I hissed. 'Remember no one must know we've been out.'

I wondered if I could rouse Mark by throwing stones at our window but that would be sure to disturb Oswyn. However, I remembered Weasel-face moaning about the ill-fitting window and the draught.

'We've got to climb up to our bedroom window,' I told Charlie.

'We can use the ivy,' he said eagerly. 'I've always wanted to do that.'

I found a stick to use as a lever for the window, put it between my teeth and we began to climb.

It would have been a simple climb in the dry, but no stone or leaf had escaped the lash of the rain. My cold fingers were practically numb by the time we reached the window. One hand clutching a branch of ivy that I prayed would hold long enough, I began to lever the window open with the stick. Slowly a small gap appeared.

Charlie wriggled in. I saw him pull off his wet clothes and slip into bed.

Sucking in my breath I began to squeeze myself through, nearly slicing my ears off in the process! I was doing well until I suddenly got stuck. God's blood, my breeches were caught on the window clasp. I was dangling, my top half in the room and my legs kicking uselessly outside. I seized the window ledge and heaved. With a dreadful tearing noise I popped through the gap like a cork from a keg of over-fermented ale. I hurtled head over heels across the floor and crashed into Oswyn's bed.

'Wassgoingon?' he muttered, sitting up.

22

I couldn't risk Weasel-face finding out that I'd just come in through the window. He would be delighted to spread the news. I did the only thing I could. In one expert move I slid under his bed. The mattress straw crackled above me. By the glow of the fire embers I could see Oswyn's bare feet rushing to the open window.

'Intruders!' he yelped. 'Robbers! Help!'

On the other side of the chamber Mark stirred. I poked my head out and put my finger on my lips. For a second I wondered if he hadn't recognised me in the dark and would join Oswyn in his panicky cries.

'Shhh, Oswyn,' he said. 'You've had a bad dream. There's no one here.' I was amazed. Mark wouldn't normally have dared to speak like that to Weasel-face.

'It wasn't a dream!' snapped Oswyn. 'The window's

wide open. Someone's sneaked in. They're going to murder me in my bed.'

I wanted to call out that this was impossible as he wasn't in his bed but I thought I'd better not.

'What's the matter?' came a drowsy voice from above my head. I was torn between admiration for Charlie's excellent acting and annoyance that he was in bed and I wasn't.

'Oswyn's had a nightmare,' called Mark, still brave in the teeth of Weasel-face's anger. 'Go back to sleep, Charlie.'

'Tell me about it tomorrow, won't you,' murmured Charlie. The creak of the mattress over my head told me he was pretending to settle down again.

Oswyn began to creep about, poking nervously into the dark corners of the room. How soon would it be before he noticed the empty place where I should have been? How long before he found me?

'I don't believe it!' I heard him exclaim. 'All this noise and Briars is still asleep!'

I lurched in surprise and nearly hit my head on the bed frame. What was he talking about? His feet were planted next to the mattress I shared with Mark and he was prodding something in it. I peered past his legs to see what it was. There was a Jack-shaped lump in the bed! Mark must have put it there so that no one suspected I wasn't around. He had covered for me.

'Don't disturb Jack,' said Mark, quite fiercely for him.

'Why shouldn't I?'

'Er . . . he gets nasty if you wake him.'

'Oh.' Oswyn actually sounded scared! He dropped his voice to a whisper. 'I've checked the room now and I think we're safe.'

I was sure I heard a faint sigh of relief from Mark as Oswyn's feet tiptoed towards me and the bed sagged.

It was only then that I realised I couldn't risk pulling the Jack-shaped lump out of the bedclothes and getting in myself, not while Oswyn was awake. I'd have to spend the night under the bed. And however tired I was, I knew I had to be up before the others so that I could get rid of dummy Jack. I silently thanked my old abbey training, which had me rising so early for services. Shivering in my wet clothes, I closed my eyes.

゜

I'd thought I was too cold to sleep but I woke with a jolt from a dream where I'd plunged my arm into solid rock, trapping myself for eternity. In a panic I tried to sit up, banging my head on the wooden slats of the bed above. I froze but no one stirred. My left hand was numb where I'd laid on it, which explained the dream. The patch of sky through the window told me it was nearly dawn. Sliding from under the bed, I crawled across to my mattress. Mark had done a good job with the dummy. I lifted the bedclothes carefully and slid out an old blanket and a cabbage.

Spreading the blanket gently over Mark I tucked

the cabbage under my arm and went down to put it back in the kitchen. As soon as Master Cromwell was awake I'd report my findings at the abbey. No doubt my master would tell the King to warn Lady Margaret that her brother-in-law had not given up his fight for the inheritance.

My shirt was still damp so I took it off and hurried through the silent passages to the alcove where I'd hidden my Norbrook livery jacket and pulled it on. I tiptoed past the important bedchambers but no one stirred.

For the first time in about a hundred years, I began to feel some warmth return to my body. The jacket was made of good, thick wool. The Norbrooks certainly did treat their servants well.

It was dark in the kitchen. As I made my way round the table, my foot caught on something and I fell flat on my face. The cabbage flew from my hands, bounced off the wall and hit me on the head. Behind me I heard a scream and then a voice.

'Don't move. I've got a knife.'

23

For a moment I thought I'd fallen over the murderer. Though I couldn't work out what he was doing sprawled on the kitchen floor. Then I realised I recognised the voice. It was Cat's.

'It's me,' I said, sitting up. 'What are you doing down here?'

'I was trying to sleep,' said Cat, putting down her weapon, 'until some galumphing idiot woke me up.'

'What's wrong with the bed you had?'

'It was Bessy's room,' said Cat quietly. 'I couldn't sleep there once she'd died.' She fumbled about and lit a candle. 'Anyway, where were you last night and why is there a cabbage on the floor?'

'I was out late and Mark put it in my bed and pretended it was me.'

'He had the right idea,' she scoffed. 'You've as much sense as a cabbage!'

'In that case you won't be interested in where I was or what I found out.'

'Have you solved the mystery then?'

'No,' I admitted. 'I followed Edward Norbrook to Franbury Abbey, but if anything I've just given myself more questions. I've still got to find out what Ruth, the monks and Edward Norbrook have been up to.'

'You're forgetting someone,' said Cat airily.

'Who?' I demanded. 'If you mean Brother Anselm, that's one thing I'm certain of. He's innocent.'

'Not him,' said Cat. 'Fulke. You know, that drunkard who came here.'

'We already know that he can't have done the poisoning,' I insisted. 'He wasn't working here then and hadn't been seen since he was dismissed. And why would he have killed Bessy if he had nothing to do with Sir Reginald's poisoning?'

'Listen to this.' Cat settled herself importantly on a bench. 'Last night at supper, Mister Brandiscombe was asking where you were and Mark said you had a pile of work to do.'

Well done, Mark Helston, I thought gratefully.

'And Mister Brandiscombe said he was glad that you were safe inside the castle as he'd seen Fulke, dead drunk as usual, shouting abuse at the gates and saying again that he was owed money and he'd be coming to get it.'

'And how does that help us?' I asked, wondering where this story was going.

'Be patient and you'll find out,' said Cat.

I could have wrung her neck!

'Then William piped up. He said he didn't understand why Fulke was going on about his money when he'd seen him coming from the castle, chinking a pouchful of coins, just before Sir Reginald took ill. Everyone was surprised at that.'

'So he had the opportunity to poison him after all,' I gasped.

Cat nodded smugly.

'We need evidence,' I said. 'I wonder where he lives.'

'Where who lives?' Charlie bounced into the kitchen.

'Fulke,' said Cat.

Charlie was wide eyed. He grabbed me by the sleeve and pulled me into the stillroom.

'Are you going after him now?' he whispered, obviously remembering that no one was to know about our nighttime adventure. 'I won't be coming with you this time, Jack. It's one thing trailing Mister Norbrook but I wouldn't go within a mile of that villain.'

'Don't worry, Charlie,' I said, 'I'm not going anywhere near Fulke.' I hoped that was true. With luck the man would be in the tavern. Mister Erskine had said he practically lived there.

'That's all right then,' said Charlie, leading the way back to the kitchen. He began to stack the fire.

'I was just being nosy about Fulke,' I said casually. 'Only Cat heard that although he demands money, he lives in a great big manor house.'

'Don't know where you got that from, Cat,' chuckled Charlie. 'He lives in a hovel on the other side of Wicken Wood. It's right under a burnt out oak.' He flapped his hand in the direction of the herb garden. 'Now I must wake Mister Brandiscombe,' he said and disappeared.

'I'm going to Fulke's house before Charlie gets back,' I said.

Cat looked at me. 'You'll stand out like a pig in a palace in your castle livery – especially with that huge hole showing half your bum.' She scuttled off and threw me a rough brown jacket and some breeches from the laundry. 'Come on. What are you waiting for? I'll mend yours when we get back.'

I knew there was no point in arguing that I was going alone. She was coming with me and that was that. I decided not to let on that Charlie had been with me last night. She'd be furious that she'd missed out and would never let me forget it!

As we went, she dived into the dairy and came back swathed in a thick cloak. She pulled the hood up over her head. She saw me looking enviously at its warmth.

'This seems to be spare,' she told me. 'It's usually hanging on the door. There's only the one – but you can share it if you insist.'

'I won't be cold at all,' I said. 'Let's go.'

Cat caught at the hem of her cloak and bunched it into one hand. 'It's a bit long,' she said. 'I have to hold it up.'

'As long as it doesn't hold *you* up,' I said.

I waited for her to make some clever answer but she caught my arm. 'Who's that?' she whispered.

I followed her gaze. Ruth was scurrying among the plants in the herb garden. She bent swiftly to pick handfuls of leaves. We watched, hidden by an angelica bush, while she furtively tucked them into her apron. Then she began to hurry back to the house.

'Why is she making such a secret of it?' hissed Cat.

'I don't know,' I answered. 'But I do know one thing. You can concoct lots of nasty potions with the right herbs.'

Before I could stop her, Cat had burst out from our hiding place. 'Ruth!' she called.

The tiring woman spun round, fear all over her face. She saw us, clutched her apron tightly to her and quickened her pace. Cat broke into a run, her cloak flying behind her.

I followed at her heels, fearing that she'd give away our intentions. I should have known better.

'I'm glad we've caught up with you,' panted Cat as we overtook Ruth on the path.

'We saw you picking something and Jack and me had a wager. Jack said it's sage for a chicken pie – his favourite – and I said don't be silly, greedy guts, it's not Ruth's job to pick herbs for the kitchen. It'll be to make her mistress's room smell sweet. Put us out of our misery. Show us what you picked.'

'I'm in a hurry,' mumbled Ruth. She tried to push

past. The leaves tumbled to the ground. Ruth gave a cry and moved to cover them with her skirts, but not before we'd seen the innocent sprigs of rosemary and lavender lying scattered on the path.

'Don't tell anyone,' she breathed, gathering them up hastily. 'I shouldn't pick anything without my mistress's say so. But these are the herbs my mother loved the most, God rest her soul. I will make a posy from them and lay them on her grave when the weather allows her to be buried.' Tears spilled down her cheeks.

She looked genuinely distressed. But I watched her face intently as Cat took her hand. 'That's a lovely thing to do,' she said softly. 'You must miss Bessy so much.'

Ruth nodded. 'And I shall never forgive myself,' she sobbed. 'I let my mother go out on her own to her death. I even stopped you accompanying her, Cat. If someone had been there with her she may not have fallen. The guilt will haunt me for ever.'

'You can't have known what was going to happen,' I said.

'That is true,' said Ruth. 'I confess I was vexed with her for she'd kept on at me for days about this poisoning story till it nearly drove me mad. I tried to tell her to forget it for I didn't want her alarming the household with her imaginings. And when she said it in front of everyone I was not as patient as I should have been. And now it's too late.'

She stumbled away, wiping her eyes.

'I've been wrong about Ruth,' I said as we watched her make her way back to the house. 'Unless she's the best actor the world's ever known, I don't think she had anything to do with the murders.'

'I'm certain she didn't,' said Cat, brushing away a tear. She shook herself. 'But we can't stand here feeling sorry for her. We're wasting time!'

We headed into the trees beyond the herb garden. A narrow path led away from the castle. We followed it, pushing aside the brambles that threatened to hide it. I was sure we were going the right way. This path would have been well trodden when Fulke worked at the castle but now the woods were taking it back.

When we came to the burnt out oak we looked for Fulke's hovel. It was so covered in creepers that at first glance it looked like a very small, lumpy hill.

We couldn't hear any sound from the house and no smoke rose from the chimney. We crept through a wet tangle of ivy and nettles and tiptoed nervously up to the door. I put my ear to the rotting wood.

'I'm sure there's no one in there,' I said.

'Hopefully he's in the tavern as usual,' whispered Cat.

Behind the house we came upon a wilderness that showed signs of having once been a vegetable patch. An old well stood here. It still had its winder and rope, under a little roof with cracked tiles. The bricks were crumbling and the bucket long gone.

We plunged into more undergrowth. I stubbed

my toe on a broken spade and steadied myself on a rosemary bush that had gone so woody it was almost a tree. Now we could see a path leading away through the brambles, thick with a pattern of footprints in the mud.

'That'll be his route to the tavern, I'll be bound,' said Cat.

I stepped forward and went flying over something hidden in the long grass. I scrambled to my feet and saw that I'd landed on bits of woven straw that had once been a beehive.

'I hope Fulke doesn't come back now,' said Cat with a nervous laugh. 'What would he do if he found you'd broken his precious skep?'

'I didn't break it,' I protested, brushing straw from my clothes. 'Fulke must have done it last summer so he could collect the honey.'

'What do you know about beekeeping?' scoffed Cat.

'Quite a lot,' I said. 'When I was at the abbey I worked with Brother Luke and his bees. He said there were two ways of collecting honey. His way was to smoke the swarm out of the skep first. That way the bees could come back afterwards. And the other way was to destroy the skep.'

'And what happened to these bees?' asked Cat.

'I don't know,' I said, 'But I don't suppose Fulke cared if they lived or died. Let's try and get inside the house. We might find something more useful than broken skeps in there.'

Cat reached out to push aside the shiny green leaves of a tall bush.

'Stop!' I yelled in alarm. She drew back her hand as if the bush was on fire. 'That's oleander,' I explained. 'It's really poisonous.' I looked around. Most of the bushes had the same leaves. 'How strange. The ground's covered in the stuff. Keep right away from it.'

'Well I wasn't going to eat it!' exclaimed Cat impatiently.

'You mustn't even touch it,' I told her firmly. 'Brother Luke told me about it. It's dangerous on your skin, deadly if you eat it and . . .' A long forgotten memory was stirring in my head. '. . . And it gives you swellings so people mistake it for the plague!'

We stared at each other.

'Fulke is either very bad at keeping bees or he put that skep next to oleander on purpose,' I said. 'Either way the bees would most likely collect the lethal nectar from the flowers.'

'Wouldn't that kill the poor things?' asked Cat.

'No,' I said. 'The bees aren't affected, but even the honey from oleander nectar can be fatal to anyone who eats it.'

'The victims at the house all took honey,' breathed Cat. 'Does this mean we've found out who our poisoner is?'

'It's possible,' I said, knowing I mustn't jump to conclusions. 'But can you imagine going to Master Cromwell and saying that Fulke is the murderer because he was seen near the castle just before Sir Reginald fell ill and he's a useless beekeeper!'

'He'd simply stare at you in that way of his,' agreed Cat. 'So we've got to prove it one way or another.'

We waded through the tangles towards the back door. I seized the handle. 'This one's locked too,' I told Cat. 'There must be another way in.'

A small rickety outhouse leaned against the corner of the cottage at such an angle it looked as if it was about to push it over.

'I'll search in here,' I said. 'There might be something that links Fulke with the murder of Sir Reginald.'

'Do you think there'll be poisoned honey there?' asked Cat.

'That's quite possible,' I said, 'but I'm not willing to test it to see if it's poisoned. Are you?'

She shook her head.

'And neither will Fulke,' I said. 'So we need to take honey back to the castle, get him arrested and ask him to taste it. If he refuses, then we'll know it's poisoned.'

'That's clever.'

I nodded wisely.

'I'll try that window and see if I can get it open,' said Cat, pointing to a filthy bit of glass high up beside the door. 'I doubt there's much holding it in place.'

She dragged a pail over and stood on it.

The ramshackle outhouse was padlocked but the metal was so rusty it broke in my hand. I heaved open the door and went inside. I doubted that the place had

146

been used for years. Apart from spiders' webs and rat droppings it was completely empty. I'd just turned to go when I heard someone coming. A man was making for the cottage. I recognised the short, powerful figure.

It was Fulke.

I was hidden but Cat was in plain sight! She seemed to have frozen. I looked desperately for a stick to defend her with. There was nothing.

The man stopped at the well. He'd seen Cat. I braced myself to leap out at him but his words took me completely by surprise.

'Good morning to you, Lady Margaret,' he called.

25

Cat stood very still. I could imagine her terror. I willed her not to turn round, for as soon as she did, Fulke would see his mistake. I cursed myself for bringing her into danger.

Then I came to my senses. I had to put my mind to my investigation. Something very strange was going on. He'd greeted Cat as Lady Margaret – he seemed to recognise the rough cloak as hers – and he was not surprised she was there. Why would her ladyship be visiting this disreputable man? It didn't make sense.

Fulke had an unpleasant smile on his face. 'Changed your mind, my lady? Have you come to pay what you owe? After all, I won't be able to give you any more of my special honey until you do. That would be such a shame. They say it works wonders.'

Cat remained frozen to the spot.

'You'll have noticed the tiny pieces of leaf I added

to the last preparation,' Fulke went on, as if he was an apothecary. 'They will have sped up the . . . effect.'

I felt sick. This man had known exactly what he was doing with his hives and its deadly produce. Had he tricked Lady Margaret into believing the honey was a cure for the plague while all the time it was poisoning anyone who ate it? Lady Margaret had been lucky to survive!

I could see Cat's hand where she gripped the window. Her knuckles were white.

'Why the silent treatment?' jeered Fulke. 'You'll soon be talking to me when you want my talents to remove your next husband and take his fortune!'

The gearwheels that were whirling in my brain finally meshed together. Fulke hadn't tricked Lady Margaret at all. She'd known exactly what she was doing when she fed his lethal honey to Sir Reginald and Joe. She knew they would die and that everyone would put it down to the plague. I was willing to wager that she'd feigned illness and none of that honey had ever passed her lips.

Lady Margaret was the murderer!

'Think you're too good to talk to me, do you?' Fulke roared at Cat. He marched up to her and took her by the arm, spinning her round. She gave a cry of terror as the pail beneath her toppled. She tumbled to the ground, legs caught in the cloak. Fulke gazed at her in shock.

'Who the devil are you?' he demanded.

149

'Don't hurt me,' gabbled Cat. 'I . . . I was sent by Lady Margaret.'

I prayed to God that Fulke had seen her in the castle kitchen and would believe she was a new servant. But then I remembered he'd been too drunk to see straight.

'Liar!' snarled Fulke. 'You were trying to break in.' He pulled her roughly to her feet, ripping the cloak from her.

I wanted to rush to her rescue but I knew Fulke would see me coming and might harm Cat before I could get there. I was wondering if I could creep round to the other side of the cottage and come at him from behind when Cat began to cry.

'I'll tell you the truth,' she whimpered. 'I made that up about your Lady Margaret. I don't even know who she is but I was scared. I meant no harm. I've walked from Tunbridge and I'm lost. I'm trying to find the abbey and I was that thirsty. I hoped you might spare some water.' She looked up at him imploringly.

Good old Cat, I thought. *Her acting would melt the hardest heart!* Surely Fulke would believe her story. But his eyes narrowed.

'I'm not swallowing that one!' he snarled. 'It's too late for excuses. You've heard more than is good for you.'

'I don't know what you're talking about,' wailed Cat. 'I'll be on my way now. . .'

'You'll be on your way all right!' shouted Fulke. He

swept her up and threw her over his shoulder. 'On your way to Hell!'

He strode off down the path.

'Let me go!' shouted Cat, beating her fists on his back.

Instinct told me to leap at him and tear her free, but reason took over. He had Cat clamped to him like a vice. I couldn't equal his strength. I sprinted up behind him and kicked as hard as I could. My foot thudded into his calf. I'd done enough fighting to know that the pain should be excruciating. With luck, he'd drop Cat as he writhed in agony.

But Fulke turned on me with a roar. 'Another sneaking worm!' he snarled. 'I might have known she wasn't working alone. I'll deal with you when I've done with your friend.'

He aimed a vicious punch at my head and swore as I ducked. 'Where are you taking me?' yelled Cat, squirming helplessly in his grasp.

'You'll find out soon enough,' growled Fulke. He turned and strode on.

In desperation I leapt and grasped him round the neck to pull him down. But the man was almost square, and as hard to topple as a rock.

Cat's frightened face peered into mine as I tightened my hold. She clawed desperately at her captor's jacket. I felt a strong grip seize my wrist. With one hand, Fulke threw me aside as if I was an annoying insect. My head thudded against a tree trunk, dazing me for a second.

I struggled to get up in the tangle of undergrowth, ripping my flesh on sharp brambles.

An icy stab of fear ran through me. Fulke was heading for the well.

Cat couldn't see ahead, but she caught my expression of horror. Fulke stormed through the bushes like a siege engine. I made after him, stumbling in my haste. I didn't know how I was going to stop him but I had to find a way.

With a horrible laugh, he lifted Cat and held her over the well. Now, at last, she knew the fate he had in store for her. Terror flooded her face.

I hammered my fists into Fulke's back. My desperate attack had no effect. He caught Cat's flailing legs and thrust her down into the well. Cat clung to the edge of the brickwork, sobbing as she tried to pull herself out.

I leapt at him again but he held me off with an iron hand.

Then he stretched the other towards Cat. For one mad moment I thought he was going to save her. But I was wrong. He slammed his fist down on her fingers. I pulled myself free of his grasp and threw myself at the well but it was too late.

For as long as I live, I'll remember her despairing scream.

And then the silence.

26

I stared down into the black hole of the well, anger burning in my belly. Even if Cat was still alive, this madman would never let me rescue her. I turned to face him. Something flashed in his hand. He had a knife.

'I'm going to spill your guts,' he snarled.

He slashed at me. I jumped aside just in time but my foot caught on a root and I fell. He gave a cry of triumph and leapt forwards. I grabbed a handful of earth and threw it into his face.

He cursed, spitting mud. I was already on my feet, charging at him, ramming my head into his belly. We crashed into the wet brambles. I scrambled onto his chest, caught his knife hand and held it with all my strength.

Fulke lifted his head and butted me hard on the chin. I collapsed beside him, the pain filling my head with shooting stars. I forced myself to stay conscious.

He grasped me hard round the neck.

'What's it to be?' he hissed. 'Would you like to choke to death or shall I be merciful and cut your throat?'

In desperation I scrabbled for more soil. My fingers connected with a stone – heavy and sharp. I swung it with all my strength into his forehead. The rough edge made a deep cut.

'You devil,' he snarled as blood gushed down, running into his eyes.

But he'd loosened his grasp. I rolled away and sprang to my feet.

Fulke got up unsteadily, trying to wipe away the blood. His face distorted with pain and fury, he plunged the knife at me. In his half-blind state I managed to dodge, knocking his arm away. He crashed down, face first, and let out a horrible gurgling groan as he hit the ground. I stood over him, ready to strike again if he moved. But he lay still. Too still. Was this a trick? I shook his shoulder, braced for a counter-attack, but still he didn't stir. With both hands I hauled him over onto his back. His eyes stared blankly up at the sky, his own knife in his heart.

Fulke was dead.

I felt as guilty as if I'd plunged the knife into his chest myself. But I had to banish it from my mind. Cat needed me. I ran to the well, trying in vain to see down.

'Cat!' I yelled. 'Are you all right?'

Nothing.

'Cat!' I called again. 'Answer me.'

I heard a faint noise. My heart leapt.

'Cat!'

And then there came a sound so quiet I thought I'd imagined it.

'Jack?' Cat's voice was weak and quavering. 'Help!'

'I'll get you out!' I yelled down, my voice echoing away into the dark.

Trembling with relief, I snatched the rope hanging from the winder and made a firm loop in the end.

'Here it comes!' I turned the winder handle as fast as I could, sending the rope down to Cat.

'Where?' Cat sounded frightened. 'I can't see it. It's as black as pitch in here.'

I could imagine her in the darkness, cold and bleeding. 'It should be with you any moment. Don't worry. I'm not leaving until you're safe with me. You'd never let me hear the end of it if I did!'

I knew that didn't make sense. I was trying to keep her spirits up – and mine.

'Got it!' I heard her faint call at last. The rope went taut. I gripped the handle of the winder and heaved. It took all my strength to turn it. The wood creaked under the strain, and my shoes slipped on the waterlogged ground. I lost my hold. Without the pressure the winder began to whizz round the other way. I heard Cat give a frightened cry.

I seized the handle, stopping it in its flow. Using my toes, I dug a hold for my feet and turned the crank again. My arms were aching. The pain shot across my shoulders but slowly I began to win.

At last I saw her head appear. She flung a hand over the brick wall, and tried to heave herself out. I let go of the rope and helped her, dragging her like a sack of turnips. She collapsed on the ground. Her wet clothing was clinging to her and her head and hands were lacerated with long scratches.

'Thanks,' she said in a faint voice. 'Seems you're making a habit of saving my life!' She started to shiver violently. I ran for the cloak that Fulke had torn off her, wrapped her in it and held her tightly, trying to share some of my body heat.

'I hit my head as I fell.' Her teeth chattered as she tried to speak. 'I must have blacked out for a moment because the next thing I knew I was up to my neck in freezing water.' She gazed round wildly. 'Where's Fulke?'

I didn't say anything but looked down to the ground. She followed my gaze and gasped when she saw the body. 'Good riddance,' she muttered under her breath. I wished I could dismiss the man's death that easily. Then her eyes filled with horror. 'It's unbelievable! Lady Margaret and Fulke. They were in it together!'

'It makes sense of Mark's story about seeing Death near to where Bessy was found,' I said.

Cat nodded. 'He said it was a tall cloaked figure. Do you think this is the very cloak that wicked woman used to disguise herself for her visits here? Or an identical one? It's not a highborn lady's garb, but Fulke seemed to recognise it.'

'I'm sure you're right. He saw a cloak he knew, and had no idea it hid a seamstress standing on a pail. He immediately thought you were someone much taller – Lady Margaret.'

'So when Bessy cried murder, it must have been her ladyship who silenced her,' said Cat. 'I wish *she* was down that well, may God forgive me.'

'She's not going to get away with it,' I said. 'Master Cromwell needs to know the truth about the King's sweet and innocent hostess. She poisoned her husband and Joe the scribe with the honey from Fulke.'

'So Edward Norbrook had nothing to do with the deaths,' said Cat, her teeth chattering so loudly now she could barely get the words out. 'And the monks at the abbey are innocent too.'

'I think so,' I replied. 'The poisoned beer was another invention of Lady Margaret's.'

A dreadful suspicion jumped into my head. 'The King!' I yelled.

'What?' Cat looked astonished. 'Surely he's not involved in all this!'

'Of course not!' I answered. 'But he could be in danger.'

'How?'

'He insisted on investigating the murders himself – and he told Lady Margaret that he and he alone would find the killer.' Fear clutched at my heart as I remembered his last words to her. 'He said he'd need to make a thorough search of the castle. She didn't seem very happy with the idea. I thought it was because she didn't want her household upset. The truth was she was scared he'd find something that proved her guilt!'

'So if she believes he's the only one who's investigating,' gasped Cat, 'all she has to do is kill him and she's safe.'

'We must get back to the castle straight away,' I said. 'Can you walk?'

'Try and stop me,' said Cat. 'I want to see my lady's face when she's found out.'

❦

We burst into the kitchen. Everyone was busy, rushing about trying to get the noonday meal ready.

'What's happened to you?' asked Mister Brandiscombe, stopping us. Luckily he hadn't noticed my borrowed garb. 'Why are you soaking wet, girl, and shivering fit to burst?'

'She fell in the pond,' I said as I darted round him and pushed my way to the door. Cat tried to follow but the cook already had a blanket round her and was steering her towards the fire. I knew I couldn't wait. I had to find the King. I dashed out of the kitchen and ran straight into Mark in the passageway.

'I'm so glad you're here, Jack,' he panted, looking askance at my battered state. 'I've been searching for you everywhere. I have terrible news.'

158

'What's the matter?' I asked, hoping not to hear another tale of the flood waters!

Mark could hardly get the words out. 'It's the Ki . . . Mister Brown, I should say. He's been taken gravely ill.'

A wave of horror nearly stopped my heart.

'First he insisted it was nothing,' Mark went on. 'He said he must have eaten too much of Lady Margaret's gingerbread last night. And that could have been true. Oswyn told me about the gingerbread. It seems Oswyn loves it as much as Mister Brown does, especially as it was made with honey, and yet he didn't get to taste one mouthful. And anyway it cannot be that, for this morning he is worse.'

'Who's with him?' I asked. I already knew but hoped desperately that I was wrong.

'Thanks be to God, he's in good hands,' Mark replied. 'They carried him to his bedchamber and her ladyship is nursing him herself. She's dosing him with honey to speed his recovery.'

27

'We must stop her,' I said desperately. I knew I could trust Mark and I might need his help. I just wouldn't tell him the whole story. 'Lady Margaret's special honey is full of poison.'

'That's terrible,' gasped Mark. 'How do you know?'

'There's no time to explain,' I said, pushing past him. 'And you cannot tell a soul about this. I must get to the King.'

I could see Lady Margaret in my head, smiling sweetly at Mister Brown while she was planning instead how to stop his investigations once and for all! She'd only had to make her gingerbread with plenty of Fulke's honey for her victim to fall ill. And now she was spooning deadly poison into his mouth to finish the job. From what Fulke had said, it wouldn't take long.

I sprinted to the Great Hall. It was empty apart

from Barnabas, who nodded to me from his post at the entrance door as I sped by. I made for the stairs, intending to go to the King's bedchamber and wrest the spoon from Lady Margaret's hands. But at that moment a tremendous thumping on the huge wooden door stopped me in my tracks. A barrage of heavy blows rattled the door.

With a frightened shout Barnabas threw his weight onto it.

'We're under attack!' he yelled.

There was no mistaking the roar of angry voices outside.

I dashed to help Barnabas shoot the bolts across and lift heavy bars into their brackets as the wood shook with its beating.

'Who's attacking?' I asked.

'I don't know.' The porter looked terrified. 'This house is truly cursed.' He reached for a rope hanging on the wall and pulled. Immediately a harsh warning bell clanged out, echoing round the stone walls.

The clamour brought Nicholas Mountford running, William and Mister Brandiscombe close behind. Frightened servants were crowding round us. Barnabas began to hand out weapons from the armoury store.

'Is it the Scots?' cried the cook.

'Bandits, more likely,' growled William.

'I bet it's pirates!' said Charlie, trying to lift a battle-axe from the floor.

Whoever it was, I had to get to the King. It would be

a hollow victory if we defended the place only to have him dying all the same. I slipped to the back of the crowd so I could creep away unnoticed.

'Surrender the castle!' came a cry from outside. 'I, Edward Norbrook, am come to claim my inheritance. I have a loyal crew of sailors, who have faced many dangers with me on the high seas. They will stop at nothing in this endeavour. Open the door now and no one will be hurt.'

The servants looked at each other.

'Master Edward?' said William in surprise.

'He always was a wild one,' muttered Mister Brandiscombe. 'Though I thought he had a good heart.'

'Surrender, I say,' came the shout again.

'Never!' I heard Charlie yell. Everyone cheered.

And now I understood what I'd overheard at the abbey. Edward must have told the abbot that he was going to take the castle by force and claim his inheritance. The abbot had tried to persuade him not to attempt it. But he was as hot-headed as everyone said and wouldn't listen. I cursed him for his poor timing.

Something crashed against the door, and splinters flew through the air, making us all leap back in alarm. The hinges creaked under the strain.

'They're using a battering ram!' shouted someone.

A frightened gasp rippled through the servants.

The next onslaught burst the bars in half.

'Open up or suffer the consequences!' came Edward

Norbrook's voice. 'We have a good strong trunk here and will smash the door in.'

The door shuddered again, the bolts straining and bending with the pressure. I couldn't see how it would survive another battering.

'Stand back.' Nicholas Mountford took charge. 'We can't stop them getting in. Make ready to attack as soon as they enter.'

It was plain that all inside were united in their purpose, ready to defend their home from whatever was coming. Cat, still pale but determined, had joined the throng, and I saw Mark too, trying not to let his nerves overcome him. His face mirrored the fear that everyone felt.

I knew I should stay and fight. But I had to defend my King from a poisoner. Fearing I might already be too late, I ran towards the stairs.

The deafening sound of splitting wood ripped through the hall. The doors crashed to the floor, bolts and bars shattered. As I reached the bottom of the staircase, Edward Norbrook burst in with a roar, leading his rabble of sailors armed with cutlasses and clubs.

The years at sea had hardened their faces. They ranged themselves around their captain and I believed that they would fight to the death for him.

I felt as if I was on the rack, being pulled in two directions. One part of me was desperate to get to the King and the other knew that the castle must be defended.

Nicholas Mountford stepped forward. 'Yield now and you may go in peace,' he said.

'I'll not be told what to do in my own home,' snapped Edward. He lunged at Mountford. I just had time to see the yeoman move expertly to one side and deflect the blow before I found a brawny man standing in front of me. His eyes, small in his bristly face, stared at me greedily. He drew his cutlass. I was unarmed and helpless.

'Catch!' I heard Cat shout. Before I knew what was happening a sword was speeding through the air in my direction. I caught it by the hilt, amazed that I hadn't missed and cut my fingers off. I tried to call to mind what His Majesty had taught me but this fierce, heaving fight was nothing like the calm of that courtyard lesson. I remembered the King's warning. These men certainly didn't keep to the rules. Well, nor would I.

As my enemy swung his blade at my head I ducked and struck him in the stomach with the pommel of my weapon. He stumbled back clutching his belly, crashed into the wall and slid down in a crumpled heap.

I could see Mountford facing two men at once and close to him was a figure I knew only too well. My master! I was amazed to find Cromwell was a skilled swordsman. I'd heard that when he was young he'd fought in foreign wars. I'd thought it was a made-up story. I believed it now.

A roar had me spinning round to face another

invader. He swiped at me with a wooden club. I dodged the worst of it but his blow caught me on the shoulder and I went tumbling across the floor.

As I struggled to my feet, he came at me again, his weapon raised to crush my skull. There was a loud clang and his fierce expression turned to surprise. Then his knees folded and he collapsed to the ground. I rolled out of his way. Charlie was standing on a table. He'd ditched the battle-axe for a frying pan. 'That'll teach him!' he yelled.

'Thanks, Charlie!' I yelled back.

I jumped to my feet, my stomach churning at the thought of the King in his chamber, all the while taking the deadly honey in the mistaken belief that it was helping to cure him. I could bear it no longer. I had to go to him.

And suddenly there he was. King Henry himself stood on the stairs, tall and strong in his borrowed clothes, his own sword in his hand. He looked truly majestic. Perhaps Mark had got it wrong. But as he came down the steps I could see he was staggering and his face was pale and covered in sweat.

I felt a mixture of relief that His Majesty was away from the clutches of Lady Margaret and despair at the sight of how sick he was. The King raised his sword and I turned to find Edward Norbrook advancing on him.

'You are making a grave mistake,' said King Henry. 'Lay down your arms now and you may be forgiven.'

'Brave words,' scoffed Edward. 'Let's see if you can fight as bravely.'

He lunged at the King. There was a clang of blades and Edward staggered back. He was on the lower stair and, as I watched, the King pressed his advantage, beating Edward down towards the throng.

But I could see His Majesty was tiring. Only his iron will was keeping him going. He needed help, and no one had seen his plight but me. I pushed through the fighting to get to him.

Edward made a vicious thrust at the King. He avoided the blow with a clever feint to one side and swung his sword at Edward. Edward parried and their weapons clashed again, their faces close. The King grasped Edward's doublet and pushed him away, sending him tottering down the steps. But it seemed to have taken its toll on his remaining strength. His knees buckled and I saw him collapse onto the stairs.

Edward gave a cry of triumph and went for him.

I dodged swords and cudgels and leapt to stand between him and the King.

Edward laughed. 'A sprat to slice in half!' he snarled.

I threw myself to one side as his blade slashed through the air at me.

With an angry growl, he attacked. Our swords came together with such a blow I thought my arm would be shaken off. He thrust again and I tried to avoid it but his sword sliced through my shirtsleeve like butter. I felt a sharp stinging sensation as the blade cut the flesh. I darted out of reach, waving my weapon to hold his attention away from the King. I didn't know how long I would succeed. I was a skinny boy who'd had one sword lesson but Edward was tall and strong and obviously well used to fighting.

Now I remembered the King's advice. He'd said a tall man cannot easily defend his legs. A low swipe with a blade could unbalance him. How to get close enough to do it? Edward would have split me in two long before.

I dodged away to a table, seized a heavy wooden dish and skimmed it across the floor as he came at me. It thudded against his legs. He yelled in pain. I raced round behind him and followed with a move I'd seen when I was playing football in Acton Village. I launched myself at him with both feet. My heels smashed against his ankles, sending him tumbling to the ground, his sword spilling as he fell.

He scrabbled for his weapon, but I was too quick. I jumped onto him, my knees pressing hard into his back.

I gripped the hilt of the huge, heavy sword as steadily as I could and held the tip to Edward Norbrook's neck. I was dimly aware of scuffling movements and muffled cries behind me but I kept my eyes fixed on him.

'Call your men off,' I said, sounding more assured than I felt. Inside I was quaking.

He didn't answer and I increased the pressure on the

blade. I had no intention of actually hurting him but I hoped he didn't realise that.

'Surrender or die!' I yelled.

Edward bellowed a command. All around us the fighting gradually stopped.

Some of the sailors lay bleeding on the floor, others were being held captive. Charlie was marching up and down waving a ladle and crowning any enemy who dared to move! Ruth was helping Mark to tie up a wound on William's leg. I tried to find Cat, but there was no sign of her.

A hand was laid on my shoulder. 'You have done well, Jack.' My master was standing beside me. 'I shall see to Norbrook now.'

'But ... Yeoman Brown!' I exclaimed. I jumped to my feet. His Majesty was lying motionless at the foot of the stairs. And I was aware of a figure coming down towards him. Lady Margaret stopped and took in the scene below her. I was sure I saw a brief flash of triumph in her eyes.

28

The gloating expression was soon gone, replaced by a look of shock that only I knew was fake.

'How could you do this, Edward?' she said. She sounded so sincere that I began to doubt that I was in the presence of a ruthless murderer.

Two castle servants dragged Edward Norbrook roughly to his feet.

'This castle is my right!' he growled through gritted teeth as he tried to shake them off. 'You have taken it from me.'

Lady Margaret appealed to Master Cromwell. 'As you can see, my brother-in-law has lost his wits. I am, as ever, grateful to you for coming to my aid when I was most in need.' Head high, she walked regally up to Edward, who stood trembling with rage between his captors. 'Reginald told me that when you were boys, you once locked him in the castle dungeon as a jest,' she said softly. 'Now it is your turn. But this time it is no game. That is where you and your miserable band of men will be taken.'

As the captives were herded together the King give a groan. I threw myself down beside him. Ruth joined me. 'He must be injured,' she said, wiping his pale forehead. 'I'll fetch water and bandages.'

'There is no need, Ruth.' Lady Margaret put out a hand to stop her. 'Mister Brown is ill but bravely insisted on coming to fight. I was already tending to him as he had woken this morning with a sickness. Help him back to his bedchamber.'

I jumped to my feet. 'No!' I shouted before I could stop myself. 'If he goes back he will die! He is being poisoned.'

Master Cromwell spun round at my tone, though his hooded eyes gave nothing away. 'No one is going anywhere,' he said coldly. 'Explain yourself, Jack Briars.'

The Great Hall was silent. Everyone was looking at me. What I was about to say would shake the castle to its foundations. I hardly dared to utter a word. Was it possible that I was mistaken?

My master must have read my thoughts. 'Do you wish to take those words back?' he asked. 'Think very carefully before you speak.'

I knew exactly what he was telling me. I had to be absolutely certain that what I was going to say was the truth. I pushed my doubts aside, raised an accusing hand and pointed at Lady Margaret.

'Here stands the one who is poisoning him,' I said in a loud voice that everyone could hear. 'She poisoned Sir Reginald and Joe – and she killed Bessy.'

Ruth's hands flew to her mouth.

Lady Margaret gasped. 'How can you say such a thing?'

'You should be ashamed of yourself,' Barnabas shouted at me. 'Her ladyship has shown nothing but kindness to you and your party.'

'He's gone mad!' This was Mister Brandiscombe.

'Lock him up,' yelled Charlie. 'Along with those villainous pirates.' Charlie's loyalty to the castle was fierce.

I looked desperately round for Cat to back me up but there was still no sign of her.

'No!' came Edward's voice. 'Hear the boy out! I want to know what happened to my brother.'

All eyes were on me again. I glanced at Cromwell, but how could he support me? He knew nothing of this. I was on my own. 'You had some very special honey, did you not, my lady?' I said. 'Made from deadly oleander nectar. You gave it to your husband and to Joe the scribe – and now you are giving it to Mister Brown.'

A murmur of disbelief went round the hall.

'The honey was supplied by your henchman, Fulke,' I finished.

'How dare you associate me with that villain?' gasped Lady Margaret, outraged. 'I wonder at you, Master Cromwell, that you allow this scribe to talk to me so. It is true I give honey to the sick. It has healing properties, as we all know.'

'Then you won't mind taking a bit yourself!' came a voice from the stairs.

Cat came down towards us, carrying a small pot with a spoon in it. 'I found this in Mister Brown's chamber.' Cat had remembered the test I was going to use on Fulke.

'Ignorant girl!' shouted Mister Brandiscombe. 'That'll be her ladyship's medicinal honey. It keeps illness away. This is all the thanks our mistress gets for her care to a guest.'

'Master Cromwell,' said Lady Margaret in a haughty tone. 'I do not understand why I am being treated in this manner. And with Mister Brown lying here so ill and needing his bed. Barnabas, help the poor yeoman to his chamber at once.'

She snatched the honey from Cat's hands and turned to go back up the stairs.

'Lady Margaret,' replied Cromwell, 'you can scotch this rumour in a moment. Take some of the honey and I will then punish the scribe for his impudence.'

I couldn't tell what my master's thoughts were. He'd chosen his words carefully.

'Wait.' This was the King, his voice little more than a croak. For one terrible moment I thought he was going to prevent the truth from coming out. He raised his head to stare intently at Lady Margaret. 'Pray do take a spoonful of your honey, my lady. After all, you claim it has healing properties. It might prevent you from falling ill as I have done.'

The King had guessed the truth! But I feared it was too late. His breathing was laboured and the sweat poured from his brow.

'Why do you hesitate, my lady?' he asked. Every word was an effort.

Lady Margaret stamped her foot. 'This is the last straw!' she snapped. 'I will not be told what to do in my own home by a jumped-up yeoman guard!'

'This is no yeoman guard,' said Cromwell. 'He put on that disguise for his own safety.'

'So who is he then?' she demanded. 'The Queen of the May?'

'Far more royal than that,' I told her. 'Forgive my impudence,' I whispered as I pulled out the seal ring on its chain from inside His Majesty's shirt, slipped it over his head and held it up. 'He is our sovereign, King Henry.'

For a moment there was a shocked, disbelieving silence. I walked round the room, holding the ring for the castle servants to see. Gradually everyone fell to their knees. Their mistress stood as if frozen.

Edward held out his bound hands.

'Forgive me, Sire. I would never have attacked the castle if I had known. I would not for the world have committed treason!'

'You will be dealt with later,' said the King, his voice barely a whisper. 'I command our hostess to take the honey.'

'Where's the harm?' added Cromwell. 'If you're innocent?'

'Very well then,' said Lady Margaret. She scooped a spoonful of dripping honey from the pot.

It felt as if everything I'd found out was about to be turned on its head. There could no poison in it. She wouldn't take it if there was.

Lady Margaret suddenly threw the pot to the ground. It smashed into pieces and honey spread in a pool over the flagstones.

'I cannot do it!' she said, her eyes filling with tears. 'I see the dreadful truth now.' She dropped to her knees beside the King. 'Your Majesty, I must beg your forgiveness for I have been badly used.'

'Explain yourself,' said Cromwell.

'That villain Fulke sold me the honey,' she said, sobbing now. 'Reginald and Joe and I all took it when we were ill. I thought it had been used up but I found the jar yesterday and put it in the gingerbread. I had no idea it was deadly. Fulke must have planned the deaths and hoped to pin the blame on me when all the time he wanted to have revenge on my husband. I have been duped by that evil man.'

'My lady must be right,' Mister Erskine put in. 'Fulke always said he'd pay Sir Reginald back for dismissing him.'

Other heads were nodding.

The King's eyes fluttered and he let out a groan.

'Someone must go to Franbury Abbey,' I cried. I

remembered something that Brother Luke had told me. 'We need charcoal to act against the deadly honey.' My mind flashed back to the almost empty physic room at the abbey. 'I pray to God they have some.'

'No need to go there,' said Mister Brandiscombe stoutly. 'We have charcoal enough from the fire.'

'That's no good,' I insisted. 'This is a special preparation to combat the poison.'

Cromwell turned to Barnabas. 'Do as he says. Take my horse and go to the abbey as fast as you can. Tell them it is for the King.'

Barnabas looked to his mistress. She nodded her head and he ran for the door.

I had to do something. Lady Margaret was winning support again.

'That doesn't explain Bessy's death, my lady,' I said loudly. 'She cried murder so you had to shut her up.'

'How can you accuse me of that?' Lady Margaret's eyes flashed as if she would turn me to stone. She was right. How could I link her to Bessy's death? There were no witnesses. 'Your Majesty, Master Cromwell, you must believe me,' she went on beseechingly. 'I am a weak woman. I would not be able to swing a stick hard enough to kill. It must have been Fulke. Stop this torment now.'

All gazed upon her with great sympathy. Lady Margaret had been too clever. She'd beaten me. She would go free, her conniving schemes unpunished, mistress of her castle. Free to marry and murder again. The only other person who knew the truth was Fulke, and he was dead.

29

Then her words sank in.

'How did you know that Bessy was killed with a stick?' I said.

I saw a flash of panic in Lady Margaret's eyes but she spoke calmly. 'Mister Brown . . . I mean His Majesty said so himself. I hope we can now turn to a more pressing matter. I wish to discover who killed my husband.'

'I already have the answer to that, Madam,' came the King's voice.

'Then please tell me, my Liege.'

'You have condemned yourself with your own words, my lady.' King Henry's voice was barely a whisper. 'I never told you how Bessy had died. Fool that I was, I wished to spare your feelings.'

'Murderer!' Ruth's shrill cry rang through the silent castle.

The tiring woman stumbled to her feet and ran from the Great Hall.

'Ruth is not in her right mind after the death of her poor mother,' said Lady Margaret. 'I shall not be hard on her. Forgive me, Your Majesty, but I fear that in your present weakness you have forgotten our conversation.' She gave a brief laugh.

'I don't think so,' I cried. 'I heard every word and it is exactly as the King says. The only other person who knew how Bessy died was her murderer.'

Lady Margaret's lips tightened. Her eyes flashed round the room. It looked as if she was searching for a means of escape. But she knew there was none. Now she was like a cornered rat – beaten but still ready to fight.

She turned to the King, her face contorted with fury.

'I curse the storms that brought you and your royal party to my home,' she spat. 'Had I been left in peace, I should now be mistress of Norbrook Castle. My husband was a foolish, trusting man, generous to all. He wouldn't listen when I told him that his good-for-nothing brother should not inherit the estate.'

'That was exactly why I quarrelled with my brother!' Edward burst out. 'I feared that he might be persuaded to change his will – for that witch had cast a spell on him.'

'Silence!' ordered Cromwell. 'You have borne arms against His Majesty. Your own future is in grave doubt.'

'I have one triumph left though,' Lady Margaret went on. 'I bested you, Master Cromwell. You thought the will was a genuine one. It was not. It was penned by my scribe, Joe, and my husband's signature was forged. You never guessed, did you? And you call yourself a lawyer.'

I saw my master's lips tighten, but he said nothing.

'Joe also copied out the letter I sent to the abbey demanding our land back – so you see that when my husband ... died, then Joe had to die too. It was easy to persuade everyone that the plague had come to the castle and I alone "nursed" the poor victims, despite appearing to be so ill myself. And then there was poor Bessy, so unsteady on her feet and half-mad. She was easily dealt with. Her skull caved in like a peach.'

Lady Margaret was the one half-mad now. She spat out her words and fixed us all with eyes that looked as if they could shoot flames.

'Take her away,' said Cromwell wearily to Nicholas Mountford. 'She can try out her own dungeons.'

'And when the floods subside,' whispered the King, 'she will go to the Tower for her treachery. Poisoners do not die easily.'

Mountford began to force Lady Margaret across the Great Hall. Her servants fell away, muttering angrily as she passed.

William shook his fist at her. 'Sir Reginald was a good man,' he cried.

'He will be avenged!' Ruth came running in, a

carving knife raised in her hand. 'And my mother too!' she screamed as she lunged at Lady Margaret.

'No!' I yelled. If she succeeded, Ruth would be burned at the stake for murder.

I threw myself at Ruth. The knife spun from her hand. 'Don't throw your life away on her account,' I pleaded.

With an inhuman screech, Lady Margaret suddenly pushed Mountford away. She snatched up the knife and before anyone could stop her, she plunged it into her own chest. She gave a shriek of agony and slumped to the floor. A pool of dark blood slowly spread round her. Her body twitched and was still.

'There dies the murderess,' said Cromwell.

'Someone help the King!' Cat's anguished cry filled the Great Hall.

His Majesty lay slumped in William's arms, his face deathly white and his breathing slow and barely audible.

'I've brought help,' shouted Barnabas, appearing at the door. He ushered a monk into the hall. It was Brother Anselm and he carried a small bag.

'I have the charcoal,' he said. 'It is specially prepared for such events but I pray I am not too late.'

30

The next morning we were summoned from the scribes' room to the Great Hall.

We'd had no news of the King and feared the worst. He'd been taken to his chamber the previous night and Brother Anselm had stayed to nurse him and forbidden anyone to disturb them. Only Master Cromwell had been allowed into the room.

A crowd of servants was standing silently around. Mark, Oswyn and I joined them. Every face showed fear of what the news might be. Cat came over.

'Have you heard anything?' she whispered.

'Not a word,' I whispered back.

A heavy footstep sounded on the stairs. Master Cromwell was coming slowly down. His expression gave nothing away. Brother Anselm followed, his head bowed. Something inside me twisted in agony. They must have the gravest of news.

Cat gave a small cry of anguish and crossed herself. I felt her hand grasp mine and hold it tightly.

Still saying nothing, Cromwell and the monk stopped at the bottom of the stairs. Then they looked up. Nicholas Mountford had appeared. Someone leant heavily on his arm, a blanket round his shoulders and his face pale and exhausted.

'God save the King!' I shouted.

Others took up the cry as we bowed deeply.

'Long live His Majesty!'

'Our prayers are answered!'

The King raised a feeble hand, acknowledging us. Mountford helped him to a chair by the fire. The King regarded us all from his makeshift throne.

'I give thanks to God, and to my loyal subjects who have saved my life,' he said hoarsely. 'I wish to hold audience. It is time for justice to be meted out.' He slumped in his chair, too tired for the moment to say anything else.

At a nod from Cromwell, the huge doors behind us flew open. Barnabas and William appeared, holding Edward Norbrook firmly by the arms. As soon as they reached His Majesty, Edward dropped to his knees and hung his head.

'You have borne arms against your King,' said Cromwell.

Edward tried to speak. 'I did not know . . .'

'So you have told us,' said Cromwell coldly. 'Ignorance is no excuse. Yet His Majesty is pleased to be lenient. Your life will be spared. Instead, you will spend the remainder of your days in prison.'

This seemed like a strange leniency to me! Edward Norbrook might be wild and headstrong, but he'd done the only thing he could think of to win back his rightful inheritance. I was sure that if he'd known who Mister Brown really was, he would never have attacked the castle. His face was ashen as he was led away.

'Mister Erskine.' The King was beckoning the steward forwards. 'How go the arrangements for the old woman's funeral?'

'Look at His Majesty's breathing,' hissed Cat. 'He shouldn't be exerting himself like that. It's not right.'

'Are you going to tell him?' I whispered.

'Not in a hundred years!' replied Cat fervently.

'Ruth has asked for Brother Anselm to do the service, my Liege,' said Mister Erskine, pointing at the tiring woman. 'A family affair.'

His Majesty looked over to Ruth. 'I have not forgotten how you tried to nurse me,' he said. 'Master Cromwell will see that all funeral costs are paid by the crown.'

Ruth bowed so deeply I wondered if her legs had given way in awe. 'Thank you, Sire,' she whispered.

'And the other body?' asked the King.

'Lady Norbrook has been dealt with,' said Mister Erskine. 'Some rough ground outside the abbey. She lies there now with Fulke.'

'Their souls are on their way to Hell!' rasped the King. He turned to Cromwell and nodded for him to continue.

'Now to happier matters,' said my master. 'His Majesty wishes to commend all those of the household who fought so courageously yesterday. Charlie, we hear you were very brave with the frying pan.'

'I was,' Charlie piped up from the crowd. 'And there's something I wanted to talk to the King about, when he has a moment.'

The King's eyes, half closed in his weak state, flew open in astonishment.

'We shall see,' said Cromwell evenly. 'His Majesty is very . . . busy. Jack Briars, come forward.'

I stepped up to the King's chair and knelt before him.

The King grasped my hand and leaned down so I should catch every faint word he said. 'You have done me another great service, Jack. I thank you for it. How can I reward you? Your sword fighting lessons will continue – with Mister Aycliffe – but there must be something else you desire.'

I knew at once what I was going to ask for. This was my chance to repay Charlie for saving me at the abbey.

'I have one thing to beg of you, my Liege,' I replied.

'Speak.'

'The young kitchen scullion who spoke up just now longs to serve you. He hopes one day to be a royal spit boy.'

'Does he indeed?' The King raised an eyebrow. 'Then such ambition should be rewarded. 'Come here, boy.'

It was a command but the tone was kind. Charlie bowed his way towards us.

'When you are a man, and taller and stronger,' said King Henry, 'you will come to roast my meat at Court. Master Cromwell will make sure of it. What do you say to that?'

For once in his life Charlie was speechless, but his huge grin answered for him.

The King looked thoughtful as Charlie backed away, bowing so deeply that his nose brushed the floor. He beckoned to Cromwell.

'The lad has put me in a mood for mercy,' he said. 'The good people here have been through much and I would see their lives return to normal. Without a master they may lose their home. Let Edward Norbrook spend some months in a cell and then release him to take his rightful inheritance.' He looked round the hall and I swear he shivered despite his robes and the fire. 'Otherwise the castle would fall forfeit to me and I have no wish to set eyes on it again.'

A pounding at the door gave me the chance to bow and slip back among the servants. Barnabas hurried to open it and Robert Aycliffe burst in.

'Thank the Lord!' he cried, at the sight of his King. He came forwards and bowed deeply. 'I am so pleased to find you, Your Majesty. I managed to cross the river by finding a bridge, more than thirty miles upstream, and have been searching for two days. I rode around deep floods and past a landslide but none had seen what had become of you.'

I saw the horror flare up in his eyes as he suddenly realised how ill his monarch appeared. It was quickly gone. No one dared tell King Henry that he was in anything but the rudest of health.

'I am grateful to you,' said the King, his tone a little impatient. 'But tell me, do you have news of Lady Anne?'

'She is well, Sire,' said Aycliffe, 'and ever eager to be reunited with you.'

The King beamed with pleasure.

'And has she been comfortably housed?'

Aycliffe grimaced. 'I would have to say it has been adequate, Your Majesty. We had to seek lodgings at the town of Otford and were several to a bed. And as for the food . . . I thank God that you've had a peaceful stay here in this castle.'

The King caught my eye and then looked at Cromwell. Poor Robert Aycliffe had no idea what he could have said to make King Henry throw back his head and roar with laughter.

Cromwell flapped his hands at us servants and we left, bowing deeply. Cat and I met out in the kitchen courtyard. A watery sun was peeping out from behind the clouds. For the first time in a week, the storm clouds weren't gathering.

'We'll be off to Greenwich the moment the King is

strong enough,' said Cat. 'I suppose you'll be forsaking our riding lessons now.'

'Why would I do that?' I asked.

'I thought you might be filling your days learning how to use a sword instead,' she said, a wicked gleam in her eye. 'You need even more practice at that!' And with a squeal of laughter, she ran back into the kitchen.

I made a vow. One day, by hook or by crook, I'd be the one to get the last word!

FATAL VOYAGE

1

'Jack Briars!' The command rang out across Deptford
Dockyard. 'Get yourself on board at once.'

I made for the gangplank. When the order came from
Henry, King of England, it would be a foolish boy who
didn't jump to it.

In truth I should have been on the ship already,
but the sight of her had stopped me in my tracks,
and the King's party had left me behind. For days His
Majesty had been boasting about the new galleon built
to honour his love, Lady Anne Boleyn. We all knew
that these were not idle boasts. King Henry would be
sure to have the most splendid of ships. And the *Fair
Anne* was an amazing spectacle. She towered over the
dockside, regal despite the wooden scaffolding around
her. Her red and white hull was painted with sea gods,
whales and giant writhing monsters. I had lost count
of the portholes, but each one had a gleaming black

cannon poking through. And just to make sure no one mistook her for anything but His Majesty's vessel, the lions of the royal pennant flapped at the top of her four masts.

I dashed onto the main deck, skidded to a halt in front of the King, made a deep bow and nearly strangled myself with the strap of my satchel.

'I thought I'd brought a scribe along to carry the ship's drawings and take notes for me,' the King boomed to the guards who flanked him. 'But when I looked over the side, there he was, gawping like a haddock. Be careful, Jack, lest someone thinks you are a fish and throws you into the Thames!'

Everybody laughed. I sheepishly took my place by my master, Thomas Cromwell, and gazed around – remembering to keep my mouth shut.

This was a different world from my boyhood at St Godric's Abbey. I couldn't imagine what Brother Matthew would have made of it all. My godfather had taught me many things but I reckoned that even the calm, humble monk would have been astounded by the *Fair Anne*. I clutched my satchel to me. The King's plans were precious and I was honoured to be charged with their safety. But it was only now I was staring at the real thing that I saw how magnificent she was.

She was like a floating palace. Well, she would be floating soon. The grand launch was to be on Thursday – just three days' time. The King had invited many important foreign guests to the palace to witness her triumphant maiden voyage. For the moment she stood propped in a long hole in the ground, or 'dry dock' as I'd heard someone say. Gryphons and fearsome eagles were carved into every bit of wood and the painters must have had gallons of gold paint. The rails, doors, hatches, everything was covered in it. The only thing they'd left alone was the rigging. Workmen were making the finishing touches, although they'd all stopped in the presence of their monarch.

The King caught me staring in awe at the towering masts and rows of cannon along the deck. 'Well, Jack,' he said. 'I warrant there weren't many such craft at your abbey.'

An image of my quiet old home flashed in front of my eyes.

'That is true, Sire,' I said solemnly. 'The carp pond was far too small.'

I didn't add that if a royal vessel had suddenly appeared at the abbey, Father Busbrig, the miserable old abbot, would probably have thought it was one of my tricks and given me a beating for it!

'You have a ready wit, Jack,' laughed His Majesty, thumping me on the back so hard he nearly winded me.

As I recovered my breath, he turned to speak to an important-looking man in a blue velvet coat. Another man, more plainly dressed, hovered nearby. I was just wondering who they were when someone gave me a nudge and I found myself looking up into the grinning face of one of the King's yeomen guard, Nicholas Mountford.

'Why isn't the Chief Scribe here in your place?' asked the giant yeoman. 'Is he ailing? Or more likely too lazy to leave his roaring fire?'

'Mister Scrope is well,' I told him. 'He's ... rather busy.'

But the yeoman had it right. When the order had come from the King for a scribe to carry the plans, old Scrope had been busy dozing in the warmth and I had jumped at the chance before anyone else could.

'Lucky for you then,' said Mountford. 'Better than sitting in a stuffy office all day, I'll warrant.'

He'd have been astonished to know that I did more than just sit in a stuffy office and write letters and copy lengthy laundry lists. *He'd* have gawped like a haddock if he'd known I was part of a network of spies, secretly recruited by Thomas Cromwell to keep the monarch safe. Not that I'd be needing my spying skills today. Today I was just a plain scribe.

'Your Majesty,' the man in the blue coat was saying. 'It is a great honour to have you on board. I can report that I've taken on extra men and all is progressing smoothly thanks to your detailed plans.'

'I am most pleased to hear it, Master Shipwright,' said the King.

In the last few days I'd copied plenty of documents from James Baker, Master Shipwright to His Majesty, so I knew that much of the design was the work of the

King himself. No one would want the shipwright's job today. If the King spotted any flaw in his new creation, it would be James Baker who answered for it.

Mister Baker waved forward the other man, who bowed until his nose nearly touched the deck. 'I humbly present John Talboys to Your Majesty,' said the shipwright. 'He is the woodcarver who has carried out your . . . extra order.'

'Ah, Mister Talboys,' boomed the King. 'This is the first time you have worked for me, I believe. I trust that the special commission I gave you has been well executed.'

The man was too frightened of King Henry to speak. Our monarch was tall and imposing and made princes gibber.

'I am sure you will be most satisfied with the result, Sire,' James Baker answered for the woodcarver. 'It will be lowered onto the foredeck, in accordance with the plan you drew up.'

'Excellent,' said the King, rubbing his gloved hands together in glee. 'And you will remember that it is I who am to guide it into place.'

'Of course, Sire,' said Mister Baker. 'A more esteemed foreman we have never had.'

'Lady Anne must not hear a word about it until the launch,' the King went on. 'Do I have your word that no one outside the shipyard knows of the statue?'

'No one, Your Majesty. Only a few have seen it and all here today are sworn to silence.'

So the mysterious surprise that the King had been hinting at in the last few days was a statue. When he hadn't been going on about his new wonderful ship, he'd been telling everyone that he had a surprise for Lady Anne, and that he personally would unveil it for her on the day of the launch. He had made it sound very mysterious. It would be in pride of place right at the front – or rather, the bows, as Mark Helston had told me.

While King Henry pointed out to his retinue the gilded carvings on the masts – just in case they'd missed them – I thought back to Mark's fidgets that morning in the scribes' office.

As soon as I'd volunteered for the task, he'd given me anxious tuition across the table. 'The front's called the bows and the back is the stern and those bits that hold the sails are called yards. Oh, and ships are always referred to as *she*. Promise you won't get it wrong, Jack. That would anger the King and it's sure to bring bad luck.'

I'd made my friend a solemn promise but he'd still told me about sailors tripping over buckets, and masts falling on the captain's head, and all because someone had called the portholes 'windows' by mistake. I remembered how our fellow scribe, Oswyn Drage, had watched the whole exchange with a sneering smile on his lips, no doubt hoping I'd commit some ghastly error in front of His Majesty and be thrown overboard on the spot. Weasel-face Drage couldn't understand why Master Cromwell had taken on a lowly abbey foundling such as me.

The King's voice cut into my thoughts. 'Come, Thomas,' he said, turning to Master Cromwell. 'We shall go up to the foredeck and welcome aboard the crowning glory of my vessel.'

'I am agog to see it, Sire,' said Cromwell dutifully. He followed the King up a steep, narrow stairway, with the Master Shipwright and carver close behind.

I scampered after them, keen to set eyes on the mysterious statue. Judging by the splendour of the rest of the vessel, it was going to be magnificent – a Roman warrior on horseback perhaps, or a mighty gorgon with snakes for hair – and the whole thing made of pure gold.

The boom of the biggest crane I'd ever seen hung high overhead. It carried something huge, swathed in tarpaulin. A man sat astride the boom, directly above it.

The workmen on the upper deck bowed low at the King's approach. 'The ship will launch in three days on the morning tide,' announced His Majesty. 'Augustus Filby, my astrologer, has studied the heavens and has found . . . Well, he can tell you himself.'

He looked back over the crowd that had accompanied him from Greenwich and were now milling about on the lower deck. 'Filby! Come up here!'

A man as round as a pig at market pushed his way through the throng. He wore a thick, plain cloak. As he puffed up the stairs, it swung open to reveal a lining embroidered with golden stars and silver moons. I hadn't come across the King's astrologer before but Mark had told me that Doctor Filby had been consulted at every turn of the ship building.

'Tell Master Cromwell why you deemed Thursday to be auspicious for the launch,' ordered King Henry.

'Well, it is most interesting.' Augustus Filby spoke in high-pitched tones, almost squeaking in his enthusiasm. 'I have drawn up your chart, my Liege, and Mars is aligned with Venus and the Sun will be in the ascendant and . . .'

He said a lot more about Aquarius rising and the conjunction of Jupiter and Saturn in Scorpio but he could have been speaking Arabic for all the sense it made to me! His Majesty smiled happily though, and my master nodded in agreement as the astrologer continued with his babble. Feeling bored, I sidled to the rail and looked along the length of the amazing crane. Its base stood way down on the dockside. It was a strong, complicated structure with pulleys, ropes and a giant wheel – and three workers close by, ready to man it.

'Reveal the statue,' commanded the King.

The man perched on the end of the boom leaned down and grasped the tarpaulin. In one dramatic move, he whipped it off and we saw the woodcarver's creation.

The carpenters and painters shouted out a

resounding cheer, and even the yeomen joined in. I was the loudest of the lot. I wasn't going to let on what I really thought. There wasn't even a hint of a warrior or mythical monster. It was a statue of Anne Boleyn. It was a very good likeness, I had to admit. The carver had got her dark hair and smile very accurately, and he'd put her in a gleaming golden gown. But it was still just a wooden woman.

The King didn't seem to share my disappointment. He beamed with pleasure. 'You obeyed my instructions most precisely,' he told John Talboys. 'I warrant she will grace the ship almost as beautifully as the lady herself. And now she must be put into her rightful place.'

Her rightful place seemed to be a blob of paint at the front of the foredeck.

'Swing the boom over,' ordered his Majesty.

I looked down to the dockside again, keen to see how the crane worked. Two of the workers below had taken hold of the wheel while the third began to rotate the creaking structure on its base. The giant statue swung very slowly over the deck.

'Careful as she goes,' shouted King Henry. 'A little further and she'll be ready for lowering.'

I could hear the excitement in his voice.

'Halt,' he called.

The boom stopped moving.

A cry rang out from the dockside. 'Let me pass!'

Someone was trying to barge through the line of

guards at the top of the steps. He wore simple clothes and had a thick beard that did not hide the anger on his face. Two yeomen quickly stood in his way, their halberds forming a locked gate against him.

'I am Benjamin Dobson, an honest wood merchant!' he yelled, shaking his fist. 'I must see the King. I speak for all of us who supply his timber. We've not had our fair pay for the ship's wood.'

'By St George!' declared His Majesty. 'What is this outrage?'

Every eye was on the intruder, who was shouting and trying to fight his way past the yeomen's weapons. I was sure everyone feared the royal fury that would burst upon him at any moment. Then something else caught my attention. It was a tiny movement of the crane. I looked up. The statue had moved. Now it was directly over the King and the man on the boom seemed to be desperately working away at something.

And suddenly the statue was falling.

2

I threw myself at the King.

I caught a brief glimpse of his astonished face as I slammed into his chest, knocking him flying. Not a second later, a deafening crash split the air. The statue fell onto the exact spot where His Majesty had stood. In the silence that followed, the only sound was the head, snapped from the broken body, rolling slowly across the wooden boards.

As the yeomen rushed forwards I jumped to my feet and helped the King up. He took my hand in a firm grasp. His was steadier than mine!

'Thank you, Jack,' he said. 'Your quick action saved me.'

'I was doing my duty, Sire,' I replied, cross with myself for the wobble in my voice.

'My Liege!' James Baker hurried between the guards and horrified onlookers to the King's side. He was ashen. 'I cannot understand how this dreadful accident happened. Our equipment is checked many times – and even more so for today's ceremony. I made the final checks myself just before your arrival. The pulley should never have failed. And Your Majesty should not have been in danger at any point during the manoeuvre. I can only believe that the men controlling the statue were distracted by the wood merchant's protest.'

'It is inexcusable, Master Shipwright.' The King now shook with fury. 'I will ensure that all those responsible will answer for it. See to it that the others are found, Thomas.' His words held a threat that must have chilled everyone who heard them.

Cromwell signalled to Nicholas Mountford who immediately led a group of yeomen off to obey the royal orders.

'Arrest the wood merchant too,' the King bellowed after them. 'He will be sorry for this day's work.'

He waved a hand at the headless statue, split in half and still fastened to the rope that had fallen with it. The pulley lay a few feet away. 'And remove this abomination from my sight!'

A group of workmen quickly untangled the body. John Talboys picked up the head, cradling it like a newborn.

'The statue must be repaired and ready for the launch,' His Majesty barked at him. 'It is to be as perfect as it was before the accident.'

The trembling man almost dropped his heavy burden

in his haste to bow. The King thundered down the steps, a shield of guards sticking close to his side. The carver waited until the royal party had stepped off the gangplank. Then he staggered from the ship and I saw him stumbling away through the shipyard, glancing left and right as if he expected to be blamed for the accident at any moment.

I didn't move.

A carpenter had already begun to repair the shattered planks where the statue had fallen. He stopped sawing and glanced up at me. 'Shouldn't you be going with His Majesty?' he asked. 'You're a hero, lad. He'll want to honour you, I shouldn't wonder.'

I nodded vaguely.

'Are you all right?' the man persisted. 'You look shaken.'

'I'm fine,' I assured him, turning away.

I *was* shaken – though not in the way he thought. Something was wrong. The words *dreadful accident* kept echoing in my head. I tried to think clearly about what had just happened. The wood merchant's shout . . . the man working desperately on the boom . . . the statue directly over the King . . . the pulley breaking. Supposing it hadn't been an accident? What if that shout had come just at the right time to distract the onlookers – so that the statue would fall while every eye was on the protesting man?

It was a terrible thought – and I knew I couldn't let it go.

Cromwell stood at the rail, watching the King's departure. I joined him.

'So, Jack,' he said. 'I must add my thanks to those of His Majesty. I cannot contemplate what might have happened if you hadn't acted as you did.' He spoke in his usual calm way but horror still lingered on his face. 'Go back to the palace and your duties. I shall stay until the guard have carried out the royal orders and we have pieced together what caused this.'

There was frantic activity on the dockside below, as a group of guards rounded up anxious workers. Others were searching through the shipyard, shouting and pushing open workshop doors with the points of their halberds.

'May I speak with you before I go, sir?' I asked.

Cromwell nodded. 'You have my ear until the guard return with the men concerned.'

'Something I saw makes me think that what happened might not have been an accident.' I told him my suspicions.

He watched me gravely. When I'd finished he was silent for a long moment. 'If what you say is true, then this is serious indeed.'

Nicholas Mountford appeared, leading two prisoners towards us, flanked by yeomen. The Master Shipwright followed, wiping his brow. A small group of workers came behind, their faces full of curiosity.

'Stay with me, Jack,' Cromwell said in a low voice.

'You may learn something. But all must believe that this was an accident. We cannot stir up fear, particularly amongst His Majesty's foreign guests.'

'The wood merchant appears to have fled in the confusion, sir,' announced Mountford. 'But I found these two.'

The prisoners shuffled forwards. They looked frightened.

'These fellows were manning the wheel at the crane's base, ready to lower the statue,' Mountford went on. 'I believe they are in no way to blame. They tell me they kept tight hold and waited for the order to lower it slowly to its place.'

'Which we'd practised many a time,' said one, a man with red cheeks.

'But the order never came,' said the other, pulling anxiously at his grizzled beard. 'We had our hands on the handle, then we heard a shout from on board and next thing we knew, the rope went slack and we saw the statue fall. There was nothing we could do.'

'Ivo was on top of the crane and Seth was moving it into position on Ivo's signal,' said the Master Shipwright. 'But those two men haven't been found yet.'

'Seth was right by us until the accident, sir,' said Red Cheeks. 'But he vanished mighty quickly afterwards. And I've never known a man climb off a boom so swiftly as Ivo did. I've seen neither hide nor hair of them since.'

'Has anyone set eyes on them?' demanded James Baker.

Grizzled Beard shook his head. 'I reckon they've scarpered. Begging your pardon, sirs, but I'd make myself scarce if I'd nearly dropped a statue on top of His Majesty.'

'Yet it will be the worse for them if they don't come back willingly,' said the shipwright sternly. 'Such good workers too.'

'That's right, sir,' agreed Red Cheeks. 'And never once shirked. It should have been Tom and Barnaby on the crane this morning but they didn't turn up for duty. So right away Seth and Ivo said they'd do the job.'

'The foreman wasn't sure, as they haven't been with us long,' put in Grizzled Beard.

'But they insisted, saying how there'd been problems with the crane,' added Red Cheeks. 'They worked with Tom and Barnaby on its construction, you see.'

'I warrant they've gone off to tell them what happened,' a voice called from the back of the group of nosy onlookers, 'and warn them what they're in for when they come to work!'

'*If* they come to work,' I heard someone mutter.

'Where are they living?' asked the Master Shipwright.

'At Mistress Bryant's lodging house in the village,' said Red Cheeks. 'Tom and Barnaby lodge next door and they've become close friends with Seth and Ivo.'

'They're always in the tavern of an evening.' Grizzled Beard took up the tale. 'And then the four of them take flagons of ale back to Mistress Bryant's and they drink late into the night.'

'I hope they're quiet about it,' called someone. 'I've heard that landlady's a right battleaxe.'

'Aye, but they've got used to creeping about when she's on the prowl,' said Grizzled Beard. 'I reckon Tom and Barnaby were too drunk to come to the shipyard this morning and the newcomers were covering for them.'

'It wouldn't be the first time,' said Red Cheeks.

'You are free to go,' Cromwell told the two men, who seemed greatly relieved to hear it and piled down the gangplank as if a demon was after them.

The others lingered for a moment but one cold glance from my master had them suddenly remembering some urgent task and they scurried away too.

Master Cromwell turned to Nicholas Mountford. 'Scour the shipyard for the wood merchant. Use all your guards. I want him found and dealt with. It will show others that they cannot disturb the King's peace and go unpunished.'

Mister Mountford looked briefly surprised. 'And the other two men, sir? Those who guided the statue. Shouldn't we round them up?'

'You will have further instructions later.' The yeoman bowed and strode away.

'Well, Jack,' said my master quietly. 'Why do you think I haven't ordered the yeomen guard to go straight to the lodging house?'

'Because you doubt the men will be there, sir,' I answered promptly. I didn't admit that for a moment I'd been as surprised as Mister Mountford that he hadn't ordered it! 'If this were a deliberate act, the perpetrators would not run home.'

'Indeed,' said Cromwell.

'Yet there might be information to be gleaned in their room,' I added.

'Which might be lost by guards tramping about.' Cromwell glanced across to the carpenter who was still at his work. 'So I will be sending someone more discreet – and more cunning,' he murmured.

'Yes, sir,' I replied. I understood the unspoken command.

As I knew I should obey my master's orders immediately and without question, I didn't tell him that I had one thing to do before I left the ship.

'Come to me as soon as you return.' My master's expression became cold and his next words chilled me. 'Whoever is behind this will wish they'd never been born.'

Thomas Cromwell was as ruthless as any killer when the safety of the King was at stake.

3

There were times when I believed that my master had eyes in the back of his head, so I waited until he'd ridden out of sight before I made my move.

'You've got a bit of colour now, lad,' called the carpenter, pausing in his repairs to straighten his back. 'I'm still shocked myself. Such a dreadful thing.'

I'd forgotten he was there. It looked as if my business would have to wait. I didn't want any witnesses to my next action.

'What will happen to the two men who were guiding the crane?' I asked, hoping for more information. 'After all, it wasn't really their fault, was it?'

'I feel sorry for Seth and Ivo,' said the carpenter. 'They're hard workers and their work is good. As soon as they joined us they offered to help Tom and Barnaby construct that special crane for the statue. In truth, they took over – and checked it again and again to make sure it was safe. I warrant they'll not get another job on a royal vessel . . . though that could be the least of their worries if they're caught!'

This was interesting. The men knew exactly how the crane was to function – so they must have known exactly how to make it fail!

'Where do they come from?' I asked. 'Are they local men?'

The carpenter shrugged. 'We heard they're journeymen, travelling around and taking employment where they can. We never knew where they hail from.' He finished his repair, picked up his tools and ambled off.

Now for my task. If I was right about the sabotage, I had to find evidence. That was going to be more of a challenge!

I gazed about as if I was overcome with the magnificence of the ship under her towering scaffolding. The crane was still high above the deck, level with a small railed platform round the top of the mast. Mark had told me all about the frightful dangers of these platforms – they were called crow's nests and many a lookout boy had been thrown into the sea from them. I reasoned that as this one had a wooden fence round it, and as we weren't at sea, I'd probably be all right. Anyway, I had no choice. Reaching the crow's nest was my only way of getting close to what I needed to check without being seen.

I wandered towards the rigging that hung like a rope

ladder from just under the crow's nest right down to the wooden boards. I tightened the strap of my satchel containing the plans. Carrying it would make what I was going to do even harder, but the King had made it clear that the plans were to be kept secret from prying eyes – so I couldn't leave them lying about. The workers on the main deck below had their heads bent over their tasks so no one spotted me grasp the rigging and begin to climb. The squares of knotted rope swayed alarmingly with each step. At last I reached the crow's nest and hauled myself over its painted wooden rail onto the platform.

From here I could see that the tarpaulin which had hidden the statue was still covering the top of the crane. But I was starting to wonder if Mark was right about the dangers. On deck I'd not noticed any breeze. Up here, the wind was strong, tossing the rigging about and slamming it into the mast. Hanging on tightly, I leaned out, stretching my fingers towards the tarpaulin. My evidence, if there was any, would be right underneath it. But it was too far away. Holding my breath, I climbed carefully out of the crow's nest, wedged my feet on the narrow rim that ran round the outside edge and tried again. The pennant above flapped wildly and the gusting wind made me clutch tightly to the rail, my stomach lurching.

The tarpaulin was still out of reach. I studied the gap between me and the crane boom. Not a great distance to jump – if I'd been on the ground. But up here with the drop almost beckoning to me, I wasn't so sure. Yet I wasn't going to leave my task half done. *What would Mark say if he could see me now?* I thought. More to the point, what would Master Cromwell say when he heard I'd been found splattered all over the deck?

I leapt. I thought I'd misjudged it. Then I felt splinters of wood stab into my palms and my fingers gripped the boom with all their strength. In one twisting movement I swung my legs and hauled myself over to sit astride it. The wind whistled round, shaking the whole structure. It made the satchel strap tug at my shoulder. I admired the men who worked on ships day after day, facing dizzying heights and a rolling ocean too!

I steadied myself, took hold of the tarpaulin and began to pull it aside.

'What the hell do you think you are doing, lad?' came an angry voice.

A man far below was glaring up at me, his hands on his hips. My heart felt as if it had sunk to the deck – and that was a long way down.

'I'm admiring the view,' I called, trying to sound young and excited. 'I've never climbed rigging before.'

'Well I'm the foreman here and you can come down this minute,' he shouted crossly. 'We've had one accident already today and we don't want another.'

Damn him! I longed to do as he said, but first I must inspect the crane. I decided to try a bit of wheedling.

'I've just saved the King's life,' I told him.

'All the more reason to stop you killing yourself,' shouted the man.

It was obvious he wasn't going to move until I obeyed. I shuffled backwards. Pretending to be scared of falling – which wasn't far from the truth – I wobbled and slid sideways, dragging at the tarpaulin as if to save myself. The foreman gave a shout of alarm, and a worker climbed quickly up the boom to rescue me.

I didn't have long before he got to me. I sat there as if numb with terror, clutching the tarpaulin. But for one fleeting moment I saw what was under it before I was hauled down to the dockside. I hardly listened as the foreman roundly scolded me for my antics. I'd found out what I needed to know.

There had been no accident here today but a deliberate attempt to kill the King.

4

I muttered apologies to the furious foreman and crept off. My heart was thudding with the horror of what I'd found. I knew that the pulley wheel must have been held firmly in place by a strong metal pin. However, the scars in the wood told a different story. The pin had been prised out at the critical moment by some sharp tool that had left tell-tale dents in the pulley casing. The weight of the statue had done the rest.

'Jack!'

I turned to see Cat Thimblebee coming down the gangway, her hair escaping from under her cap like a halo of red fire.

'Well don't just stand there gawping like a gudgeon!' she laughed.

God's oath! It was the second time that day I'd been likened to a fish. I might have to take it from my King but not from a seamstress – even if that seamstress had proved herself a loyal friend and assistant in my secret work.

'I'm not gawping,' I insisted. 'It's just that I wasn't expecting to find you on board. I thought all the sewing was finished long ago.'

'Don't get your breeches in a twist,' answered Cat. 'His Majesty wanted some more falcons and all sorts of fancy stuff embroidered on Lady Anne's cushions.' She waggled her sewing basket at me. 'We would have done them in the workshop at the palace but the King insisted they had to be kept on board in case he wanted to inspect them. And everyone else is running about like headless chickens trying to get the courtiers' best outfits ready when there's only three days till the grand launch so I told Mister Wiltshire I'd come.'

I don't suppose her master had had any say in the matter!

Cat jerked her thumb at the ship.

'She's a magnificent thing and no mistake. I've been all over. The King has a chamber especially for banquets, and a gallery for archery and even a tennis court on board! Anyway, there I was minding my own business, finishing off some peacock feathers when I heard a loud thud. Someone rushed in and told me you'd bowled His Majesty over. How clumsy was that!'

I was about to protest that she'd got it wrong when I saw that the irritating girl was shaking with laughter.

'I know,' she went on, 'you're the hero of the hour really. Everyone's been talking about it. But I'm betting that's not the end of the matter. I'm betting you have to sniff about and find out how the accident happened. Am I right?' She didn't give me a chance to reply but winked and tapped her nose. 'I can see I am. Count me in. What are we going to do next?'

I couldn't believe it. Not only had she guessed the truth, but she was muscling in on my mission as usual.

'No time to explain,' I said, quickening my pace. 'And you have to get off to the palace, I expect.'

'Not yet,' said Cat airily. She turned and thrust her sewing basket at one of the passing palace servants. 'Rick! Take this back for me. Tell them I'll be along later. Important work for His Majesty. Mark my words, Jack,' she said when the astonished man had gone, 'you'll need my help and it's no good telling me you won't. Where are we going?'

I gave up. Trying to keep Cat at bay was like trying to turn back the tide. She'd proved very useful in the past but I wasn't going to say so – though she often did!

'I don't believe that what happened to the King was an accident,' I said quietly, as we passed through the dockyard gates.

I checked no one was lurking nearby and told Cat my suspicions.

'So those two men were actually trying to kill His Majesty!' she gasped.

I nodded. 'And they've got away. We have no idea who they were working for but I'm going to search their lodgings to see if I can find anything out.'

We reached the village green. A bustling market filled the space between cottages and the church. Although not much selling was going on. Everyone was talking excitedly of the unexpected arrival of the King that morning and his unexpectedly hasty departure!

'Now where does this Mistress Bryant live?' asked Cat, looking around.

'I don't know,' I said. 'We need to find out . . . '

I was talking to the air! Cat had marched up to a man mending a wheel. She marched back, a satisfied smile on her face.

'It's down there,' she said. 'Last house on the left.'

She headed off along the road. I had to run to catch her up.

'You can't come,' I said.

'Why not?' she demanded.

'Because I'm in livery so I can say I'm on official business,' I told her. 'I can't say "oh and by the way, I've brought a seamstress along for company".'

'I suppose you're right,' she muttered reluctantly. 'I'll have a look round the market while I wait.'

The row of shabby dwellings were battered and leaning and I could imagine that a breath of wind would blow them down. A large woman was sitting on an upturned barrel outside the door of the last one. Even if a passing man hadn't nervously called out, 'Good morrow, Mistress Bryant,' I'd still have guessed that this was the fearsome landlady.

Unsmiling, the woman nodded to him. Close to, she

put me in mind of a large toad about to swallow a tasty fly. I straightened my shoulders and approached.

'What do you want?' she snapped before I'd had a chance to speak.

'I'd like to go in and pick up a tool of Seth and Ivo's please,' I said politely. 'They sent me from the shipyard to get it.'

Mistress Bryant gave a harsh chuckle. 'Is that so? I didn't know the shipyard was dressing its workers in royal livery these days.'

'That's to say, I came from the palace today – with the King – to see his new ship.'

'With the King, eh?' said Mistress Bryant. 'Seth and Ivo are moving in very high circles if they can get a royal servant to do their bidding!' She heaved herself to her feet and plonked her considerable bulk firmly in the doorway. 'Think you can hoodwink a weak and defenceless woman, do you? Royal servant, my foot. I don't believe a word of your story. You've stolen that outfit. Be off with you before I let the dogs loose.'

She gave a shrill whistle. In answer came a volley of deep vicious barks and three huge dogs hurtled round from the back of the house.

5

The chains snapped tight round the beasts' thick necks. They strained on their leashes, slavering and snarling inches from my face.

I retreated hurriedly to find Cat trying on a pair of fine leather gloves.

'Not quite my colour,' she told the stall holder, putting them down. She pulled me to one side. 'You're back quick. What did you find out?'

'Mistress Bryant wouldn't let me in. And she's got guard dogs.'

'Leave it to me!' And before I could stop her, Cat had marched off down the road. I followed at a distance, keeping out of sight. There was no sign of the dogs.

'Mistress Bryant?' demanded Cat.

'Who wants to know?' growled the landlady, towering above her.

'That's for you to find out,' said Cat cheekily. 'I've

come to tell you that Peg up at Limehouse said you were a bad-tempered old witch and she'll tell you that to your face if she ever sees you.'

'What?' thundered Mistress Bryant.

'And I said I'd pass it on cause I agree with every word!' added Cat.

'You little minx!' The landlady swung a beefy hand at her.

Cat dodged the blow and put her thumb to her nose, waggling her fingers. 'Can't catch me!' she taunted, skipping off down the road.

With a roar, Mistress Bryant lumbered after her. As soon as they'd disappeared round a corner I crept to the door as quietly as a ghost. I had no intention of alerting the hellhounds to my presence.

I raced across the floor of a poky little kitchen and up a narrow staircase. The dogs were growling outside, their chains clanking as they prowled about. I prayed Cat would keep their owner away long enough for me to do my job and get away.

I came to a chamber on the first floor and listened at the crack of the door. When I heard no sound I carefully opened the latch. The gloomy little room was filled with an unmade bed and a table by its side. A huge corset hung from the bedpost and I doubted it belonged to either Seth or Ivo.

A flight of even more rickety stairs took me to a room in the eaves of the house. I listened again, then opened the door slowly, my heart pounding, suddenly feeling I might be wrong, and that the two men would be here after all. A splintered shutter covered a rough window in the front wall. Chinks of light cut through the gloom, enough for me to tell that the room was empty.

Outside, the dogs had begun to bark. Had they sensed that there was an intruder?

There wasn't much to see in the bedchamber. The floor was bare, with no rushes to hide the dirt, and the boards were covered in dark stains. A couple of lumpy straw mattresses lay against one wall. An old wooden chest stood in a corner and a collection of empty flagons stood next to it, amongst scattered boots and a bag of tools. The room stank of drink and I would wager it was strong ale, Dragon's Milk or Dagger Beer, guaranteed to make a man drunk quickly. But there was something else mingled with it. Something that caught in my throat and almost made me choke.

I went to the window to take a breath of fresh air. The floor sloped towards the front wall and with every step I took, it creaked so badly I feared I'd fall through. I wondered if it was only its neighbour that was holding the house up. The shutter swung lopsidedly on one hinge as I eased it open. I didn't like what I saw down in the street. Mistress Bryant was storming back to the house! I quickly closed the shutter and began to search for clues about the men who'd operated the crane. I picked through the few ragged clothes I found in the chest, then rifled through the bag. Nothing there but a hammer, saw and chisel – ordinary carpenter's tools.

Footsteps on the stairs had me whirling round. I was torn between composing some feeble excuse and jumping out of the window. But to my huge relief, it was Cat's cheeky face that poked round the door. I was cross with myself for not recognising her light, running feet that couldn't have been the heavy lumbering of Mistress Bryant. Cat took one glance at me and burst out laughing.

'You thought I was that old baggage!'

'Of course I didn't,' I insisted. 'But I know she's on her way.'

Cat made her way gingerly over the dilapidated floor and peered through a crack in the shutter down into the street. 'I'll keep watch. She's stopped to talk to someone.' She chuckled. 'No, I'm wrong. She's not talking, she's yelling at them and if I'm any judge, she'll be a little while.'

'I don't think I'll need much longer,' I told her. 'There's no sign of anything suspicious. Just give me a hand to check under the mattresses and we can be off.'

No sooner had we moved the first, than the strange, choking smell became stronger. I hesitated. A cold sensation hit the pit of my stomach.

We seized the other mattress and pulled it away. The smell rose up, making us both gag.

Two men lay, tossed down like discarded dolls. Their faces showed horror and each had a red gaping wound across his throat looking for all the world like a second mouth. The dark stains I'd seen on the floor were pools of their dried blood.

Cat grabbed my arm and clung on tightly.

'Lord have mercy,' she whispered.

6

We gazed down at the grisly sight.

'The poor souls,' whispered Cat, crossing herself. 'But I don't understand. How did Seth and Ivo get back here – without Mistress Bryant seeing – and be murdered and cold and all in an hour or so?'

'These are not the men I saw working the crane,' I said.

'Then who are they?' gasped Cat.

'Tom and Barnaby is my guess,' I said. 'It fits in with what I heard at the shipyard. Seth and Ivo came to work on the King's ship with one thing in mind – killing the King.'

'And when they heard about the King ordering the statue it must have sounded like the perfect chance,' said Cat.

'Exactly,' I agreed. 'So they offered to construct the crane, and deliberately befriended Tom and Barnaby so it was easy to get them to come here last night for one of their drinking sessions.'

'They got Tom and Barnaby blind drunk and slit their throats,' finished Cat. 'How terrible.'

A door banged.

'What is it, my lovelies?' There was as much menace in Mistress Bryant's distant voice as in the snarling and barking below. 'Who's in my house?'

We heard footsteps and scrabbling claws on the stairs.

'They're coming!' hissed Cat, 'and there's no way out.'

'Oh yes there is,' I said firmly. I shut the bedroom door and heaved the chest against it. 'The roof. I'll go first.'

Cat nodded, her eyes wide with fear.

I flung the shutter open and scrambled onto the rotting window ledge. I wished I could be rid of the King's plans. The satchel strap caught on a loose bit of wood and sent it tumbling into the street. Luckily no one noticed. I suppose they were used to Mistress Bryant's house falling to pieces!

A loud pounding started on the door.

'Hurry!' squeaked Cat as I hauled myself onto the sloping roof above.

The clay tiles were cracked and loose, with moss growing over them. In places they were missing, showing wooden slats and crumbling plaster. I clung to the slats as if they were a ladder and hoped they

225

weren't full of woodworm. The roof rose steeply. If I missed my footing I'd plummet to the ground and if I survived that, the dogs would be sure to have me for supper. I pushed the grisly thoughts away and reached out a hand to grasp Cat's. She suddenly pulled back.

'I can't,' she breathed. 'It's too high. I'll fall.'

'You've got no choice,' I insisted.

Cat gave a muffled squeal as I dragged her towards me, her legs kicking wildly. We crouched on the ridge of the roof, terrified, listening to the sound of the chest being pushed across the floor as the door was forced open. There was a pause, and then a deafening shriek.

'She's found the bodies,' whispered Cat.

'And by the sound of it, so have the dogs,' I whispered back.

'Help!' bellowed the landlady through the open window. 'Murder!'

We heard doors opening and puzzled shouts from the street.

'Fetch the constable!' shrieked the landlady.

The cry was taken up.

'We've got to get out of sight,' I whispered.

We scrambled towards a ramshackle chimney. There was a crunching sound and I felt my foot smash between slats and plaster.

Mistress Bryant gave a screech. 'The murderer's coming through my ceiling!'

Her cry didn't go unheeded. 'The constable's on his way,' rang out from the street below.

Cat and I slithered and scampered around the chimney.

'Someone bring a ladder,' ordered Mistress Bryant. 'He's on the roof. I'm sending the dogs out. The villain will be trapped until we're ready for him.'

We slid over the next ridge while the crowds gathered around the house. A ladder crashed onto the eaves behind us. We looked back. The head and shoulders of a portly man had appeared. He was panting as his beady eyes searched round.

'The constable,' gasped Cat.

We ducked out of sight and turned to make for the slope of the next roof. There wasn't one. We'd run out of houses. In front of us was a long drop to the cobbles below.

Cat gulped as we stared down. She looked terrified. 'We're stuck!'

There wouldn't be a happy ending if we were caught.

'We're in luck,' I told her. 'I can see a soft landing.'

Cat followed my gaze. 'You must be joking!' she hissed, staring at the horse and cart standing in the street.

'It's full of hay,' I argued.

'Stop in the name of the law!' The cry came from the constable and he sounded very close.

I turned back to see Cat leaping into the air with a yelp. She landed in the hay.

I landed at her side. Cat scrambled on to the driver's bench.

'Hang on tight!' she yelled.

I clung to the wooden sides, the hay not enough to cushion the bumps as the cart moved off at speed. Above the clatter of the wheels on the rough cobbles, I heard something else – a vicious barking.

The dogs were after us. They pounded along, their breath steaming from their muzzles as they howled and snarled.

'Go faster,' I yelled. 'They're catching us up.'

The old nag between the shafts seemed to think it was young again. It flattened its ears and put a spurt on. I was sure that Cat would claim she'd done something special but if I'd been a horse with three slavering hounds on my tail, I think I'd have bolted too.

We lurched forwards. One of my hands lost its grasp and I nearly tumbled off the back. As I struggled to save myself, I was confronted by three sets of sharp, snapping teeth.

7

I used the only weapon I had. I kicked half the contents of the cart into the dogs' faces. For a moment all I could see was a bundle of churning hay full of snouts and claws. Then we swerved round a corner on two wheels and left them behind.

When we reached the bridge over Deptford Creek, Cat reined the horse in. She jumped down and came round to the back.

'You can let go now!' she laughed.

I released my grip on the side of the cart and clambered down, brushing hay off my livery and checking my teeth were still in place after the jolting journey. I was relieved to find the satchel still across my chest. I couldn't imagine trying to explain to His Majesty that I'd lost the royal plans on a rooftop!

'What are we going to do with the nag?' I asked.

Cat went to the horse's head and led it round to face

back towards the village. 'I reckon this old dobbin can find his own way home,' she said. 'You are a fine steed and I thank you.' She stroked its neck and patted its rump.

The nag nodded as if it understood and plodded obediently off. I felt a pang of envy at the way Cat handled horses. Every time I had dealings with the four-legged fiends, they always seemed to be in charge.

'What are you going to do now?' asked Cat as we headed for the palace.

'Whatever Master Cromwell instructs me to,' I said. 'I'll go and tell him what I've found out and it'll be up to him.'

'You can't present yourself to him like this,' said Cat. 'I've seen chimney sweeps look cleaner.' She brushed me down, rather fiercely. 'Luckily it was just dust and moss,' she said as she gave me a final whack.

We passed the smokehouse and reached the gate to the kitchen vegetable plots. Cat peered ahead through the fading afternoon light. 'I reckon you'll find your master in the Knot Garden,' she said.

She waited for me to congratulate her on her detective work. I didn't. I could hear the voices and music coming from there just as well as she could.

'I can't stand around like a lazy lollop,' she declared. As usual, she managed to make herself sound more important than me. 'I'll see you later,' she called over her shoulder as she left. 'I want to hear what you're going to do next. Whatever it is, I'm sure you'll be needing my help!'

I was just thinking up a rude retort when I realised she'd gone.

I stood at the edge of the Knot Garden. The welcome glow of torch flames reminded me that the King had ordered a feast for his guests tonight. Mark had told me all about it in a whispered conversation over the scribes' table early that morning. He'd claimed that they'd be taking their dessert in the new Banqueting House in the grounds. I hadn't seen any building work going on at Greenwich and thought he must have got it wrong, but I hadn't had time to ask. Oswyn had piped up at that moment, complaining that we weren't doing any work and nervous Mark had refused to say another word.

As I approached the Knot Garden, I saw that its patterns of low hedges were lit by a vast array of torches, all burning with different coloured flames, and interspersed with intricate wooden models of ships on marble stands, perfect in every detail. The King was determined to show his foreign visitors how grand and important England was. The paths led to a huge white tent erected in the centre. Silhouettes moved across the glowing canvas and I heard conversation and laughter from inside. Courtiers were pouring from the palace towards its open door, which was swathed in gold cloth and hung with royal pennants. So this was the Banqueting House. And I knew where my master would be. I only had to make my way through all the guests crowding round the King and I'd find Cromwell loyally by his side.

I squared my shoulders and prepared for battle. And a battle it was, squeezing my way through all the courtiers and guests, invited for the launch of the *Fair Anne*. I might not have had a sword but my bony elbows were the next best thing and caused a few indignant comments as I fought towards my goal. I soon found myself squashed against a trestle table that heaved with wonderful puddings. There were raisin tarts, gingerbread galleons, platefuls of jumbles and marchpane ships set inside bright wobbling jelly. Everyone around me was eating – and I hadn't had a bite since breakfast.

Reluctantly I ignored the growling in my stomach and continued with my search for Cromwell.

I finally found him standing with King Henry beside an ornate fountain that spewed red and white wine from the mouths of stone lions. Lady Anne was with the King. She certainly didn't have the smile the carver had given her statue. And she certainly wasn't wearing a golden gown. She would never choose to outshine His Majesty. She looked pale and anxious and the King was patting her hand. I'd bet the livery off my back that he was trying to soothe her fears about the accident. The news of the falling statue had spread quickly, for everyone was talking about it. But I doubted anyone had dared tell Lady Anne that the object which had nearly dropped on her beloved's head was a wooden version of her!

Cromwell saw me and came over at once.

'Well, Jack?' he said. 'I see you have something to tell me. Although I cannot fathom why it should have taken you so long to visit a lodging house.'

'I . . . did a little more than that, sir,' I said.

He watched me in that grave way that gave me the feeling he was reading my thoughts but he kept silent. I took it as permission to go on.

'The pulley was deliberately sabotaged.'

Before he could ask how I had found this out, I told him about the discovery of the dead men. Although I assured him that no one had seen my face – I thought I'd leave Cat out of it – I saw a hint of annoyance in his eyes that I'd taken the risk of being recognised. Easy for him. He hadn't had to run for his life over slippery roofs, carrying a bag full of precious plans.

When I finished, my master was silent for a moment. 'The deaths have occurred within the Verge of Court so they will be investigated by the coroner as are all fatalities so close to the King,' he said finally. 'We have other aspects of this case to deal with. Have you any theories about who is behind the attempt on His Majesty, Jack?'

I knew he had plenty of theories for himself. He was just testing me, getting me to use my brain and think about the investigation.

I paused for a moment.

'Seth and Ivo might have decided to kill the King on the spur of the moment,' I said. 'For some foul purpose of their own. But the arrival of the wood merchant which distracted everyone was too convenient so I believe that the three of them were involved. It must have been thought of a while ago because Seth and Ivo needed time to befriend the murdered men and get taken on for the King's ship. And . . .' I paused. I'd let my thoughts run away with me. Was I barking up the wrong tree?

'Go on.'

'It seems a complicated plan for two carpenters and a wood merchant. I believe they are more likely to be conspirators in a larger scheme.'

'So do I, Jack,' said Cromwell. He looked over the guests again, here from all corners of Europe. 'A plot to overthrow the King of England.'

8

'What are your orders, sir?' I said. I imagined there would be plenty for me to do with such a dire threat hanging over His Majesty.

'For now, your part is done,' said Cromwell. 'I have placed men in the crowd, listening to the talk. Take those plans and put them away.'

Fighting down the feeling of disappointment, I cast my eyes about to see if I could spot anyone who might also work for my master. A foolish idea – they were all too skilled to behave suspiciously. I was always in awe of Cromwell's network of spies – simply because they were invisible. I knew of only one other, Robert Aycliffe, a young lawyer in training, but a fully-fledged agent. I saw him now. He appeared to be having a pleasant chat with one of the King's gentlemen but I knew he would be listening to all that went on around him. I wished I was allowed to stay and help. I thought of pleading my case with my master, but Cromwell had gone.

I went to do as he'd instructed but was stopped by a slender hand on my sleeve.

'I wish to thank you, Jack,' said a voice. I turned and bowed quickly. Lady Anne was gazing down at me. She looked as if she'd been crying. 'I hear you did me and the country a great service today.'

I tried to find the right words. 'I would give my life for His Majesty, my lady,' I burbled at last.

'As would every one of his loyal subjects,' said Lady Anne fervently.

At that moment I caught sight of a foreign nobleman staring through the crowds at her. The venom in his eyes took me aback. I knew I had to return the plans but the spy in me also knew I couldn't ignore such hatred directed at the King's great love. I remembered a saying of my godfather's when the abbot was looking more vindictive than usual – 'his face would sour milk'. That exactly described this man's expression. I took a pitcher of wine from the fountain and walked towards him as if looking for goblets to fill.

I stopped at a respectful distance. The sour-faced nobleman's lip curled as he murmured something to his two companions. He was obviously important, splendidly dressed in fur-lined velvet. The plump, round-faced gentleman on his left wore a hat so full of feathers that he looked as if he'd stuck a chicken on his head, a chicken which bowed in deference to his master. On his right stood a stiff little man. His doublet was immaculate and adorned with chains. But instead of precious jewels, each one had some sort of amulet on it. They made me wonder if he was an astrologer, like Doctor Filby. He was nibbling delicately at a marchpane sweet and wiping his pinched mouth with each bite.

I moved towards them and cursed myself that the only foreign tongue I knew was Latin. Sour-face was speaking Spanish.

This must be the imperial ambassador, Eustace Chapuys. I knew a little of Chapuys. He was the ambassador to Charles, the King of Spain and Holy Roman Emperor. Emperor Charles was the nephew of Queen Katherine. There was bad blood between him and King Henry because the King was trying to divorce Queen Katherine and marry Anne Boleyn in her place. No wonder Charles's loyal servant was barely hiding his dislike for Lady Anne. My heartbeat quickened a little. Had this bad blood led to the attempted murder of the King?

But whatever suspicion I had, I'd learn nothing from their foreign words. I stored it in the back of my mind and was about to leave the Banqueting House to return the plans, when His Majesty came and greeted the ambassador.

'I am sure you would like to know about the *Fair Anne*,' he boomed. It was as if the incident at the dockyard had never happened.

'Indeed, Sire.' The ambassador managed to look as if he wanted nothing more than to talk about the King's new ship. He indicated the small man with a wave of his hand. 'My deputy, Bolivar, and I were only just saying we are looking forward to the grand launch.'

So not a man of the stars after all but the second most important Spaniard at Court.

'You can imagine I am also very eager,' beamed the King. 'We will process from the palace in great state to the shipyard. The tide will be at its highest at ten o'clock and that is when the *Fair Anne* will take to the water.'

'I'm sure it will be a magnificent sight,' said Chapuys.

'It will,' crowed King Henry. 'She will be the finest galleon ever to sail the seas. I'll warrant your emperor has nothing that compares!' He rocked back on his heels, enjoying the men's discomfort at the slight to their master. 'And that's all I shall say for I do not want to spoil the glorious moment.'

I was impressed that the ambassador showed no sign of the irritation he must have felt at the King's teasing.

'I was most concerned to hear that there was an accident today, Your Majesty,' he said smoothly. 'And most relieved to see you have come to no harm.'

His entourage nodded in earnest agreement. I was sure they were play-acting.

I had just turned to slip out of the tent when my shoulder was clamped by a gloved hand, covered in rings. I nearly toppled backwards with the force.

'Here you see my saviour,' said the King, spinning me round to face his listeners. 'Were it not for this lad's quick actions, I would not be alive to tell you about the wonders of the *Fair Anne.*'

Every one of the ambassador's party turned to stare at me. I wondered if some of them would gladly have dropped a statue on *my* head for saving my sovereign. However, they merely showed polite interest.

'Indeed,' said King Henry, 'were it not for my foresight in taking a royal scribe with me to carry the ship's plans, events would have taken a tragic turn.' I was amused at how he was now congratulating himself for the rescue!

'Your Majesty, we would be honoured if you would allow us to see your drawings,' said Deputy Bolivar, his English more heavily accented than the ambassador's. 'They say the ship was built to your own design. We know you to be a most gifted man but can such an achievement really be true?'

I realised the Spanish were hoping to sweet-talk the King into showing them everything.

The King looked delighted, as he always did with compliments. 'Give me the plans, Jack.'

I fumbled with the clasp of my satchel and pulled out the scrolls. Bowing, I held them out, surprised that after all my fears about losing them and letting out their secret, His Majesty was going to show them to anyone who asked nicely!

But of course I was wrong. The King opened one,

handing the others back to me in a tight roll. It showed a coloured picture of the outside of the vessel – and no more.

'His Majesty is truly gifted!' crooned Chapuys. 'Look, Bolivar, at this perfect draughtsmanship.' He turned back to his royal host. 'It is the finest in Christendom, nay, in the whole world.'

I could see he was overdoing the flattery – but the King preened himself like a royal parrot. However, he quickly rolled the parchment up and thrust it into my hands.

'May we see what you have designed for the interior?' asked Chapuys. 'I imagine it is even more marvellous.'

'No.' His Majesty almost snapped the word.

I fumbled about, trying to get all the papers back into the satchel as quickly as possible.

The King flashed a smile to soften his bluntness. 'I wish to keep that for the launch. My Lady Anne is to feast her eyes on its delights before anyone else.'

Chapuys bent his head in acknowledgement, no doubt grinding his teeth at the mention of Anne Boleyn. While I fastened the satchel, I kept a close watch on him. I know I didn't imagine the brief flash of anger in his eyes, as if he'd been thwarted. I was certain he'd wanted to examine those drawings.

'You look hungry, young scribe.' King Henry was beaming down at me. 'Choose something from the table there.'

I didn't need telling twice.

Helping myself to a custard tart, I tried to eat quietly but it was hard not to gobble the delicious yellow filling.

I'd just bitten off a very large piece of pastry when the King pulled me to one side. I desperately tried to hide my bulging cheeks and prayed I wouldn't have to reply to any questions.

'Listen well, Jack. I have a commission for you.'

I swallowed the mouthful, nearly choked, and nodded, looking attentive – I hoped.

'I would have you go to the dockyard tomorrow with all haste.' He bent towards me, and his next words were whispered right into my ear so that no one else could possibly hear. 'Tell the carver that as he repairs the statue, I command him to fashion a gold crown for the image of my love to wear. It will be her *crowning* glory.' He wheezed with laughter at his own joke. Then he caught sight of a figure in the crowd. 'Filby!' he boomed. 'You must draw me a new horoscope for the launch. I wish to know of any inauspicious omens.' And he strode away towards the stout little astrologer.

I turned my attention back to the ambassador and his men who were talking earnestly together. There were times when it was very useful being a servant because servants appear invisible to their masters and things are said in front of them that shouldn't be said.

Unfortunately, even if they were scheming to paint the wine fountain blue I'd never know as they spoke in Spanish again. It sounded as if they were angry. But then that might just have been how they always talked. I remembered when I first came to Court and heard a delegation from the Prince of Moscow jabbering away. They'd sounded fierce and I'd been sure they were plotting a murder until they burst out laughing and I realised that they'd been telling a joke.

However, these three men didn't burst out laughing. Instead they spoke in low voices, throwing occasional glances at my satchel.

I thought about Eustace Chapuys and his interest in the King's ship. Incredible design or not, the *Fair Anne* was nothing more than a royal pleasure boat!

Yet, something in his expression told me that the plans were very important to him.

9

I had to report my suspicions to Cromwell. I scanned the Banqueting House but there was no sign of him. I slipped out of the tent and set off across the Knot Garden. I hadn't gone far when I heard a voice calling from behind.

'Excuse me, boy. A moment please.'

I turned. The portly Spanish gentleman with the chicken on his head was smiling at me.

He beckoned for me to approach. It was dark now and the torches stuck among the bushes gave a fierce flame.

'My name is Adalberto Donis,' he said. He spoke English with very little accent. 'I am secretary to the ambassador. You are a hero, saving your King's life today.'

'Not really,' I muttered. Something was shrieking in my brain to be careful and not trust this man. 'I just happened to be in the right place at the right time.'

'You are as modest as you are clever,' said Señor Donis smoothly. 'And I'm sure a clever young man like you could explain those ship plans to me as well as your monarch. In fact . . .' He produced a golden coin and held it up in front of me. '. . . I'd warrant that it might be worth your while to let me look for myself.'

The man was bribing me! I wanted to tell him what to do with his money but suggesting such a painful and undignified thing to a foreign guest might cause a diplomatic incident. Instead I bowed politely. 'I would be most pleased to oblige you, sir,' I began, and saw the man looking hopeful, 'but I'm sure you will understand that I cannot disobey my King's orders. Besides, in three days' time you will see the ship for yourself. Why spoil the surprise?'

Donis pressed his lips into a thin line. He was clearly not pleased. Perhaps he'd had his own orders, and didn't wish to fail in his task. But orders from whom? I was willing to wager that Chapuys was behind it. Donis flipped the coin into the air. It looked newly minted and caught the light as it spun. Such money would make a deal of difference to a scribe and Donis knew it. It fell at my feet with a clatter.

My hand clutching the buckle of the satchel, I picked up the coin to return it to him.

Donis gave me a nod. 'It's yours. Go on. Who would know?'

Just for a second I felt the tug of temptation before my loyalty crushed it dead and left a wave of anger and disgust washing over me.

Without a word I dropped it into his hand and turned on my heel. I heard Señor Donis give an impatient grunt and stride away.

'I saw what happened,' said a low voice. Master Cromwell was standing in the shadows. 'Well done, Jack.'

'Thank you, sir,' I replied.

'Do not be too hard on yourself,' my master went on, looking intently into my face. 'We all have moments of weakness.'

I was stunned. As ever, Cromwell seemed to have read my mind.

'But you did the right thing.' He paused. 'Why do you think Señor Donis wanted those plans?'

'I think Chapuys might well have sent him to me,' I said, glad to take my mind from the bribe. I told him my suspicions about the ambassador. 'There are two possible reasons why he wants to see the drawings. He wishes to find out the dimensions and features of the *Fair Anne* so that the Emperor can build an even more impressive vessel, not for battle, for he must already know it is no warship, but just to show off that he has better than our King.'

'And the other reason?'

'The other reason is much darker,' I replied, 'for which he might need very detailed knowledge of the ship. It is possible that the Emperor's men are behind the failed attempt on the King's life and are seeking a new way to kill him. If that is the case, the ship is somehow central to their plans.'

'I understand you are to carry out an errand for His Majesty,' said Cromwell.

I nodded dumbly, wondering if there was anything that my master didn't make it his business to know.

'I have an errand for you too. When you have finished with the carver, go to the Master Shipwright's office and ask about any bills of sale connected with Benjamin Dobson, the wood merchant who made the fuss. You might be able to verify his tale . . . or prove it to be the falsehood we believe it is.'

'Yes, sir,' I said.

'And no acrobatics this time.' There was a slight smile on my master's face.

'Of course not, sir.' God's teeth! The man did know everything!

'Did you make any notes on the plans that the King might want to see tonight?'

'No, sir. There was no time before the . . . accident, and His Majesty had other things to think of afterwards.'

'Then take them to his apartments and hand them to one of his Gentlemen. They will be safe there.'

I knew he meant from the prying eyes of the Emperor's men.

He walked back to the Banqueting House, leaving me feeling very pleased with myself at being part of the investigation again. I turned and almost collided with Oswyn Drage.

'Just the boy I wanted to see,' he said. His voice oozed smug satisfaction. 'I've been sent by Mister Scrope especially to find you. There is a heap of work and he said that it's time you did your share, no matter how late it is.'

'I shall be along very soon,' I replied. 'But I have one errand to carry out before I return.'

'Don't you think you'd better do as you're bidden directly?' snapped Oswyn. 'Really, Briars, if I didn't know better I'd say you're up to something. You've been gone nearly all day from the scribes' room, and yet the King and his party have been back for hours. And all you've been doing is carrying a bag of drawings.'

I remembered how, earlier that day in the scribes' office, he'd looked ready to stab me dead from jealousy when I'd grabbed the job.

'I have been about His Majesty's business, Oswyn,' I assured him, keeping my tone light. 'When that is finished, I shall return to work.'

'That was this morning.' Weasel-face leaned down until our noses were nearly touching. 'What I want to know is, what have you been doing all the hours since?'

'My duty,' I said shortly. 'Ask Master Cromwell if you really wish to know.'

'I suppose he wanted more of your wonderful handwriting that Scrope goes on about,' scoffed Oswyn. 'Private letters was it?'

'You can ask Master Cromwell that as well.'

I knew he wouldn't.

Oswyn's mouth tightened and he marched off without another word.

'Come one, come all!' A brightly clad acrobat came running past. More entertainers skipped after him, all joining in the cry. 'Pray join us in the Presence Chamber where we will tumble for your delight and amazement.'

I wished I could go and see them. The King's tumblers always had the audience gasping in wonder and no doubt they'd have been told to dazzle the foreign dignitaries with an even more splendid performance than usual. But I had the ship's plans to deal with and a heap of work waiting for me. Cursing inwardly, I headed across the Inner Court to reach the King's apartments. Unfortunately this was also the route to the Presence Chamber and it seemed as if every courtier in the palace was off to see the acrobats. It was like being in a fast-flowing river. I was swept along and buffeted from side to side. I tried using my elbows to battle against the tide but it was hopeless.

Someone at my back stumbled into me, knocking me off balance. I toppled forwards and fell. The surging crowd behind had no chance to stop. I heard shrieks and oaths as several people landed on top of me. It was some minutes before I could pull myself free of the heap. One lady was on hands and knees picking up broken beads, another was wailing about her torn cloak. Two gentlemen were arguing about who'd caused the disaster.

I struggled to my feet and felt for my bag but it had fallen from my shoulder. As the crowd began to move away I snatched it up. Heart racing, I looked inside. I frantically thrust my hand in and felt every seam. It was hopeless. The bag was empty and the plans were gone. I searched the ground around. Nothing to be seen but some ribbon and a flattened headdress. I scanned the courtiers, hoping someone had picked them up. There was no sign of them.

And then, in the distance, I saw a hat festooned with chicken feathers bobbing along. Señor Donis was clearly in a hurry to get away. I was willing to wager that tucked into his cloak were the plans of the King's ship.

I knew I couldn't challenge him – but I had to follow and somehow get them back. I darted into the palace. The courtiers were surging off towards the Presence Chamber. The chicken feathers were going in the other direction – at speed.

I set off after them.

10

'Jack Briars!' came a peevish voice. 'That is not the way to our office. And that is where you should be heading.'

Mister Scrope blocked my path – as much as a thin scrawny man could block anyone's path. I smelt the gravy on his robes where he'd spilled his lunch.

God's wounds! I was losing my prey! The chicken feathers disappeared round a corner.

'Didn't Oswyn pass on the message? I'm going to have to tie you to your seat if you carry on like this,' grumbled the Chief Scribe.

'I'm sorry, sir,' I said. 'The King . . .'

'I am well aware that you had an important job to do for His Majesty,' said Mister Scrope irritably. 'However, I'm sure you've finished looking after his plans by now.'

Little did he know how true his words were!

'I was just . . . going back to work,' I answered, feeling desperate inside, 'but it was so crowded that I decided on a different route.' It sounded a feeble excuse, even to my ears, but I had to say something to get away.

'Well, hurry up,' he grunted.

I went to do as he said but he caught my arm with his bony fingers.

'You will see Oswyn and Mark no doubt. I told them they may watch the tumblers. It's their reward for working so hard. Don't be tempted to go with them. You have too much copying to catch up with.'

Señor Donis was long gone. I trailed back to the gatehouse and climbed wearily to the second floor. As soon as I pushed open the office door Mark leapt to his feet.

'Where have you been, Jack?' he gasped, his thin face twisted with anxiety. 'Mister Scrope expected you back ages ago.'

'I know,' I groaned. 'I met him just now. He gave me my orders. You're going to the entertainment and I'm to stay here and do some work.'

Oswyn pushed a tall pile of parchments across the table. 'And here it is,' he said, scarcely bothering to hide his triumph. 'Come on, Mark. We must leave the poor boy to his labours.'

But I found it impossible to sit and copy out letters while the King could be in jeopardy. There was a chance that the Spaniards only wanted the plans to build a better ship for their emperor, but in my fevered imagination they were at this very moment pouring over the drawings, trying to find some weakness that would help their plot to kill the King succeed.

I made myself think logically. All the foreign delegations were expected in the Presence Chamber for the entertainment. It would be noticed if their seats were empty. So that was where Donis would certainly be by now, with the rest of his party. Yet I was sure that he would have put the plans somewhere safe first. And the most likely place was the ambassador's apartments. I had to get there before they returned . . .

I jumped to my feet, but stopped as the door swung violently open. A small redheaded figure bustled into the room.

'What's the matter with you?' laughed Cat. 'You look as if you've seen a ghost!'

I opened my mouth to explain but she hardly let me start.

'I've come to find out how you're getting on with' – she looked round conspiratorially – 'our mission. I went off to the Presence Chamber first because I thought you'd be watching the tumblers. I wasn't really meant to be in there but I grabbed a kerchief I'd mended and sneaked in pretending I'd just picked it up and was looking for the owner. Clever, don't you agree?'

'Very,' I said, 'but I'm in a hurry . . .'

'Anyway, the acrobats were performing,' Cat went on, oblivious. 'I wish you'd seen them. Their Tower of

Babel was amazing. When they all fell down in a heap I confess I screamed. But then, all the ladies did – so no one noticed.'

'Good,' I said, only half listening. 'Now I must . . .'

'I bet you're wondering how I knew you were up here.' Cat was relentless! 'Mark told me. After a lot of stammering and stuttering. I don't know why that boy's so scared of me, I really don't . . .'

'I've got to go!' I managed to put in.

'Go?' said Cat. 'But Mark said you were working this evening.'

'It'll have to wait.' I made for the door. I knew I should explain, but my head was full of the lost plans and one thought – how to get them back.

Cat followed. 'But you haven't told me what's happened about the King's statue or those two men or anything. What have you found out?'

'Nothing,' I said impatiently. 'And nor will I if you don't let me get on! I'm off to Ambassador Chapuys's rooms. You don't need to come with me. I know the way.'

As everyone was in the Presence Chamber watching the acrobats, the passages were unusually quiet. I hurried along. I could hear drums and gasps of amazement even from here.

Cat caught up with me. 'I *am* coming with you,' she panted. 'I can always hide while you're talking to the foreign gentlemen. I'll listen in and then I'll know what's happening!'

It was no good. To stop her flow I had to tell her the full story. Cat gawped as I told her about the King's missing plans.

'So let me guess – you're going in to Mister Shappooee's rooms to find them while he's not there,' she said when I'd finished. 'That sounds risky!'

'And the longer I leave it the riskier it gets,' I replied. 'He's sure to go back there as soon as the entertainment's over.'

'You'll be in trouble if he finds you,' said Cat helpfully. 'However, I've got a plan. I'll see you outside his chambers – behind the sculpture of the man-eating Cyclops. I won't be long.'

With that she disappeared. Bemused, I strode on. Cat was right – it would be very serious if I was caught sneaking about in the rooms of the King's important guests. I wondered what she had in mind that was going to keep me safe. I came to the statue – a gruesome bit of marble showing a greedy-looking Cyclops tucking in to a rather surprised peasant – and squashed myself behind it to wait. Down the passage were the three ornately carved doors of the ambassador's apartments.

Cat popped up beside me, carrying a skirt, a cap, a shirt and a bodice.

'What are you doing with those?' I asked her. 'I thought you had a plan.'

'I have,' said Cat, smugly. She held out the bundle of clothes. 'They're for you. Put them on.'

I stared at her in disbelief.

'A scribe can't go sniffing around in the ambassador's apartments,' she went on, 'but there is someone who can. I've thought it all through. It's no good you being a seamstress – you wouldn't recognise a bit of mending if you fell over it – but if you're caught as a laundry maid you can just pretend you're collecting the bed linen for washing. I'll do all the talking and you can be my assistant.'

'No one will believe I'm a girl,' I protested. 'I'm better off being a log boy or something.'

She gave me a knowing smile. 'And you've got some log boy's clothing with you? Where is it? Up your livery sleeve? Under your cap? I thought you were in a hurry to find the plans.'

I reluctantly took off my jacket and hat. Pulling the clothes on over my shirt, I stuffed my uniform behind the Cyclops's bum.

Cat yanked the linen cap down over my forehead and tugged the apron into place. Then she looked me over. 'You'll do,' she said. 'I've delivered mending here plenty of times, of course, but don't you start worrying that they'll remember I'm not a laundress. All that work and they've never noticed me nor pressed a coin into my hand. Too high and mighty with their foreign ways.'

It was only a few steps to the nearest door but it wasn't easy walking in a skirt. It wrapped itself round my legs and I nearly went headlong. I wondered how Cat managed to stay upright.

She knocked loudly at the door and waited but no one came to her summons so she boldly swung it open. Like most rooms in the palace, it wasn't locked.

'No one here,' she announced. 'I'll just check the other rooms for you – in case someone's stayed behind and not gone to see the tumblers.' She was soon back and planted herself like a sentry outside the room. 'You're safe. Go in here. You can get to the other rooms from inside. If anyone comes, I'll cough loudly. But you must play your part. If we're caught, remember what I said. We're just laundry maids going about our duties.'

'I hope that works,' I muttered.

She gave me a push. 'In you go.'

I hesitated. When I stepped across that threshold, I would be making a grave intrusion into the chambers of an honoured guest. If I got caught then no one, not even Thomas Cromwell, would be able to help me.

11

It was as quiet as the tomb inside.

The first chamber was small and plain. A fire blazed in the grate. It was obviously where the servants slept. I'd soon checked under each of the mattresses and inside the single chest. A curtain concealed the entrance to the next room. I hoped to have more luck there. This was even hotter and better furnished, with two large beds – for Deputy Bolivar and Señor Donis, I decided. It was easy to see which bed was which. A garland of rue and lavender hung beside one. Old Father Jerome at the abbey had sworn by lavender to keep evil away. And if that wasn't enough, amulets etched with strange runes were scattered over the pillow. That would be the superstitious deputy's bed for sure. But for all the boxes and caskets and clothes presses, there was no sign of the King's plans.

I slipped through the curtain into the last chamber.

I didn't need to be a spy to know I was now in the ambassador's own room. Rich velvet hangings were draped all over the bed, tapestries of dramatic Bible scenes hung on every wall and a huge fire blasted out heat. Mark had told me that the foreigners always complained about the cold and damp in England.

Papers were piled on a large oak table. At a quick glance they looked like bills, official documents and letters with the seal of the Holy Roman Emperor. I rifled through them, although I thought it doubtful that the plans would be so poorly hidden. They were more likely to have been put into one of the grand, inlaid chests that stood under the window. However no ship's drawings came to light, although I unfolded every silk shirt and embroidered cloak that I found inside.

I reasoned that the plans could still be with Donis. They could even be stuffed under his chicken hat. And short of knocking it off his head, there was no way I'd find them. I had a sick feeling at the pit of my stomach, as if I'd eaten something bad. The plans were lost to me.

'You nearly finished?' demanded Cat pushing through the curtain to join me. 'Only I can't hear the music any more so they might be back any moment . . . God in Heaven!' She marched over and gawped at the floor. 'The sen-yors have got a carpet. I've not seen that before.'

'What's so special about it?' I asked, peering at the large, elaborately woven square of wool by the bed. 'The abbot at St Godric's had them hanging all over the walls of his rooms.'

'Exactly,' said Cat. 'Hanging on the walls away from muddy boots. I thought only His Majesty was wealthy enough to put rugs on the floor.'

To my astonishment, she whipped off her shoes and strutted up and down on the carpet. 'It's so soft,' she murmured.

'It doesn't stop the floorboards squeaking though,' I said. 'Come on, we must go before someone comes along and hears you.'

Cat gave one last prance. I winced at the creaking sound. And then suddenly I was on my hands and knees, cursing my stupidity. I'd looked everywhere except under the floor! I pulled the rug aside. Sure enough, one board was loose. I lifted it up and we both peered inside.

'What's that?' asked Cat.

In the dust and mouse droppings lay a long thin shape. My hopes soared. I'd found the plans. It looked as if Señor Donis had hurriedly wrapped them in a rough piece of paper and stuffed them in here. He must have thought they'd be safe until he could show them to his master.

I snatched up the parcel – and my hopes crumbled to ashes.

'That's not exactly the plans of the King's ship!' said Cat.

We both stared at the plain brown shirt that tumbled out of the wrapping.

'I don't understand!' I said angrily. 'Why would anyone want to hide *this*?'

'I can't imagine,' replied Cat, picking it up and inspecting it. 'I'm surprised the foreign gentlemen have got anything this coarse. I've mended plenty of their shirts and they're all silk. They're very fussy about what goes next to their precious skin – even their servants wouldn't wear this sort of thing.'

I was just about to put the parcel back into its hiding place when I noticed there was something else under the floor. Some sheets of paper. I picked one up.

'This shirt *must* belong to one of them,' I exclaimed. 'Here's the bill. It's from some tailor's shop in Greenwich Village. But it's no help. It just says "supplied one shirt, payment on receipt" but it doesn't say who it was supplied to.' I grabbed the other papers. 'Someone here has a lot of bills from the same place. Shirts . . . hose . . . hats . . .'

'Now that is another odd thing and no mistake.' Cat sounded intrigued. 'It's well known that the ambassador and his men never buy English clothes. They have them sent over and make a fuss about it, saying that our fashions are not good enough.' She broke off. 'I thought I heard something . . .' She tiptoed to the door which led to the passageway outside and poked her nose out. She coughed loudly.

I felt icy cold despite the roaring fire. That was the signal. Someone was coming.

12

I stuffed the shirt and bills back under the floorboard and had just pulled the carpet over it when a pile of sheets was thrust into my arms.

'There you go, Jacquetta,' came Cat's voice from beyond the white mountain. 'Bring these to the laundry for me and be quick about it . . . Oh, good evening, sirs. I didn't see you there.'

I peered round my burden to find Ambassador Chapuys and Deputy Bolivar frowning down at us. I felt an immense anger boiling up inside. Thanks to their thieving, I could soon lose my job. But I quickly remembered that I'd lose it all the sooner if they discovered who Jacquetta really was!

'We'll be out of your way in a tick, your worshipfulnesses,' said Cat cheerfully. 'Got any more washing before we go?'

Chapuys waved an irritable hand at her. 'Leave us,'

he muttered. 'I am too busy to give my time to such things now.'

I was sure he spoke the truth. No doubt he wanted us gone so they could pore over the stolen plans as soon as Donis brought them along! Cat bobbed a curtsey and steered me towards the door.

'Wait!' Chapuys rapped out the order. 'Come back.'

We stopped and turned. I buried my face in the bed linen.

'As you are here, you will take these too.' I felt something being thrown on top of my load. It overbalanced and, helpless to stop it, I spilled the whole lot on the floor. I crawled about gathering them up, hoping that all he saw was the top of my cap.

'You clumsy clot, Jacquetta!' said Cat. 'I'm sorry, your ambassadorship and your sen-yorship. Jacquetta's new and she isn't the brightest button on the breeches.'

'It is most odd that you are here,' I heard Bolivar say. There was suspicion in his voice. 'You mended a doublet for me the other day, girl.'

'Not me, sir,' said Cat quickly.

'Yes, you did. I am certain of it. Why are you collecting dirty washing when you are in truth a seamstress?'

So Cat hadn't passed unnoticed after all. Was this to be our undoing? I staggered to my feet, keeping my face well hidden. My palms grew sticky with sweat. I wondered whether, if I threw the laundry in their faces, we might get away.

'A seamstress, your honourableness?' said Cat as if

in great surprise. 'No indeed. I wish I was. I'm just a laundry maid. You must be thinking of my twin sister, Kitty. She's always been the lucky one.'

'Is that so?'

'Indeed, your noblenesses. There were ten in our family but of all of us Kitty got the best jobs. Ever since she was born she . . .'

'Enough. We do not need a family history. Go.'

I wobbled with relief. Cat grabbed me by the shoulders and steered me out of the door. She apologised to the passers-by and berated me as my feet caught in my skirts and my laundry pile swayed from side to side. I heard the words 'clodpole' and 'halfwit' repeated so often that I itched to throw the whole lot on top of her.

'Where are we going?' I asked. It felt like a very long journey.

'The laundry, of course! We can't leave those sheets just anywhere or we'll get someone into trouble – and they were due for washing anyway. Can't you be more careful with them? There's a lot of folk about now the tumblers have finished.'

I could have told her that. I'd bumped into most of them! She steered me down a narrow stairway. Now we were alone.

'Listen,' said Cat, striding on ahead. 'I've had a thought . . .'

I staggered along behind her, only half attending to what she was saying. My mind was firmly on the missing plans. How was I ever going to break the news to my master that I'd failed to keep them safe? The King could be in even greater danger now.

Cat's voice brought me out of my anxious thoughts. 'It's a proper mystery!'

'Too right,' I groaned. 'Those plans might be anywhere in the palace. And there's nothing I can . . .'

'Never mind the plans,' said Cat dismissively. 'I'm talking about the shirt. I can't understand why any of those foreign gents would have that rough old thing – or anything English.' She stopped so suddenly that I barged into her. 'That's why it was hidden, of course. The man who bought it was ashamed to be seen with such poor quality stuff so he shoved it under the floor, together with the bills for all the other English clothes he bought.'

We reached the laundry and Cat took the bundle from me and went inside. I wondered what excuse she'd make for presenting them to the surprised workers in there.

'I tried to tell the ambassador that I'm a seamstress,' I heard her say, 'but he'd have none of it and thrust his dirty washing into my arms.' She was as good as a worm at wriggling out of a difficult hole.

Then she was back. She clearly hadn't finished with the subject of the wretched shirt. 'Why buy such a common thing in the first place?'

'It must be easier to go to somewhere local like Fettiplace's shop than send to Spain,' I said, remembering the paper I'd found with the stockings.

265

This didn't exactly satisfy Cat. In fact she was even more astonished. 'Fettiplace? He got it from Fettiplace? I don't believe it.' She rounded on me. 'Are you sure?'

'I read his name on the bill,' I told her.

'I know all about that tailor,' said Cat. 'No one from the palace goes near him – not even the servants, if they've got any sense. That man is a swindling swine and they say he knows every villain around. He'd sell his own grandmother if he got a good price for her. You must have seen his shop in Greenwich Village. It's next to the baker's – more's the pity for the baker! It's the one with the broken shutters and the cracked windows.' She looked at me. 'I can tell you're not listening to a word I'm saying.'

Nothing was further from the truth! Her words had opened up a new trail for me. One question drummed in my head. What was the connection between Chapuys and his men and a villain like Fettiplace?

13

'I'm sorry you didn't find what you were after,' Cat went on. 'I do wish I could help.'

'You've been more helpful than you can imagine,' I said to her surprise, and swept off, leaving her guessing. I was pleased that for once it was my turn to make the grand exit and not hers.

I'd only gone a few paces when I realised that I was still dressed as a laundry maid. I couldn't possibly go back to retrieve my livery from the statue outside the imperial apartments without hiding my face – not now the whole Court was milling about. Knowing I was going to have to eat humble pie I turned and caught up with Cat.

'I thought you'd be back,' she said, grinning smugly from ear to ear.

'The thing is,' I mumbled, 'I have to go and report to my master, and . . .'

'. . . You'd rather be Jack than Jacquetta,' said Cat. 'I can see it would be a problem if he gave you his smalls when you appear.'

Cat soon returned, but refused to hand me my clothes until I'd told her how she'd inspired my next move. I was forced to repeat several times how clever she'd been.

Exhausted, I got away at last.

I was relieved to find Master Cromwell still at his desk. The courtyard clock had just struck ten and I'd been worried he might have gone to his home at Austin Friars as he sometimes did. His office was always dark and mysterious, even by day, but at night he was almost a shadow beside his single candle.

'Yes, Jack?' he said, his eyes glassy in the flame. 'You have something to tell me?'

There was nothing for it. I launched right in with my confession about losing the plans. He heard me out and then stood and paced up and down his office.

'This is very worrying,' was all he said.

'I've been trying to find them,' I burst out. 'I searched the ambassador's rooms . . .'

My master spun on his heel. 'What?'

'That is to say, Jacquetta, the . . . new laundry maid, had a look round while she was fetching the dirty sheets.' I thought it best not to tell him that Chapuys and his deputy had come across Jacquetta.

The glimmer of a smile appeared on his face. 'I'll be bound that she was assisted by a certain seamstress?'

He became grave again. 'You took a huge risk. This is something only my most experienced men would be instructed to do – in extreme circumstances. Had you been caught spying in the ambassador's chamber it would have made waves that would have rippled throughout Europe.'

'But not as big as the waves that killing King Henry would cause,' I dared to interject.

'I share your passion for the King's safety, Jack,' my master said firmly. 'But I have cautioned you before not to go beyond your instructions. You sail too close to the wind.'

I feared he was about to send me away in disgrace, never to be entrusted with anything important again.

'On this occasion, however, you got away with your actions, reckless though they were. If His Majesty asks for his designs, I shall respectfully suggest that they are safer hidden here at Greenwich until after the launch. Meanwhile, I shall instruct some of my people to scour the entire palace and discover where they are and what the Emperor's men are up to. If they are indeed behind this plot, then I pray we find out before it is too late.' He sighed. 'I fear that the theft of the plans could be connected with another attempt on the King's life.'

'I am truly sorry that I was not successful in my search,' I told him. 'But I did find a link with Fettiplace, a tailor in Greenwich.'

'Did you indeed?' said my master. The name obviously meant something to him. 'Tell me more.'

I was encouraged by his tone. 'With your consent, I wish to investigate his shop. It would be easy to go on my way back from delivering His Majesty's message to the woodcarver tomorrow morning.'

Cromwell sat heavily at his table. 'I am relieved to hear you asking my permission this time,' he said dryly. 'Although I suspect you would be tempted to do it anyway. Before I allow it, you must heed my warning. Fettiplace is known to me and to my other agents. He is a dangerous man who mixes with many criminals, from cutpurses to cutthroats.'

'I will be careful, sir,' I answered.

'You must be wary of all who cross your path tomorrow.' My master looked at me intently. 'We know little about who is involved in this dreadful plan to harm the King. If any one of the plotters gets wind of your involvement, they will be quick to silence you.'

14

The next morning, I got up at first light and hurried through the work that I'd put aside the night before. I longed to go in search of the missing plans. It didn't sit well with me that I was forced to leave it to others, especially if there was going to be another plot against the King. In truth, my guilt at losing them was making it hard for me to think straight.

Mark and Oswyn were still asleep, or so I thought. I hadn't taken into account the scratching of my quill. Oswyn raised his head from his privileged sleeping position by the fire.

'I thought we had mice in the wainscot,' he said, peering blearily at me. 'I was wrong. It's a miserable little rat.'

'I hope Mister Scrope doesn't set a trap,' I retaliated. 'There's more than one rodent in this office.'

I waited for him to snap back at me but he didn't.

I felt pleased my silly retort had shut him up for a moment. He ignored me and shook Mark awake.

'Breakfast time for us two, Helston. But sadly not for Jack. We'll leave him to catch up with his copying.'

Mark gave me an anxious look as he pulled on his livery jacket and trooped off out of the door after Oswyn. I was sure he expected to find me starved to a skeleton on his return. I wouldn't have been surprised myself. I was so hungry I felt as if my belly was touching my backbone.

I was just finishing the last letter when Mister Scrope came in, a great chunk of manchet bread in one hand and a tankard of beer in the other. For one glorious moment I imagined they were for me, but he plonked himself down by the fire and began to eat and drink with alternate mouthfuls.

'The documents from last night are all done, Mister Scrope,' I announced, getting to my feet. 'And now I must run an errand.'

'What!' The Chief Scribe spluttered beer into his lap. 'Like you managed to do all day yesterday? Certainly not. I don't care what it is but your little chore can wait.'

Mark and Oswyn appeared at the door. Mark scuttled to his chair. I waited for Oswyn to put in some remark about how I was always shirking but he just took his place and reached for a quill. I wondered if he was ill but wasn't going to waste any time on him. I nodded as if agreeing with Mister Scrope.

'Of course, sir,' I said. 'If you'll just grant me leave to go and tell the King that I can't do his bidding after all.'

I watched as the words sank in. 'The King?'

'He wanted me to deliver a new order for the carver but I'm sure he'll understand . . .'

'Go!' shrieked Mister Scrope, turning pale at the thought of offending his monarch. 'Get yourself there now!'

I made for the door.

But before I undertook my errand I had something more to do. I went off to seek out old Mrs Pennycod, the pastry cook. I was hoping she'd insist on giving me something tasty to keep me going on my errand. After all, if I fainted from hunger before I'd even left the palace walls it would not serve the best interests of His Majesty. I had my excuse for visiting her. I'd ask her if she knew where the carver's workshop was. I didn't really need to know – I could easily enquire at the shipyard gates.

Everyone in the kitchen was busy with preparations for the noontide meal even though breakfast was only just finished. I got some friendly nods as I made my way over to a familiar figure busy with a rolling pin at the large table in the centre of the huge room.

'Jackanapes,' beamed Mrs Pennycod, expertly flicking the prepared pastry over a pie dish and pressing down the edges with barely a glance at her work. 'I've been hearing all about how you saved the King.' She looked hard at me. 'I've a feeling you've come here for something.'

'You are a mind reader, Mrs P,' I laughed. 'Doctor Filby had better watch his step or you'll be taking over his job.'

She gave a snort of derision. 'That wastrel! I watched him once doing this and that with some chicken entrails saying that they were telling him all sorts of things. Well, all they were telling me was that they'd make a tasty broth once he got his grubby paws off them! Anyway, you deserve a reward for saving His Glorious Majesty.' She pressed a thick slice of pork into my hands.

'Thank you,' I managed between mouthfuls.

'So what can I help you with?' she asked.

'I have to take a message to Mister Talboys the woodcarver,' I told her. 'It's from the King himself.'

'Lordy, Jack!' Mrs Pennycod shrieked in delight. 'You're well in with His Majesty now! He'll be wanting you sitting on his council before long, I shouldn't wonder.'

'And you'll be pie-maker-in-chief to Sir Jack Briars,' I laughed.

'That would be wonderful,' she cackled. 'Oswyn Drage would have to bow to you.' She peered at me keenly. 'Is he giving you trouble again? He looked like the cat who'd got the cream when I last saw him.'

'He's the same as always,' I said. 'And I'm just a scribe – a scribe who has to go to the carver's workshop at the shipyard. I came to ask you if you know where it is.'

'You're in luck, Jackanapes,' said Mrs Pennycod eagerly. 'Jacob the gardener told me that his cousin works in the coopers' store at the shipyard. He said his cousin went on and on about His Majesty's new vessel. His cousin said she was finer than anything he'd seen before. I'd give anything to see her myself – and I've heard that some of the servants are going to watch the procession. Not us, alas. We'll be here preparing the feast that will follow. And we've so little time with the launch being in two days.'

Mrs Pennycod opened the oven door in the wall and slid her pie in. 'Anyway, Jacob's cousin said that the carver has recently taken a little workshop there. It's right next to the coopers' storehouse,' she finished triumphantly.

'And whereabouts is the coopers' storehouse?' I asked.

'Lord bless you, I've no idea!' cackled the old lady. 'I've never set foot in the place.'

She delved in a jar and passed me a lump of marchpane. I thanked her and bit into the sugary treat as I left.

JP

A man at the gates of the shipyard gave me clear instructions how to find the woodcarver's workshop.

I passed a jumbled mass of storehouses and

workshops where shouts and hammering battered my ears. I skirted round men mending sails, the canvases stretched across the ground, and came up to a pile of barrels waiting to be loaded onto a cart outside the coopers' store. Next to it stood a small, simple building. As I walked in I saw the head of the wooden Anne Boleyn lying on a workbench. The carver was in the corner, working on the two halves of the statue's body, and helped by a large, brawny man, who looked up and smiled warmly. But the carver's behaviour was very different. He nearly jumped out of his boots when he saw my livery.

'The statue's not ready,' he gabbled. 'Tell the boy, Gilbert.'

His assistant laid a reassuring hand on his skinny arm. 'Calm yourself, Mister Talboys,' he said. 'Let's hear what the lad has come for.'

I told them about the King's demand for the statue to wear a golden crown. The carver's skin went pale and his mouth twitched uncontrollably.

Gilbert frowned so hard that his eyebrows made a black bushy forest above his eyes. 'That will be tricky. But if it's what His Majesty wants, then who are we to argue?' He turned to his master. 'Come now, sir, don't take on so. In all our years together have we ever failed? It's as well you sent for me after the accident to help repair the statue. I can stay and help you with this too. Your apprentices back in Lambeth will cope without me bashing their heads together for a few days.'

'I hope so,' said Talboys, trying to get a grip on himself.

The assistant led his master into a small back room where they started an earnest discussion. I waited, fearing that the carver might have a fatal apoplexy and imagining how I would break the news to His Majesty! I thanked the stars that the assistant seemed to be a sensible man.

As I stood there, listening to the anxious mutterings of the two men, my mind flew back to the attempt on the King's life. I wondered whether the carver had ever had dealings with the wood merchant, Dobson. He might even know something of Seth and Ivo. I'd have to be casual in my questioning though. I had no idea who was involved in the plot and couldn't risk being thought anything but a nosy royal scribe.

It seemed to me that the carver's jitters made him a very unlikely plotter. If he was party to an attempt on the King's life, he would surely have hidden his nerves for fear of being suspected. But I wasn't going to let him off the hook yet. Mister Talboys' behaviour might be designed to throw everyone off the scent.

I wandered around the workshop, looking at the carver's work – fat-cheeked cherubs, grand majestic lions and the fearsome bust of Neptune in the corner. I wondered if they'd been made for His Majesty's ship but there hadn't been room for them. As I gazed at the king of the sea with his thick curly beard and jewelled crown perched on top, I had an idea.

'Excuse me, Mister Talboys,' I called through the door, 'but perhaps Neptune's gold crown would do for the statue?'

The carver scuttled out. 'Do you think so?'

'It's a beautiful crown,' I assured him. 'I'm sure it would be perfect.'

Mister Talboys nodded. 'It should only need a little adjustment . . .' He peered at me closely. 'I thought you looked familiar. You're the boy who saved the King . . .'

'The boy who saved the King?' Gilbert had joined us, making the carver jump again. 'My master told me all about that. If it hadn't been for you, His Majesty would be dead.' He sounded as if he was pleased to be sharing the same air as such a hero as me. 'How was it that you saw the danger when no one else did?'

The carver had no idea how helpful he'd been. He'd brought up the very subject I wanted to ask about.

'I spotted the statue falling and acted without thinking,' I said.

'And please God you and your sharp eyes will be at his side again for the launch,' Gilbert went on, 'you being like a lucky bodyguard for him.'

'If His Majesty commands it, I will of course be there,' I said, knowing perfectly well that His Majesty was unlikely to think of me as a bodyguard!

'Then we'll be seeing each other again,' said the jovial assistant with a beaming smile. 'I am to accompany my master. It will be a privilege to witness something so spectacular.'

'I don't think any wood merchants will be invited,' I joked, turning to the carver. 'Have you had any dealings with the one who dared to yell at the King?'

Mister Talboys shook his head. 'I'd never seen him before. My wood comes from other suppliers.'

'All in all, it was a dreadful morning,' I went on. 'Everyone at the palace is talking about it. An angry wood merchant, the near accident for the King, and then two shipyard workers found murdered. The word is that those two men were friends of Seth and Ivo and that it should have been them operating the crane.' I paused as if something had just occurred to me. 'Don't you think it's strange that they were killed and then the crane went wrong? If they'd been there, the accident might never have happened.'

Mister Talboys stared at me, a tic pulsing in his cheek.

'Enough of this,' he said sharply. 'You may not be very busy, young sir, but I am. I'd be grateful if you'd let us get on.'

And with that, he ushered me out of the workshop and shut the door with a bang.

15

I wondered if I'd been wrong to discount Mister Talboys as a possible accomplice. Then I remembered that I'd just given the man a task that had to be completed in very little time and from an impatient master. He was probably letting his panic do his talking. The King's errand was complete but I still had one from Cromwell.

I hurried through the acrid smoke of a boiling tar barrel towards the Master Shipwright's office. I pushed open the door of a large room full of scribes bent over their work. Mister Baker came over. He had looked worried when I last saw him and now he looked positively ill.

'You're the lad who saved the King,' he said nervously. 'Why are you here? Has His Majesty sent some order?'

I felt sorry for the Master Shipwright. I'd heard the King say that he would have to answer for the terrible accident. He must have been hourly awaiting arrest.

'I'm here on business from Thomas Cromwell,' I told him. 'Nothing more.'

I did not imagine the relief that passed over his face. 'Of course, of course,' he said.

'Is he truly the boy who saved the King?' asked an elderly man who had stopped in the middle of adding up some figures.

Mister Baker sighed. 'Jack, would you be kind enough to relate your great act of courage to those here? They've been pestering me for the story.'

He looked as if he'd rather have dealt with me straight away and sent me packing but he was the only one. Eager faces watched me as I repeated my tale. I kept the details brief. One boy clapped when the King was saved. I turned to the shipwright before anyone could bother me with questions.

'Master Cromwell sent me to ask you about the wood merchant who protested yesterday, sir,' I said. 'He has not been found yet. Can you supply information about his dealings with the shipyard?'

'He is Benjamin Dobson,' James Baker told me. 'He doesn't have much business at Deptford but he did supply some of the timber for the *Fair Anne*.' He searched through a ledger until he came to the name. 'I will get a copy of his dealings sent to your master. His outburst did seem strange. He knew the price would be low but that's what the King pays and I remember Dobson having no gripe with it at the time.'

'The other day he confessed he had obligations to meet,' said the elderly scribe. 'He was worried.'

'Obligations?' I wondered what he meant.

'His daughter was getting married and he needed the money for her dowry.'

'Begging your pardon, sir,' called the boy who'd been delighted with my tale, 'but he was selling you a line. I've heard that he doesn't have a daughter.'

I made sure I didn't react to this interesting news. Why had the wood merchant lied? I got my answer soon enough.

'He'd have wanted the money to buy his ale,' laughed the scribe seated next to him. 'That's the only obligation Ben has – to get drunk every night. He'd chop off his arm for a pint of rum or a flagon of Mad Dog ale.'

'I reckon he's skulked back home to Gravesend,' said the boy. 'I've not seen him since.'

'Good riddance,' said his neighbour. 'We won't shed any tears over him.'

'Not like poor Tom and Barnaby,' agreed the boy. 'That was sad. Who do you think did that?'

'You must be the only one who doesn't know,' the elderly scribe told him. 'According to Mistress Bryant, it was a vicious assassin, two yards high who escaped over the roof, grew wings and flew away.'

I was surprised to find myself grateful to the landlady whose exaggerations had got Cat and me off the hook.

I thought about the snippets of information as I left

the Master Shipwright's office. They were beginning to make sense. Now I was almost sure Benjamin Dobson had been involved in the attempt on the King. He was a loner – he would have been an easy target for plotters to recruit without drawing attention to themselves. I could imagine them approaching him with the lure of more drinking money if he performed his part well.

By my reckoning, Dobson had not gone to hide at his home, but had scarpered along with Seth and Ivo.

It seemed that every worker at the shipyard knew me. Each one I passed on the way to the gates smiled or shook my hand and thanked the Lord that I'd been sent to save His Glorious Majesty. I managed to get a few men talking about the wood merchant and Seth and Ivo, but each one repeated the same as I'd heard before. There seemed to be no connection between the two carpenters and the merchant – and all accepted that it wasn't odd that the three had vanished. Every man said that he'd have done the same if he'd nearly squashed his sovereign. Some, like the carver's assistant, asked if I'd be at the launch to protect His Majesty again. They said I'd make a good guard, and the youngest the King had ever had. I could imagine Cat snorting at that idea!

I finally managed to find a quiet route by a couple of large rectangular ponds. I set off along the edge of the first, past a pile of long tree trunks. More trunks floated in the murky pond. These were tied together like rafts. The water was mostly still but every now and then a breeze stirred the surface and the rafts knocked together. I remembered Mark telling me about mast ponds, where wood had to be soaked before it was fit to use for shipbuilding.

I picked up my pace as the missing plans jumped into my head. Where were they? I had to get back and look for them. I tried to work out a way I could get inside the ambassador's apartments again.

I thought I heard a footstep behind me.

I looked back but there was no one there. I walked on, quickening my pace.

Suddenly an ominous noise filled the air. It was like the hoof beats on the cobbled yard when the entire Court was setting off on a hunt. I whipped round. The tree trunks were tumbling off their pile!

They were rolling, relentless and unstoppable, and I was in their path.

16

The rumbling thudded in my ears. I had no hope of escape. I did the only thing I could. I dived into the pond. The cold water hit me like a blow. Logs piled in over my head, forcing me into the depths.

More and more wood came thundering down and I was overcome with the terrible panic of being trapped far from the surface. Then, through the dark I caught a tiny flash of light, and thought that I might be able to push my way up into the gap, but the logs quickly crashed together. I knew my breath wouldn't hold for long. There had to be an escape. I clawed my way along the bottom of the pond, kicking up swirls of mud. My hand hit the sheer side. I pulled myself up the rough bank until I felt the logs above me. I tried to heave them aside with my shoulders. But nothing gave. My heart was thumping with the painful effort. Soon I would have to take a breath – a fatal gulp of water.

Something drifted in the murk below me. I swam down towards it, hoping to find a piece of timber to wedge between the log rafts. The shape was just out of reach, and difficult to make out in the gloom. I grabbed at it. It spun in my grasp and I was confronted by a bloated face, its dead eyes bulging. Despite the disfigurement I recognised Benjamin Dobson, the wood merchant! My thoughts reeled as I pushed the corpse away. He couldn't have just fallen in. His usefulness at an end, he'd been discarded.

I felt a surge of anger, kicked hard and thrust between the timber and the earth wall. The logs moved a little. It was enough. Cold air filled my lungs at last.

The bank rose sheer, too high for me to reach the top, too hard to allow my fingers to get a grip. A tree root was sticking out a few feet up. It looked strong. I shot out a hand to grasp it. It was beyond my reach.

I needed something to hook over the root. *If only I had a rope*, I thought desperately as I thrashed about, trying to keep my head above the surface. Yet all I possessed were the clothes on my back. They were more of a hindrance. Saturated and heavy, they were dragging me down.

And then I had the answer. My clothes could save me – at least, my belt could.

Treading water, I slipped it off and fastened the buckle again to make a loop. I swung it at the root. It missed. My legs were getting tired and I took in mouthfuls of dirty pond slime as I tried again. Small waves were washing over my head and the logs jostled me, threatening to take me under.

I swung the belt a third time – and felt it tighten. I'd done it! Bracing my legs on the wall, I pulled myself up. My hands were slipping and my muscles screaming with the effort but my shoulders were out of the water. I pushed with my feet, grabbed the root, and thrust my knee into the circle of the belt.

I paused, my heart racing in terror. My attacker might be lurking, poised to force me back in and finish me off. Cautiously I raised my head. I could see no one around. I heaved myself out and lay gasping on the bank. Slowly my brain began to click into action. I remembered what Master Cromwell had told me. *'If any one of the plotters gets wind of your involvement, they will be quick to silence you.'* Someone had not liked me asking about Seth, Ivo and Benjamin Dobson. Why else would they want to get rid of me? And it had to be someone who worked at the shipyard. Unless, of course, one of Chapuys's men had found out that I'd been snooping in their apartments, and followed me here.

As I buckled my belt on, a wind blew up round the shipyard, making my wet clothes cling to me like icy sheets. But something else was sending chills through me. Supposing my attacker came back to make sure I was dead?

I crept along, keeping to the shadows and ducking behind crates. Every nerve in my body jangled until

I'd slipped past the man at the gate and was away from the shipyard. I ached to go straight back to the safety of the palace and huddle in front of a blazing fire, but I had to stop at Greenwich Village. The attempt on my life could only mean that I was getting close to a terrible secret that someone was desperate to hide. I must not delay my investigation into Fettiplace.

His shop was just as Cat had described. The broken shutters and cracked panes of glass stood out like a putrid carbuncle. I came to the bakery first, a neat establishment with a glorious warm smell of baking bread that called to my empty belly and chilled limbs. I thrust away the thought of the roaring oven inside. Instead I sheltered, shivering, in the alley beside the tailor's hovel and considered my next move. A boy in royal livery would look very odd marching through the front door of such a place – and a dripping wet one would be even more curious. But there might be another way in.

I slipped down the alley. Luckily the back of the shop was in even worse repair than the front and the door hung on one hinge. I made my way round a pile of smelly, rotting food and listened at the crack. No sound came from the dark little back room beyond so I inched the broken frame open, hoping the whole thing didn't come away in my hand, and squeezed myself inside. I picked up faint voices through another door beyond. Luckily it was closed. From what I could hear, the tailor was busy with a customer.

The room reminded me of Cat's workshop, only hers was clean and orderly and this was dirty and untended. Several bolts of musty cloth stood rolled against one wall, and skeins of thread were heaped on a table, next to a pair of huge scissors, a few scattered pins and a half-eaten pasty.

It didn't look as if Mister Fettiplace did much tailoring. His real skills lay elsewhere, no doubt on the other side of the law. I checked that I wasn't leaving wet footprints on the filthy floor and searched quickly, not knowing how long I had before the tailor came in. Ignoring my chattering teeth and thudding heart I forced myself to think logically. I reasoned that if Fettiplace had a link to the imperial ambassador's staff then there might be bills, or notes, something written that told more of the story. Perhaps a hidden stash of weapons, held for the plotters? Or signs that this shabby shop was a meeting place? In a corner, a pile of clothes lay next to a dusty old chest. I lifted the lid cautiously, half expecting a rat to pop out. A few rough shirts and plain linen caps lay at the bottom.

I found two dirty scraps of paper with bills written in the same scrawly writing that I'd seen in the ambassador's rooms at the palace. But that was all the chest held.

As my eyes grew more used to the dark I noticed a shelf, too high for me to reach. A single box had been put there, pushed to the back. Perhaps it was here that the tailor kept anything he didn't want others to see. I climbed onto a rickety stool and reached up to it.

There was a deafening crack and the stool gave way beneath me, sending me toppling into the bolts of cloth. They thudded to the ground, knocking pins, thread and the pasty off the table. There was an angry oath from the shop and the customer bade a hasty farewell. I dived for the one hiding place – the old chest. I'd only just shut the lid when I heard the door open. The chest was battered and broken and through the gaps I spied the figure of Mister Fettiplace, holding a candle. The tailor was surprisingly well-dressed, strangely at odds with his shabby surroundings.

'Who's there?' he said quietly. His voice was soft but held more threat than I could have imagined from such a small, skinny man. I shivered, and not because of my damp clothes.

Cromwell's warning loomed into my head again. I knew that if I was discovered it would end very badly for me. I could hardly defend myself by throwing caps and shirts at the tailor.

Fettiplace put his candle on the table, heaved each bolt of cloth back to its place and brushed up the pins, muttering under his breath. As he kicked the crumbled remains of the pasty aside I caught the words 'damned cats' and 'skin them alive'. I silently thanked the heavens – though why a cat would want to touch the rancid pasty I'd seen beggared belief, even if it was starving! I waited for Fettiplace to return to his shop but he made no move to leave the room.

Instead, he started to sweep the floor. Dust flew into the air, blowing in through the gaps in the chest. I covered my face, trying not to breathe it in. One sneeze and he'd know he wasn't dealing with a cat! He came closer and closer, then suddenly threw his broom to the floor and scooped up the pile of clothes that lay next to my hiding place. I saw his hand reach for the chest clasp. I pulled one of the shirts over me, desperately trying to hide myself.

But I heard the creak of the hinges and knew with dread that I was about to be discovered.

17

A scratching at the back door stopped the tailor in his tracks.

Saved by the cats again! I thought with relief.

Fettiplace dropped the lid, put down his load and flung the door open. A young boy in a torn jacket and ragged breeches stood outside. His face was filthy but that didn't disguise his fear. Fettiplace hauled him into the room by his collar. The boy's cap tumbled to the ground. He timidly picked it up and stuck it back over his matted hair.

'How many times do I have to tell you not to linger outside?' he growled.

The boy seemed too terrified to speak.

'Where have you been?' The tailor lowered his voice. 'I told you there would be an answer to be delivered by noon.' He hurried through to the front and was quickly back with a package. 'This comes from the palace like the ones yesterday, so no one else must see it. Now get going.'

From the palace! Could these be the missing plans? I prayed they were. The parcel was big enough to be holding them. The trembling boy nodded and put it under his shirt. Fettiplace pushed him out of the door and heaved it shut.

A voice called from the shop.

As soon as he'd gone to deal with his customer I climbed out of the chest. Fettiplace must be involved in some mysterious chain that linked him to the palace – and the boy would lead me to the next link.

I opened the back door as silently as possible, listening with each groan of the woodwork for the tailor to burst in. Soon I was out and running along the alley. I looked up and down. The small figure was scuttling away in the distance, in a stooping run. I tailed him as he took the road that led towards St Alfrege's church and Greenwich Palace. That was strange. The tailor had said the message came from Greenwich Palace. Yet here was the boy, heading in that direction. However, when the royal buildings came into sight he veered away from them, making for the river. He moved furtively, and I soon saw why. The banks were being patrolled by what looked like an army of yeomen guard. Their halberds at the ready, they stood surveying the water and the land around. The usual number who watched over the palace had been doubled – if not trebled. Master Cromwell would be behind the increased security. No doubt people thought it was to ensure the safety of the King's foreign guests at the palace.

Little did they know the real reason.

A few courtiers were strolling up and down the bank. Among them I spotted Robert Aycliffe. I was willing to bet that this was no pleasant walk for him, however much he might appear to be having a casual chat with friends.

The boy sneaked along towards the river's edge. Now I saw his target – a small rowing boat tied to a post on the bank. I quickened my pace. Once he got away, I'd have no means of following him.

One of the yeomen gave a shout. The boy broke into a run, threw the package into the boat and fumbled with the mooring rope. Guards descended on him. In desperation he dived into the water. I saw him fling up his arms as he was swept along by the strong currents. Soon the Thames had swallowed him completely.

Even though the package was safe, I couldn't stand by and watch the boy drown. Cursing myself for not being able to act the cold, calculating spy, I dodged the guards and ran for the bank. I was about to throw off my jacket and plunge in after him when I felt a strong hand on my shoulder, pulling me back. I turned to see Aycliffe glaring at me.

'Don't be foolhardy, Jack!' he snapped. 'The river's treacherous. You wouldn't stand a chance.'

He didn't need to tell me. I'd escaped from its clutches once before – and only just.

'But he'll die!' I exclaimed, trying to shake him off.

'And you will not.' Aycliffe held on to me firmly. 'You are . . . necessary to us.'

I began to wonder if I would ever become unfeeling about human life, like Robert Aycliffe seemed to be. Suddenly I saw my place in Cromwell's network with unforgiving reality. Aycliffe wasn't looking at me as a person. I was merely useful, as a worker ant is to the nest. If anything happened to me, no tears would be shed. The important thing was the safety of the King.

I forced myself to banish the image of the helpless boy taken by the river.

Aycliffe called to the approaching guards. 'Nothing to concern you here. The lad was just a common thief. Good riddance to him!'

The yeomen went back to their posts. Now I wasn't on the move I found myself shivering violently.

'Judging by the state of you, you've already had one swim today, Jack!' said Aycliffe, pulling at my wet sleeve. 'What have you been up to?'

I hauled the boat's mooring rope towards me and took the parcel from the bottom of the boat. 'I fell in a pond,' I said simply. 'I hope you'll excuse me. I must take this to Cromwell.' I knew to keep my activities secret, even from a man who also worked as a spy for my master.

'Why were you after that boy?' asked Aycliffe. I hesitated at the direct question.

He laughed at my silence. 'I'm sorry, Jack. I should have explained – Master Cromwell has told me about your investigations following the . . . accident yesterday. I too am involved in this. While you went to the shipyard and the tailor's today, I have been ingratiating myself with Ambassador Chapuys but I discovered nothing out of the ordinary.'

I was relieved that I could speak freely. My first thought was to ask him if he had any news of the missing plans but I pushed that aside and told him all that had happened that morning. 'What I overheard makes me believe that Fettiplace is involved in some way,' I finished, 'and that he was giving something significant to the messenger when he handed over this parcel.'

Aycliffe took the package from my hands, which were shaking with cold. He threw his cloak around my shoulders. 'You need to get into the warm, lad. I fancy that Mister Scrope would not be best pleased to hear that one of his scribes was dead of pneumonia! We'll go together to see Master Cromwell. He will be very interested in what you've found.'

18

I stood at Cromwell's table, grateful for the warmth of the fire and hoping I wasn't steaming too much. My livery jacket and breeches certainly were, propped on a chair near the grate. I was still wrapped in Aycliffe's cloak. The remains of a meal sat temptingly on a platter in front of me, but I didn't dare remind my master that I hadn't eaten for hours. Instead I related my tale. My master's eyes narrowed when I told him about my plunge into the mast pond.

'We must not underestimate the plotters,' he said gravely. 'If they are willing to dispose of any nosy boy who asks uncomfortable questions, then they are surely desperate.'

'And then we saw the urchin approaching the river.' Aycliffe finished the story while I undid the string of the parcel. In my fevered imagination I was about to find the King's missing plans for the *Fair Anne* and I would finally be free of the guilt that had been weighing me down.

Inside the wrappings lay a shirt, a plain, ordinary shirt, very like the one I'd found in the ambassador's apartments. I felt as if a bucket of cold water had been tipped over my head. A small piece of paper fluttered out onto the table. I read aloud the roughly scrawled words. 'Item – one linen shirt supplied by the tailor Fettiplace to Mister Harry Hoggett in respect of which he must pay two shillings.'

I knew I had to hide my disappointment and concentrate on what this could mean. But it didn't seem to mean anything! 'It's just a shirt and a bill from Fettiplace to a man called Harry Hoggett,' I said, showing it to Cromwell. 'I don't understand. Fettiplace told the boy that this parcel came from the palace, but why would a shirt be sent *from* the palace *to* the tailor – with the tailor's bill in it? Surely it should be the other way round. And why send a shirt and a bill anywhere in such secrecy?'

'I have my theories,' said Aycliffe, stroking his beard.

'What do *you* think, Jack?' asked my master.

He was testing me, just as he had at the Banqueting House. I was determined not to show myself a fool but my brain felt as thick as the mud in the mast pond. Playing for time, I put on what I hoped was an intelligent and thoughtful expression and paced the room.

'Well?' said Aycliffe impatiently.

298

What had I got to go on? A shirt and a piece of paper. Whoever sent them must have wanted this Harry Hoggett to know something.

'The parcel is a message,' I declared. 'The person who receives it knows that it's a signal of some sort.' I could come up with no other explanation.

'You may be right, Jack,' said Cromwell to my relief. 'Hoggett is well known to us and is an associate of Fettiplace. He owns the New Ship Inn at Rotherhithe. He's been a useful source of information in the past. It's the only thing that keeps him from the hangman's noose. He'd do anything for money – so it would come as no surprise that he's involved in a plot to kill the King.'

Then another possible solution came to me. I seized the bill and examined it minutely. 'Is there a code in these words?' I ventured. I felt that if I was right, I would be able to use the decoding skills that Brother Matthew had taught me in games back at the abbey – skills that I'd used before in the service of the King. 'It must be a very short message – there are so few words to hide it in.'

Cromwell looked amused at my confusion. 'Try reading between the lines.'

I wanted to shout, 'Just tell me the answer!' but knew I'd never learn if I didn't work things out for myself. I held the bill closer to the candle. Perhaps there was something written there that I hadn't seen.

'You're getting warmer,' said Aycliffe, laughing.

I certainly was. My fingers were so close to the heat they were almost burning. But there was still no message that I could see. I was about to remark that a fiendish code in Latin would have been easier, when I saw that something was happening to the paper. Dark brown marks were slowly appearing on the blank parts of the bill. They were forming words!

'How . . . ?' I stuttered stupidly.

'Take the paper from the flame,' Aycliffe warned as an edge began to curl. 'I lost a whole message once through carelessness – and ruined a fine shirt cuff.'

I laid the paper on the table and considered carefully. 'I'll discount witchcraft,' I said. 'I don't suppose those involved in the black arts need to send parcels! There must be some substance on that paper that only appears when it's hot – but I can't imagine what it might be.'

'Lemon juice,' Cromwell told me. 'The perfect way to create invisible writing. Our men use it regularly. Tell us what it says.'

I held the paper back to the flame, more carefully this time. Lines of writing were now visible. I peered at the brown words, clearly written in a smaller, neater hand than the bill. 'I do not like your threats,' I read. 'However I will meet you at the usual place tonight at three. You will get your reward for the part you have played.'

'This tells us nothing,' I exclaimed. 'There's no mention of dropping statues on His Majesty!'

I felt like tearing the paper into pieces. Had I helped

300

drive a boy to his death in the river just for this? I stared angrily at the writing. There had to be more. I went through what I knew. The tailor, Fettiplace, was involved in some underhand business with the Emperor's men at Greenwich Palace and with a certain Harry Hoggett – that much was clear. They communicated by sending or receiving items of clothing with innocent-looking bills holding hidden messages. The business must be important for all that effort. A voice inside my head was shouting at me that this had to be linked to the attempt on the King's life. My eyes were drawn to a small mark in the bottom right hand corner. I hadn't put this edge near the flame – for one good reason. My fingers had been holding it. I turned the paper and thrust it out to the candle.

'Don't burn it, you fool,' shouted Aycliffe. 'Even if it's no good in this case, it means there is something going on in the palace that will need investigating . . .'

He stopped, and we stared silently as more words slowly appeared.

'. . . Only when the King is dead!'

19

'You will get your reward for the part you have played only when the King is dead.'

I repeated the words slowly, struggling to keep the horror from my voice.

'I must congratulate you, Jack,' said Cromwell. 'Although you acted rashly, I have to concede that had you not gone into the ambassador's room, you would not have led us to this discovery.'

'And now what do we do?'

'First we need to find out where the meeting is to be held,' said Aycliffe. 'Then we have a chance of hearing what new horrors the plotters have up their sleeves.'

Cromwell nodded, his expression grim. 'It won't be at the New Ship, if I know Hoggett.'

'But will the meeting still take place?' I asked. 'Surely when the tailor's messenger doesn't get to Hoggett with the expected parcel, Hoggett will suspect that the boy has been intercepted.' Even as I was saying this, the answer came to me. 'Of course. It must still be delivered!'

'Exactly so.' Cromwell was staring at me intently. I didn't like what I read in his expression. This was going to be my job. And if Hoggett was anything like Fettiplace, I was being thrown into the lion's den.

'Do we take it that you're volunteering, Jack?' asked Aycliffe. 'After all, you're about the same height as the unfortunate boy. And we know how good you are at taking on a part.'

I'd hoodwinked Aycliffe once by becoming Simkins, a hunchback pigboy – and he wasn't going to let me forget it.

'It will be my pleasure,' I said. I tried to push down a sudden swell of fear. 'I'm sure I can find some ragged clothes and turn myself into the tailor's messenger.'

'I applaud your enthusiasm,' said Cromwell.

I suspected he knew my real feelings. I was never able to disguise my thoughts from him.

'You will make your delivery and leave, then wait and follow Hoggett to the meeting, listen to all you can and return to report to me. And yes, you may help yourself to the chicken pie that you've been eyeing.'

I opened my mouth to protest that I hadn't even seen it, but as he and Aycliffe were chuckling loudly I gave up and filled it full of pie instead.

'What will you do with the information I bring, sir?' I asked when I'd swallowed the last bit of pastry.

'That is not for you to ask your master,' said Aycliffe. 'You should know that, Jack.'

'Robert is right,' added Cromwell. 'I would remind you that if these plotters were to discover who sent you, they would use fair means or foul to "persuade" you to give them information. The less you know, the less you can tell.'

A thought suddenly struck me. 'The King's plans!' I exclaimed. 'They could be with the plotters by now. Unless your men have already . . .'

'They have not been found,' said Cromwell. 'And you will not jeopardise your mission by trying to find them. You will obey my orders and nothing more.' He rose and went to a cupboard in the corner. 'Before you go,' he went on, 'there's something that needs doing if the deception is to work. I'm sure you know what that is.'

I looked at the hidden message. The words were still clear on the page. Hoggett would know it had been intercepted. 'It will have to be copied, won't it?' I said. This time I was happy to offer my services. 'But Hoggett might notice the difference in the paper. Fettiplace has used a cheap, thin sort – and I've not seen anything like it here at the palace.'

'A good point,' said Cromwell, opening the cupboard. 'Luckily we are ready for that. It is by no means the first time my men have had to forge unusual documents.' He put a piece of paper and a pot of quills in front of me, together with a bottle of ink and another of a clear liquid. The paper looked and felt almost identical to the one I was to copy from. 'Be as quick as you can, Jack.'

I reached for the knife that lay on the table to trim my first quill. Studying the words of the bill carefully, I could see that the letters had been formed with a jagged, scratchy nib, so that some were faint and others had a double line. I hacked into the point of one of the quills to make it as rough as I imagined Fettiplace's had been. It would be more difficult to work with, but it would be accurate. When I'd done, I turned to the hidden message. The script was small and careful, written with a finer quill and, I'd wager, not by Fettiplace. This was going to be more difficult – and I didn't have time for mistakes. As I cut my second quill, I briefly wondered what my godfather would make of this. It was he who'd given me my skill in lettering, little thinking what I would use it for.

The sharp smell of the lemon juice hit me as I opened the bottle. It was strange seeing each letter I copied being sucked away into the paper and disappearing. By the time I'd finished, the gut-wrenching fear of my mission had gone. Of course it might have been that my belly was now full of pie, but I was almost looking forward to my journey even though I knew I'd have to row the messenger's boat. I didn't tell Cromwell that I'd never lifted a pair of oars in my life!

'That is very good indeed,' my master said when

I showed him the forged bill. 'We must always keep Jack on our side, Robert. Imagine what he would do to us if he ever turned traitor!'

'I can imagine it only too well,' replied Aycliffe with a wry smile.

Though this was high praise, their words horrified me. 'I would never . . .' I began.

Cromwell dismissed me with a wave of his hand. 'As soon as darkness falls, get yourself to Rotherhithe. On your return you will, I hope, have knowledge of the plotters' intentions and who is involved. If I had my way I would keep the King locked in the palace until the villains are under arrest but I know His Majesty would never countenance that. However, I will set a watch on the ambassador and his men and take all measures to safeguard the King.'

'Will you send guards to the inn?' I asked.

'I cannot run the risk,' replied Cromwell. 'We must not have any of the birds getting wind of our actions and flying the coop. It's up to you, Jack.'

I tucked the bill into the shirt, tied the parcel up and pulled on my damp jacket and breeches. Then I bowed and took my leave, feeling like Daniel in the Bible, about to be thrown into the lion's den.

I headed for the sewing room. I needed a good disguise, and who better to help me than Cat? As long as she didn't find me another skirt.

The passage outside was bustling with courtiers heading to the Presence Chamber for the evening's entertainment but I barely paid them any heed. I was thinking back to when Cromwell had seen my moment of weakness in front of Donis. Did he have a worm of worry about my loyalty? Did he suspect that I hadn't lost the plans but sold them to the Spanish? Was that why he'd mentioned me turning traitor? I pushed the thought away. My deeds would prove me loyal.

Cat looked up to see me standing in the doorway of the sewing room with my parcel in my hand.

'Good,' she said, laying down her work and getting to her feet. 'I hope that's my new threads you've got in there, Jack Briars. Come with me so I can see them in what's left of the daylight.'

'Er ... yes, these are for you,' I said, marvelling at how quickly she'd found an excuse to leave the room.

Once in the passageway she pulled me through a small door and out into a deserted courtyard.

'So?' she said, her voice bright and eager. 'What's in the parcel? What's the news? And why are your clothes wet?'

Her eyes grew round when I told her about the mast pond. They were as big as cartwheels when I got to Fettiplace and the message from someone in the palace.

'So I need another disguise,' I finished.

'What's it to be this time?' asked Cat. 'Though I think you're mad for going. I can do you a nice milkmaid, or

307

a tiring woman – or a high-born lady if you don't mind a gown with a big rip down the back.'

'That won't be necessary,' I told her. 'Sorry to disappoint you but I'm to be a boy – an urchin.'

'Shame.' She dragged me back inside and took me off to a storeroom.

'Have a look in the poor box,' she said, showing me a crate in the corner and backing off quickly. 'Though rather you than me. Some of those clothes are a bit musty.'

I squatted down and picked through the pile. Not for the first time, I silently thanked my godfather, who'd taught me to be so observant. I had a clear picture in my head of the messenger boy.

'Where's the urchin got to go?' Cat asked as I held some ragged breeches up against me.

I told her about the new threat to the King. She let out a gasp. Then I explained my mission.

'Harry Hoggett's known all over London!' she exclaimed. 'You won't come out alive from the inn let alone go to any meeting place!'

'Thank you for your comforting words,' I said, shaking mouse droppings out of a tattered jacket and tearing one arm at the shoulder to look like the boy's. I knew what Cat's next words would be.

'You're not going alone,' she said. 'I'm coming with you.'

I stood up to face her. 'You can't,' I said.

'Oh, yes I can,' said Cat firmly. 'You can say I'm your

long-lost sister. We'll go on Diablo and be there in no time – as long as you're not in control of the horse. I've lost count of the lessons I've given you and you're still struggling to hold the reins properly—'

I cut across her insults.

'Harry Hoggett is expecting a boy to turn up – on his own. He won't be expecting any sisters, long-lost or otherwise! And certainly not on one of the King's fine horses.'

She was right though. We would have got there in no time on Diablo – the devil horse that she made me ride every time I had a lesson.

'I'm sorry,' I said seriously. 'Thanks for the offer – it was very brave.'

To my surprise, Cat shrugged.

'Never mind,' she said. 'I have an idea how I can help while you're away.'

'Dry my clothes?' I suggested.

'I'll do that if I have time.' Cat picked them up and held them at arm's length. 'I thought I might just slip back into the ambassador's apartments and . . . find some mending that might need doing . . .'

'You are not to look for those plans!' I said firmly, although I suspected that whatever orders I gave, my bold friend would take no notice.

Cat grinned. 'Who said I would?' Then her face fell. 'I wish you weren't going,' she said in a small voice. 'What if you don't come back?'

'No doubt Master Cromwell will send soldiers to

309

scour the area for me.' I knew full well he wouldn't. He'd never risk alerting the plotters and scuppering the investigation for the sake of one life.

Cat knew it too. Her next words sent shards of ice down my spine.

'That'll be to pick up your dead body!'

20

I soon found out that rowing a boat was not as easy as I'd thought. For a start, I had to sit with my back to where I was going. And the oars seemed to have a life of their own, splashing me into the bargain. My hands were sore from the effort of pulling them through the water and not losing them overboard. And the pain in my shoulders was running my hands a close competition. But I'd never been scared of hard work and I was finally moving along nicely when I hit a current and was at once heading for the bank. I'd only just got back on course when the wash from a barge sent me rocking so violently I thought I'd overturn.

But eventually I found my rhythm and Rotherhithe drew nearer instead of getting further away. At least I guessed it must be Rotherhithe. The few buildings on the shore were just shadowy lumps. But Aycliffe had told me that if the turrets of the Tower of London were ahead of me, then the New Ship wouldn't be far away. The inn finally came into sight. I reckoned that the ship it had been named after must have sunk a long time ago because the tavern was very ramshackle. In fact I might have rowed on past if it hadn't been for the tatty sign banging against the wall. By the dim light of one of the dirty windows, I was just able to make out in the paint the shape of a hull and some white blobs which I took to be sails.

As I moored the boat and went ashore, a church clock struck eleven. I ambled up to the door, practising the boy's stooping walk and hoping that this Harry Hoggett didn't know Fettiplace's messenger very well. It would all be over if he smelt a rat.

I paused outside, remembering I must imitate the boy's worried face and anxious, darting movements. An image of him came into my head. God's blood! I could have struck myself for being a fool. I'd forgotten his filthy face and matted hair. I smeared mud all over mine, in huge thick globs. I'd challenge even my godfather to recognise me under this smelly mask. Now I poked my head timidly round the door. The room was small and dark, lit by one guttering candle above a fireplace where a single log burned feebly. A couple of customers sat at a table in a shadowy corner. No one else seemed to be about.

But all of a sudden there was an angry roar, and a tall, brawny man strode towards me. I found myself cowering without having to act the part! The man whipped the parcel from my hands.

'What took you so long?' he snarled as he slammed the door shut behind me and cuffed me round the head. 'Trying to get out of doing your chores as usual? And you look as if you've been rolling in the mud. I've a good mind to give you a beating.'

Even as I quaked, a small corner of my brain managed to reason that this was Harry Hoggett and that the mission was going to be even harder than I'd thought. The boy was not Fettiplace's servant – he was Hoggett's! I prayed fervently that my disguise was good enough to fool a man who must know his boy well. There was only one hopeful sign here. The innkeeper wore a pair of very thick glasses, and I noticed that he squinted short-sightedly through them. They didn't fit him very well and he took them off now and rubbed the bridge of his nose where they'd made a red mark.

I made myself focus on my mission. I certainly couldn't leave and then hide and tail Hoggett to the meeting place as instructed by Cromwell. I was playing a new role now – one which would need all my cunning.

But how to glean the information I needed from this fearsome man? Was I supposed to be in on his plans? Perhaps I could bring him round to talking about them when he'd read the message. I waited for him to open the parcel.

But he dropped it among the flagons and tankards on a long table and swung round to face me again. I kept my head down, making my eyes dart about as the boy's had done.

'Well, you miserable worm,' he sneered, a nasty smile spreading over his stubbly cheeks. 'Aren't you going to say anything? Has the cat got your tongue?'

I broke into a cold sweat as I suddenly remembered that I hadn't heard the messenger speak. I had no idea what his voice was like. Why hadn't I thought of this earlier? Hoggett might be short-sighted but it was too much to hope that he was stone deaf too! All I could do was pretend I had a very sore throat.

I opened my mouth to croak that the boat had sprung a leak and I'd had to mend it, when I heard raucous laughter from the two customers.

'The cat certainly has got his tongue,' snorted one of them.

'A big cat called Harry!' chortled the other. 'Your knife taught him not to tell lies.' His laughter turned to a gravelly cough and he swigged at his drink. 'He's never told a single one since that day!'

'Aye,' said Harry, 'and I'll do even worse if he doesn't watch himself. I only keep him because he can't argue – nor give away my secrets!'

I tried to make sense of what I'd heard. Why did the boy no longer speak? Had Hoggett terrified him into silence with his knife? I remembered that he hadn't said a word at Fettiplace's.

314

Then the truth hit me and my stomach turned to lead. Harry Hoggett had just been goading me with his question. He didn't expect an answer. He knew there wouldn't be one from a boy whose tongue he'd cut out.

21

Harry Hoggett marched towards me. He was holding a long pole with something on the end and for a moment I thought he was going to beat me with it. I backed against the door. But instead he thrust it into my hands. In my terror I hadn't seen it was a broom.

'Don't stand there like a dishclout!' he snapped, cuffing me round the ear for good measure. 'Get the sweeping done.'

I took the broom and set to work in the darkest corner of the inn, the furthest I could get from the innkeeper.

'You're lucky I keep you on,' he shouted after me. 'There's many a lad would want your job.'

This sounded unlikely I thought as I swept up the filthy rushes which smelt worse than the palace jakes on a hot day.

'I reckon you're feeding him too much,' said the man with the gravelly cough. 'I'd swear he's grown!'

I kept on sweeping but my eyes frantically searched for the nearest exit. After all this was I still going to be discovered? If not by Hoggett, then at least by his customers. I hoped the dingy light would keep me safe.

'That's the trouble with boys,' said Harry Hoggett. 'You can stop them talking but growing is another matter – unless you chop their legs off.' There was a long, terrible pause. 'He's still of some use,' he said finally.

He topped up the drinkers' tankards, argued with them about payment and then made for the table where the package lay. I was instantly on the alert, hoping my forgery was good enough to fool him.

He took the parcel off to an alcove out of sight. I heard the sound of flint on a tinderbox and a small candle flickered into life.

I made myself busy, sweeping round a drunken man who I discovered snoring on the floor. Pretending to be working at some thick dust under a chair, I took a quick peek at the innkeeper. He was holding the paper to the candle. When the message appeared, he took off his glasses, clutched it close to his nose and peered eagerly at it, mouthing every word.

At least my writing hadn't let me down. Hoggett hadn't 'smelt a rat'. As he came to the end, the door clattered open and a bunch of men bundled in demanding ale. Harry Hoggett thrust the message inside his jerkin, stuck his glasses back on and called out a rough greeting.

One of them motioned to Harry and drew him aside. They sidled over to the fire. Head down, I took my broom towards them. I melted into the deep shadows in a nearby corner. I wanted to hear every word of their talk.

'I did as you asked, Harry,' said the man. I concentrated on the scene in front of me. The newcomer, an ugly man with a jagged scar down his cheek, spoke quietly and I only just caught the words. He glanced about furtively and then delved into his coat. Something changed hands. For a moment I wondered if it was another message but then I heard the chink of coins as Hoggett thrust them into a pouch hanging from his belt.

'You got a good price, I hope,' Harry murmured.

The man nodded. 'And you've got your share, you old rogue.' He rocked back on his heels. 'I sold the earrings to a lady of the Court!'

'You fool!' hissed Harry, giving him a thump. 'They were stolen from a lady there in the first place.'

'Hold your horses,' snarled the scarred man. 'She was only too pleased to have them and asked no questions.'

Harry Hoggett nodded. 'There'll be a right cat fight if the previous owner spots them,' he said at last.

'Aye, it would be worth seeing.'

'Harry!' called another of the men. 'Are we going to die of thirst before you serve us?'

Harry hurried over and began to fill tankards from a jug.

So this was nothing to do with the plot against the King – just the general villainy that Master Cromwell had told me about.

I was sworn at by one of the men as I didn't stop my sweeping quickly enough when he thrust an empty tankard at me. It appeared that the mute was a whipping boy for all. And not one called me by name.

'Serve the gentleman, you imbecile!' snarled Hoggett.

No name but a string of insults instead. I ran to do his bidding before he cuffed me again. I'd served at table at the palace but I didn't know where anything was here in this stinking inn and I soon earned more curses for being too slow.

For hours I swept and cleaned pots and poured drink after drink. All the time I kept a secret eye on the innkeeper to make sure he didn't slip out unseen. And every second, my guts were twisting with the fear that Harry Hoggett would find me out before I'd got the information I needed and escaped from his clutches.

The man with the scar rose unsteadily and tottered to the door. 'That's two by the church clock,' he called as he went out. 'I'm away to my bed.'

Hoggett called me over. I walked slowly up to him, ready to duck any blows. But the innkeeper was busy pulling on a coat and packing a satchel with bread and meat.

'I'm off out,' he told me in a low voice. 'Important business.'

I could hardly conceal my excitement. Hoggett must be going to the meeting! If he didn't name the location I would just have to sneak out and follow him.

He waved something in my face. I was horrified to see that it was an iron manacle on a long chain. 'And I'm going to make sure you stay here. I can't have you running away from your duties. Remember what happened last time you did? I warrant the skin on your back has only just healed.'

He looped the chain round a stout beam and clamped the manacle on my ankle, locking it and putting the key into the pouch on his belt. I was trapped. His voice was loud in my ear and I felt his spittle on my cheek.

'Now finish that floor. The chain's long enough.'

I was shackled like an animal and I had no idea how to open the manacle without the key. Hoggett took off his glasses, placing them on a stool while he rubbed the red patch on his nose where they'd pressed.

'And the rest of you can disappear,' he growled at his customers. 'The inn's closed for the night.'

Grumbling, the drinkers tipped back their tankards. One man sneaked a swig of his neighbour's. They fell into an argument as they rolled towards the door. Hoggett peered short-sightedly in their direction.

'Who's making that racket?' he muttered to himself, groping for his glasses. I hadn't realised quite how much he depended on them. Without them he was almost blind. He wouldn't be able to venture out at night without a guide to help him over any rough ground and get him safely to his secret meeting place! And surely the only guide who wouldn't be able to give away its location was the mute.

As his customers lurched unsteadily past him, I stuck out my unfettered foot and kicked the stool over. As I'd hoped, Hoggett's glasses clattered to the floor.

'Who did that?' roared the innkeeper, lashing out at the nearest man with his fists. 'Find my glasses, boy.'

The customer let out a slurred oath and swung a punch at the innkeeper. He missed and went tumbling to the ground. Hoggett kicked him. With cries of delight, the other men left their beer and came over, egging the fight on.

The glasses lay by the upturned stool. I edged round the shouting men and ground my heel into the lenses. Then I picked them up.

Hoggett had the drunk by the scruff of his neck. The man was barely conscious.

'Where are my glasses?' the innkeeper snarled at me, dropping his victim to the floor. 'I've wasted enough time.'

I pushed them into his hand and he put them on.

His eyes were barely visible behind the cracked lenses. He tore them off, sending them spinning across the floor.

'The devil!' he bellowed, seizing my shoulder in a hard grip. 'Did you do this?'

22

I stared up at him, desperately trying to think how to escape, shackled as I was. Then one of the drinkers came to my rescue.

'I'd wager it was Dan Trott's fault,' he laughed. 'Must have trodden on them with those big feet of his when he knocked the stool over.'

'Where is the milk-livered maltworm?' snarled Hoggett.

'He's lying right in front of you!' chortled the drinker. It sounded as if he was hoping for more fun.

A sick feeling rose in my throat. Someone else was going to be punished for something I'd done. But to my relief Hoggett just aimed another kick in the drunkard's direction.

'Get him out!' he ordered. 'And you tell him from me he's not to show his face in here again.'

The man was dragged away by his friends. Soon the tavern was empty.

My new master fumbled for the key in his pouch and undid my shackles. 'We're off to the meeting . . .'

My plan had worked! But Hoggett hadn't finished.

'. . . And you're going to lead me there so I don't get lost.'

Cold reality washed over me like a shower of rain. I'd foolishly imagined that he'd only need me to guide him round rocks and potholes along the way, not to give directions too! How was I going to take Hoggett to a place that I knew nothing about?

'Pick up my bag,' snapped the innkeeper. As soon as I'd brought it he clamped his hand back onto my shoulder. 'Go!' he ordered.

I stepped out of the door and hesitated, pretending to fiddle with the bag. I felt him push me in the right direction. So far so good.

'I'm going to get a new pair of glasses,' growled Hoggett as we stumbled along a narrow lane lined with overhanging trees. 'They'll be expensive – made specially for me, not like those old ones that . . . fell into my hands. And do you know where the money's coming from?'

Was I about to hear the name of the plotter? I was so intent on not missing his next words that I nearly steered him into a ditch.

'From him we're seeing tonight.' He gave a nasty laugh. 'He'll be paying up soon enough.'

323

God's oath! He could at least have given me the man's name. And then when we reached our destination, I'd have bolted back to Cromwell with the information. Hoggett wouldn't have had a hope of following and would have thought the boy had simply run away again.

I was just imagining my return at the head of a platoon of yeomen guard when we came to a place where the path divided. To the left in the distance lay the river. To the right, the way led between dark hedges. I hesitated as if I'd forgotten which way to go. Hoggett already considered his boy to be a brainless idiot, so I hoped my behaviour wouldn't seem suspicious. But a flicker of terror was dancing in my insides.

'Why have you stopped?' he growled. 'Don't mess me about.'

I had no idea what to do. If I chose the wrong path we'd never get there. If I didn't move I would pay heavily for it.

'Damn my eyes!' Hoggett muttered under his breath. 'He's got no tongue and no brain. Can't even remember where we are.' He stuck his face close to mine. 'Have we reached a fork in the path?'

I nodded vigorously.

'Then go right!' he ordered, adding a clip round the ear for good measure.

We stumbled on. Each time there was more than one way we could go, I stopped and Hoggett gave me a clout and an instruction. We came to an open field.

'Where are we?' snapped the innkeeper, digging his fingers viciously into my shoulder. 'Look around, you dolt. There'll be a light in the window. It's the only house in these parts so even you can't get it wrong.'

I longed to run from this cruel, heartless man. He certainly wouldn't be able to catch me. Yet I knew I must overcome my fear. I had to see this through. However dangerous my mission was turning out to be, the King's life might depend on it.

And the King's life was far more important than mine.

Unbidden, Cromwell's remark about me turning traitor jumped into my head. As the hours passed would he think about that again? Would he wonder even more about the missing plans . . .

I strained to pick up a light but trees grew thickly around the field. I had no idea which way to go. Then I smelt something. Wood smoke. If the meeting place was at the only house around, then it must be coming from there. I felt a slight breeze on my left cheek. That would be bringing the smell. I set off towards it.

As the trees gave way to a tangle of bushes I saw with huge relief that a light shone dimly ahead. The outline of a house and barns loomed dark against the night sky. I guessed it had been a farm once. A broken trough leaned against the remains of a fence, beside a heap of hay. I could hear shuffling sounds nearby and made out the shape of two horses tethered to a peg in the ground. Other people were already there. I led the innkeeper up to a battered door.

Hoggett thumped on the wood, making a rhythm like one of the drummers at Court. This must be a signal. I heard a faint movement inside.

'It's me,' he growled.

Bolts were shot and the door opened a crack. Hoggett prodded me through.

A meagre candle flickered, showing a rough room, little better than the outside but the light was enough for me to recognise the man who'd let us in. It was Seth. The one I'd seen guiding the crane boom from the shipyard dockside.

Upturned crates were arranged like seats round a small fire. Another man sat there, his hands stretched out to the flames. I wasn't surprised to see it was Ivo. It was a good hiding place for two men who had tried to kill the King.

'What are you doing here?' he called.

'I had a message from the gentleman,' said Hoggett. 'He's coming at three.'

Seth nodded his head to me. 'Did you have to bring him?'

'You know the lad can't give anything away,' growled Hoggett. 'There's bread in there for you.' He threw the bag of food down and told the men – with plenty of swearing and cursing – about his glasses. I was glad I'd finished off Cromwell's pie. It was clear I wasn't going to be fed at this place!

I shrank back into the shadows, hoping Seth and Ivo had been too busy dropping statues on the King to notice the boy in livery who'd saved him.

'I'll warrant it's almost time,' said Hoggett. 'And the gentleman is usually punctual.'

'I hope he'll be rewarding us for all this extra work,' grumbled Ivo.

'He'd better if he wants us to do anything more,' said the innkeeper looking uncomfortable. As well he might. I'd seen the message and knew they were getting nothing when the gentleman arrived.

They huddled round their food like animals. It wasn't long before I heard hoof beats, then the signal of raps at the door.

'That'll be him.' Seth left his food and cautiously slid the bolts across. A figure swept in, his dark cloak and hood hiding his identity.

The other two men were on their feet, silent now. Hoggett came forward, peering short-sightedly at the new arrival.

'It's good of you to come to see us, sir,' he said in a toadying voice.

'Your demand for a meeting left me no option,' snapped the stranger. He spoke with a heavy foreign accent. I knew that voice. The 'gentleman' was Señor Bolivar, the amulet-adorned deputy to Ambassador Chapuys.

Had Cromwell guessed the terrible truth? Was there indeed an imperial plot to kill the King of England?

My master had said the ambassador and his staff would be watched. Therefore anyone leaving the palace at this time of night would be kept under surveillance. Was one of Cromwell's spies outside at that very moment? I fervently hoped so.

The Spaniard flung off his cloak. His finely decorated clothes looked strange in this rough room. He fixed the plotters with an angry glare. I shrank back. If I'd worried that Seth and Ivo might recognise me, I had much more reason to keep my face away from Bolivar. I'd been presented to him as His Majesty's saviour! I hoped the mud on my face would be enough.

'It was not so easy to leave King Henry's palace,' he complained. 'There are always yeomen everywhere and I did not want anyone to notice my departure. I had to be very cunning.'

God's blood! He'd got past the watchers. No one had followed him. I was on my own again.

'There was one who saw me go.' Bolivar sounded very pleased with himself. 'He saw my face so I couldn't risk leaving him behind.'

'Did you slit his throat?' asked Seth eagerly.

Bolivar gave a shudder. 'That task is beneath me. I brought him here for you to do the deed although it slowed me down. I tied him to my servant's pony and tethered the reins to my horse's saddle. The sneaky little worm is shut in the old barn.'

I wondered which of Cromwell's agents it was. I shuddered at the fate that awaited him.

Ivo got up and drew out his knife.

Bolivar turned pale. 'Not now!' he snapped, wiping his mouth with a silk handkerchief. 'I do not wish to hear his screams. Wait until I am gone. It will be soon.'

'Why are you in such a hurry to get back to the palace?' asked Hoggett. 'Aren't you safer here?'

'He wants to see the royal blood being splattered all over the ship,' smirked Seth.

'Enough!' Bolivar looked as if he was going to be sick. He was squeamish for a man who was plotting murder. 'Of course I must go back to Greenwich. If I am found to be missing there will be immediate suspicion. I only came because of Hoggett's pestering messages. If you remain here and manage not to get anything else wrong, I will bring your money tomorrow. You will have plenty of time to deal with my prisoner when I leave.'

'We will see to it, sir,' said Hoggett.

'So when do we get paid?' put in Ivo.

'You'll be lucky to receive any payment after your pathetic failure with the statue,' snapped Bolivar. 'In fact I have been too lenient so far with your mistakes.'

He left the threat unfinished.

'Don't start blaming us.' There was a nasty edge to Seth's voice. 'We did as you instructed. So did Fettiplace. Even that drunkard Dobson played his part.'

'My plan should have been foolproof!' Bolivar shrieked the words. 'King Henry should be dead – and he would have been if it wasn't for you idiots.'

'It wasn't our fault the servant saw the statue fall,' growled Ivo.

'He ought to have been looking at Dobson like everyone else,' hissed Bolivar. 'You must have been careless and drawn his attention.'

'Not me,' said Ivo sullenly. 'It was just bad luck. And it will be his bad luck if I ever see his face again.'

23

'You won't be seeing the meddling servant again,' said Bolivar, with a cold smile. 'I received a message. The boy turned up at the shipyard yesterday asking questions. But he didn't leave.'

'Pleased to hear it,' said Ivo, 'though I'd like to have done the job myself.'

The Spaniard sat himself in front of the fire, taking all the heat. 'My new plan has been set in motion. And it will succeed this time – even though I heard this evening that the King has changed the day of the ceremony. The *Fair Anne* will not be launched tomorrow after all. She is to set sail on this morning's tide.'

The breath caught in my chest. I barely had time to raise the alarm if the launch was in just a few hours.

'Why's he done that?' asked Hoggett.

'Because he thinks it will bring him good luck!'

Bolivar exploded with laughter and couldn't speak for a few moments. Finally he wiped his eyes. 'Apparently his astrologer has predicted that Wednesday is now the most auspicious day for the launch.' He pulled out a chain from under his doublet. A gold lizard, some dried herbs and an elf shot hung from it. He lifted the pointed flint to his lips and kissed it. 'I have greater protection than His Majesty with my amulets. That fool Filby must have been looking at *my* horoscope and not the King's. Whether it be today or tomorrow, my plan will succeed.'

It dawned on me that Bolivar spoke of the plan as being his own. Was he working alone? His next words confirmed it. 'The Emperor will reward me when he finds out what I have achieved. He'll see that while Eustace Chapuys has done nothing but toady up to King Henry, I have taken the action of a good loyal servant to the empire. When the King is dead, Emperor Charles is sure to make me ambassador to the new monarch, Queen Mary. I will be a hero. I will be able to ask for anything I want.'

I had a brief moment of relief knowing that this was the plot of just one fanatic. The relief quickly died. The King was still in deadly danger – whether it was from an empire or a madman.

'How's your new scheme going to work?' asked Hoggett. 'You might need some extra hands now the launch is only a few hours away.'

I'd warrant he was angling for more money but his

question did me a service. I tried not to look too eager for the answer.

'You do not need to know,' sneered Bolivar. 'All I will say is this. The ship will slide smoothly into the Thames to the cheers of the crowds. The wind will carry her downstream until the moment she reaches Greenwich Palace. And the beauty of this plan is that it only needs one man on board to carry it out.'

'How are you going to manage that?' asked Hoggett. 'No one can get through the yeoman guard – and no one's ever tried to bribe a yeoman and lived to tell the tale.'

'And you haven't got two helpful carpenters this time,' added Seth.

'I have a man who can get on board without raising suspicion,' boasted Bolivar. 'One who will not let me down. It was he who dispatched the nosy scribe. And as he is known to all as the woodcarver's man he is allowed to attend the ship's launch with his master.'

So, it was the cheerful, smiling Gilbert who'd tried to drown me in the mast pond!

He must have been forcing the woodcarver to let him pose as his assistant. No wonder Mister Talboys had been so nervous when I'd visited his workshop. Why hadn't I seen through Gilbert's friendly act? I cursed myself for being such a poor spy.

My next move was clear – get back and warn my master before the King left Greenwich Palace. I tried to push away the thought of Cromwell's poor man locked up in the barn.

I was just inching towards the door when we heard the tap of the code, this time very faint.

'What is going on?' asked Bolivar suspiciously. 'We are not expecting anyone else.'

Seth crept over and peered through a crack.

'Well, this is interesting,' he said. To my astonishment he turned in my direction and gave me a smile that a wolf might give a sheep. It spelled danger. Seth flung the door open and a thin figure stumbled in and collapsed on the floor.

'Who is it?' demanded Hoggett, gazing blindly over.

Seth whipped round, thrust my chin up and stared into my face. 'The question you should be asking is who is *this*?'

'What are you blathering on about?' growled Harry Hoggett. 'You know I can't see.'

'You haven't got two lads who can't speak, have you?' asked Seth. 'Let's check.' He forced open my mouth. 'Just as I thought. The one you brought with you has still got his tongue.'

'By the devil, that's impossible!' roared Hoggett.

'Take a look.' Seth dragged me over to the innkeeper.

'What's your game, pretending to be my boy?' demanded Hoggett, shaking me so hard I thought my eyes would pop out.

'No game, sir,' I squeaked. 'I . . . stole the package and

. . . and I knew where the boy was heading. I thought you might pay me for delivering it.'

My story sounded lamer than a horse that had lost all its shoes. I waited to be challenged about how I could have possibly known it was for the innkeeper when Bolivar cut in.

'A likely tale!' he snorted. 'It doesn't matter who he is. He's seen and heard too much. Wait a minute.' He snatched my cap from my head and started in surprise. 'He seems familiar. Fetch water and a cloth.'

Ivo hurried out and I heard the creak of a pump. He was soon back. Seizing my chin, he washed my face roughly with a wet rag. I saw a sudden flash of recognition in Bolivar's eyes as the mud was scrubbed off. My heart pounded like a bird trying to escape a cage. But amazingly the Spaniard seemed more scared than me. He shrank behind Hoggett, giving a little moan of terror.

'What ails you?' exclaimed the innkeeper.

'It's a ghost,' quavered Bolivar, pointing at me with a shaky finger.

'He's no ghost,' scoffed Seth.

'But he has to be,' said Bolivar faintly. 'Gilbert drowned him in the mast pond.' He clutched at his chain of amulets.

'He's as alive as you and me,' said Ivo. 'And here's the proof.' He clouted me hard, making me yelp.

'Who is he then?' said Hoggett.

Bolivar produced his handkerchief again and wiped

his brow. 'The scribe who saved the King and then went asking questions. Gilbert assured me he'd been dealt with.'

'He soon will be, sen-yor,' rasped Harry Hoggett. 'We can't have him blabbing, can we?' He grasped me by the throat and peered at me with his small mean eyes. 'Want to play my dumb servant, do you? Let me help. I'll cut your tongue out.'

24

I struggled desperately, but I was no match for Seth's iron grasp. He forced me down onto the floor. I heard the sickening sound of a blade being pulled from its sheath as Harry Hoggett bent over me. I tried to clamp my jaw shut, but the innkeeper forced his fingers into my mouth and I felt the cold steel against my tongue.

'No!' The order came from Bolivar. His voice sounded strained, as if he was gagging. The two men paused and looked up. 'You can do that later – when I am no longer here to witness it.'

I thanked the Lord and all the angels in heaven that the man was so squeamish. If I hadn't already been on the floor, I would have slumped to it in relief.

'In any case, we have more important things to discuss,' Bolivar went on. 'Lock him up with the other prisoner. You can see to them both at the same time.'

For a moment, I thought that Harry was going to

carry out his threat in spite of the Spaniard's order. But instead he slowly slid the knife out of my mouth and put it to my cheek. 'Here's a promissory note,' he muttered in my ear. I flinched as I felt the blade cut my skin and a warm trickle of blood run down my neck.

'Take him from my sight!' shrieked Bolivar.

Seth hauled me to my feet and dragged me out of the door and round the house to where a ramshackle barn leaned against the back wall. In the light of his lantern, I could see the double doors were fastened shut with a stout wooden bar kept in place by a bracket on each door. As soon as he'd pushed me in, I heard the bar being dropped back into place. I threw myself against the wood but it held fast. Cold air on my face and a tiny strip of moonlight told me there was a gap but it was too narrow for my fingers.

I had a moment of desperation. I had to get out. The launch was in a few hours and if I didn't get back to Cromwell in time, the King would step aboard his ship and die.

There was a muffled groan in the dark behind me. The prisoner that Bolivar had brought was in here too. Another groan came. It struck me that whoever it was had been gagged.

'I'm coming,' I said, stumbling blindly across piles of dank, stinking hay towards the sound.

I almost fell over the kicking legs of my fellow captive. If this was a man, he was very small. Of course, I might not be the only boy who worked for Cromwell.

'I'm going to help you,' I told him. I dropped to my knees and felt for the knot of the gag. It was tight. The prisoner thrashed his head from side to side.

'Keep still!' I hissed.

He obeyed and at last he was free.

'About time!' said a familiar voice.

I gasped in astonishment. My brain struggled to understand that this was not one of Cromwell's spies at all. 'Cat? Is that you, Cat?'

'The same,' she said. 'And it's a good job I'm here. It looks like you need me.'

I was too dazed to retort that she was the one tied up.

'What happened?' I asked as I felt for the ropes around her wrists. 'Why are you here?' Although I thought I knew. 'Bolivar caught you snooping around the apartment, didn't he?'

''Course not!' Cat snorted. 'I thought of something better.'

'And I'm sure you're going to tell me about it,' I said, wrestling with the bonds at her ankles. 'But keep your voice down. Our captors are only on the other side of this wall.'

I didn't add that those very captors were going to slit our throats once Bolivar had gone.

'Well I knew that one of those sen-yors had written that message you told me about so I thought if I hung around the stable, whoever it was would be sure to need his horse. I was going to follow on Diablo.'

339

'But he caught you.' I struggled with the stubborn knot.

'The thing is, I was just sneaking up to see who it was and some dunderhead had left one of the empty stall doors open. I only brushed against it but it creaked something rotten. It gave the villain a proper fright. I'm sure he thought I was a ghost and so I just stood really still. But then he swung his lantern round and saw me. It was that Sen-yor Bolivar and he's surprisingly strong for a weedy little rat! He had me tied up and thrown over an old pony before you could say pincushion.'

'There's one thing I don't understand,' I said, pulling the rope away at last. 'Bolivar talked as if he'd caught a man – or a boy at least.'

'You can't see my clever disguise in this dark.'

I didn't need any light to know she would be looking smug.

'Anyway,' I went on, 'I've got really important news. The launch is going to be this morning instead of tomorrow.'

Cat snorted. 'Surely we've got more urgent things to worry about than whether we get to wave at the ship or not.'

'You don't understand. Bolivar's planning for something to happen when the ship sails past the palace. Something fatal to the King.'

I heard her sharp intake of breath.

'And there's nothing we can do to stop Gilbert,' she

whispered when I'd told her the little I knew. 'We're stuck in this evil-smelling place.'

'We can't let ourselves be stuck,' I said. 'We have to get to the palace and stop the King setting out.'

'Oh yes?' scoffed Cat. 'And how are we going to do that? You may not have noticed but there are no windows and those doors are barred.'

I stumbled across to the doors. 'If we could find something thin enough to poke through the gap, I might just be able to raise the bar.'

I could hear Cat coughing as she rummaged through the smelly hay. I dropped to my hands and knees, searching for anything that would do as a tool. I came across a bundle of rags and a broken chair. The splintered legs were far too thick to use as a lever. I also found evidence that this place had once been used as a cow byre.

Minutes later I heard Cat swear under her breath. 'There's nothing here.'

'Keep looking,' I urged, trying to keep the despair out of my voice. Despair for the King's fate – and for ours when Ivo and Seth got their hands on us.

As I spoke my elbow caught something hard that leaned against the wall. It fell and I waited for the clatter to bring the men running. There was a soft thud and I thanked the stars for the dung-ridden hay.

'What was that?' hissed Cat.

'I think I've found something,' I replied.

My fingers felt round a piece of curved metal, the rust crumbling at my touch.

'It's a scythe,' I said with triumph.

I felt Cat grasping my arm and we made our way slowly to the little strip of moonlight between the doors.

I slipped the scythe into the gap. The heavy bar gave a clunk as it began to lift. I stopped, fearful that someone had heard. After an agonising wait, I continued with my task. The blade grated against the wood. A small sound that still seemed to me to shout out into the night. Our captors gave no sign of hearing anything. I moved the scythe higher still and felt the bar move at last. Slowly I eased it upwards until I could tell that one side had come clear of its bracket.

'Nearly there,' I breathed. 'Push open the doors.' Cat pushed. 'Slowly,' I urged but it was too late. The bar slid to the ground with a clatter. We froze. At first there was silence.

'They must have heard that,' I whispered. 'We've got to get away before they find us.'

'I'll take you on the sen-yor's horse,' Cat whispered back.

But a door slammed and a flicker of light shone around the side of the house. I knew we'd be seen if we tried to run. There was only one chance for us – and it depended on the two men coming into the barn. I pulled Cat into the darkness and we flattened ourselves against the rough wooden walls.

I knew from their voices it was Seth and Ivo.

'I warrant it was nothing, Ivo,' came a shout from Hoggett. 'No one knows about this place.'

'I'm telling you I heard something,' Ivo shouted back.

'Better make sure,' said Seth.

'Whatever you say,' called Hoggett. 'You'll miss out on the last of the rum.'

My heartbeat was drumming so hard in my ears I thought my head was going to explode.

'Here!' cried Seth. 'The barn doors are open.'

I heard feet running towards us. Bright flickering light flashed into the barn. The men were carrying flaming torches.

'No use looking in there,' I heard Seth growl. 'They'll be gone.'

I felt for the scythe, got my hand around it and slung it into the back of the barn, hoping it wouldn't fall noiselessly into the hay. There was a loud, satisfying thump as it crashed into the far wall.

'They're still in there! I can hear them.' That was Ivo.

'Let's finish them off now. Bolivar needn't know.'

I heard knife blades being drawn. Cat twitched beside me.

They rushed in past us, waving the light into the far corners.

Before they could turn and see us, I grabbed Cat's hand and pulled her out of the barn, slamming the doors shut.

'Go for the horse,' I hissed as I heaved the bar into place.

She scampered ahead of me. Now I could see that she'd been right about her clever disguise. If I hadn't known it was her, I'd have thought she was a boy in her tattered breeches. Her long hair was hidden under a rough woollen cap, the straps tied tightly under her chin.

Behind us the two men were pounding on the door. The wood wasn't thick or strong but I hoped it would hold them captive long enough for us to get away. I guessed they'd be cursing their torches. One false move and they'd set the whole place alight!

Cat reached Bolivar's horse and I saw her releasing it from a small pony that had its reins tied to the ornate saddle. I was about to follow when the farmhouse door opened and a bright lantern flooded the ground with light. I was picked out like a deer under the archer's aim. Then I realised that it was only Harry Hoggett, squinting blindly out.

'Find them!' Bolivar's voice screeched from inside. 'Kill them. They know too much.'

I began to creep silently away. But now Hoggett had the mute by the collar.

'Be my eyes,' he rasped. 'Can you spot the villains?'

The boy looked straight at me. I backed into the shadow of a tree.

A splintering crash told me that Seth and Ivo would be upon me in an instant. Yet to my terrified mind, it felt that time had stopped.

'Where did he go, boy?' demanded Hoggett, giving the mute a vicious shake. 'Tell me or I'll skin you alive.'

As if I was watching in a dream, I saw the boy raise a hand.

I shrank into the darkness. A sense of hopelessness threatened to wash over me. But to my astonishment the boy took Harry Hoggett's hand in his and pointed it in the opposite direction to where I was hiding. He was daring to trick his master for my sake. I hoped the brutal innkeeper never found out.

'What are you waiting for, you useless pair?' demanded Hoggett as Seth and Ivo skidded into sight. 'Get after him!'

The boy pointed again, tugging at Hoggett's hand, and the men ran off in pursuit.

'They'll catch the varmints,' grunted Hoggett.

'Tell them that I will pay them well for killing the rats,' came Bolivar's voice from inside the house.

Hoggett bellowed this offer after the two men. 'Take me back in!' he ordered the mute boy, giving him a shove towards the door.

Silently Cat beckoned to me. She was already in the saddle. The horse snorted and pranced impatiently on the spot. I was glad Cat was with me. On my own, I would have given it a wide berth and taken my chances on foot! I ran to her and she hauled me up behind.

I'd only just got my arms clasped around her rough boy's jerkin when we were off.

'Which way?' Cat asked. 'That sen-yor had me bundled up like a sack facing the pony's bum.'

I looked round, hoping to get sight of the river in the moonlight. All I could see was the first glow of dawn in the sky.

'That way,' I cried, daring to let go with one hand and point to where the sun would soon rise. 'The palace is east of us.'

Cat wheeled the horse round.

Now we were thundering towards a hedge.

'Hold tight!' she called.

I closed my eyes and said a silent prayer as we sailed into the air. Then we were down and speeding over the muddy fields.

I gradually became aware of a sound above the pounding of the stallion's hooves. Unless our steed had suddenly grown extra legs, there was a horse coming behind us.

I risked twisting to look behind. I didn't like what I saw. Two horses, coming at a fast lick. They weren't near enough yet to distinguish the riders but I knew it must be Seth and Ivo.

'They're after us,' I cried. 'Can't you go any quicker?'

'We're going at full pelt now,' Cat called over her shoulder. 'It's not so easy with a passenger. How come they've got such good horses?'

'Stolen, no doubt,' I answered.

Shouts reached our ears. Angry curses, full of nasty promises of what they were going to do when they caught us. Our journey to Greenwich had become a race to stay alive.

Cat kicked the stallion's flanks. But slowly and surely they were catching up and the land around was too open to keep us from their sight. Cat suddenly changed direction. Ahead was a hill, covered in a dense wood.

'What are you doing?' I yelled. 'This isn't the way to the palace!'

'I've got an idea,' she replied grimly. 'You won't like it.'

She clicked her tongue and the stallion gave a spurt of speed. We pounded up the hill and crashed among the trees, our pursuers charging along behind.

'When I say jump, we jump off!' she shouted. 'It's our only chance to escape and save the King. I'm hoping the horse will lead them away.'

I wanted to refuse. It was a desperate plan. But it was all we had.

I swallowed curses as branches caught and scratched my legs, knowing that the pain was nothing compared with what we were about to do. As we got to the thickest part of the wood Cat yelled, 'Jump!'

I crashed against a trunk and slid to the ground, winded. I raised my head just in time to see our riderless steed disappearing through the trees, its stirrups flying. Ignoring the pain in my bum and legs and every other part of my body – even bits I didn't know I had – I dragged myself behind a bush. I couldn't see Cat anywhere.

I'd barely got my breath when Seth and Ivo galloped past in a whirr of hooves.

Sending a silent plea to the stallion to lead them far away, I hauled myself painfully to my feet and began a frantic search for Cat.

'What have you lost?' said a voice from above.

I could just make out Cat sitting on a branch above my head. She leapt down beside me.

'Come on,' I said before she could boast about her acrobatic skills.

Leading, I sprinted off the way we'd come – trying to keep my sense of direction in the darkness of the forest. When we reached the edge of the trees I was relieved to see the winding river below me. Father Thames would be our guide back to the palace.

'That's the way we must go,' I told Cat.

She nodded. 'Though there's nothing to shield us from view. We're going to stand out like pilchards in a pigsty.'

We tore across the open land. I feared a shout at any moment but the only noise was the cawing of crows in the high branches. My spirits began to lift – especially when I thought of Bolivar in his fine clothes, having to ride all the way back to the palace on his servant's pony.

We reached the water and ran alongside the bank. In the distance, the roofs and flags of the palace were clear against the sky. The sun was rising. It must be six already and we still had a long way to go. The high tide would be an hour earlier today than tomorrow. So the launch would be at nine o'clock.

'Faster,' I panted.

The palace would be up and about ready for this important day. I could imagine the fear on Mark's face when he found I was gone. And the delight on Oswyn's when he reported my disappearance to Scrope. But I had something more important to worry about. Cromwell must be wondering why I had not returned. His remark about me turning traitor suddenly flashed across my mind. Might he truly believe that I hadn't lost the plans at all but had joined forces with the Spanish?

I forced myself to keep up the pace. *Save the King*, I repeated over and over, hoping that my legs and lungs would obey. Cat ran at my side, staring doggedly ahead, her breath coming in harsh gasps.

Across the land I heard the sound I'd been dreading. The trumpets of the harbingers were blasting out to announce that His Majesty had left Greenwich Palace. He was on his way to Deptford – and his death.

26

Only a scribe and a seamstress stood between the King and his terrible fate.

'New plan,' I managed between gasping breaths. 'Stop the procession. We make for Deptford.'

Cat nodded, breathing hard.

I didn't tell her my worry. If I'd thought it would be difficult to stop His Majesty leaving the palace, it now seemed impossible to halt the might of a royal procession. But there was no choice. Even if I had to throw myself in front of his horse.

My legs were pleading with me to slow down but I tried to go faster. Above my thudding footsteps the harbingers were loud and clear now. I guessed they were heralding the King's arrival at Deptford. We were nearly there.

As we entered the village I realised that I'd be lucky to get anywhere near His Majesty's horse, let alone throw myself in front of it. The green was awash with stalls, flags and bunting. Crowds of people were lining the road to the shipyard. News of the early launch had travelled fast.

'Genuine Royal Launch pomanders,' sang out a woman thrusting an orange stuck with cloves in our faces. 'Buy them in honour of the King's new ship.'

'You won't make any more sales now, Molly,' growled a stall holder. 'His Majesty's almost here.'

He was right! The harbingers were being drowned out by the cheers of the crowd.

We stopped, unable to speak at first for panting.

The procession must be coming close if the volume of the cheers was anything to go by. I could just spot the royal pennants approaching. The line of onlookers stood four deep. Where had they all come from? I couldn't believe there were this many people in Deptford. I got my bony elbows ready to barge through.

'Found you at last!' came a nastily familiar voice behind me.

I spun round and my stomach turned to lead. Seth and Ivo stood there, like hungry hounds at the kill.

'Going somewhere?' asked Seth.

'I don't think so.' Ivo gave a nasty chuckle. 'You gave us quite a run around. But we guessed you'd come here in the end. We'll just get you out of the way and then we'll deal with your little friend, wherever he is.'

I looked round with sudden hope. To my huge relief, Cat had slipped away. Seth lunged at me but I was faster. The crowd scattered, letting out shouts of protest as I barged through them.

I forced my way round sheep pens, boxes of eggs and piles of vegetables, ignoring the curses and oaths of the stallholders behind me. I slipped past people carrying baskets and others trying to get a glimpse of their monarch.

A fanfare of trumpets suddenly filled the air. The onlookers roared in delight and called 'God save His Majesty'. I knew the King must be in sight!

But out of nowhere, Ivo stepped into my path. I swerved to avoid him and went sprawling over a crate of cabbages.

'Oi,' came an angry shout. 'You pick them up, you clumsy oaf!' A man carrying another load of cabbages started towards me but then a fearful expression spread over his face. He edged away quickly.

I looked back to see Seth and Ivo advancing. Their faces spoke of murder.

Old Brother Jerome at the abbey always used to say desperate times call for desperate measures. I snatched up one of the cabbages and chose my target – a large burly man watching the procession. The cabbage hit him squarely on the back of the head.

'What the hell?' he shouted, spinning round.

'It was him,' I yelled, pointing at Seth.

The man roared and charged, sending Seth flying into a stall of toy ships. It collapsed, and the galleons went rolling into the mud. I couldn't see Ivo now. He seemed to have run at the first hint of trouble. The stallholder dragged Seth to his feet, shouting about his ruined wares.

The big man with the sore head hadn't finished with him either. He rolled up his sleeves and took a wild swing at him, missed and hit the toy stallholder. Soon everyone was fighting – even Molly the pomander seller.

The King was passing now. I caught sight of him over the heads of the crowd. He was riding slowly along, swathed in a golden cloak and flanked by the royal guards. Now was my chance. I turned and ran – straight into a coarse woven waistcoat. I looked up into the face of Ivo.

27

Before I had the chance to escape, Ivo grasped me by the arm. He wore an expression of vicious triumph. But to my amazement, he suddenly bucked at the knees and crumpled in a heap. Behind him stood a small figure wielding a large horseshoe. She dropped it with a thud. For a moment I wondered if I was being confronted by my guardian angel – an angel with an annoying grin and muddy breeches.

'Thanks,' I managed to croak.

Cat poked Ivo with her toe. 'I'm guessing this is one of the men who chased us.'

I nodded.

'Where's the other one?' she said, holding up her horseshoe, ready to smite Seth if he dared to show his face.

'I'm hoping he's too busy fighting,' I said.

We ran, dodging through the spectators who lined the

way until we could see the dockyard gates. The last of the procession was approaching them and lines of well-armed guards were standing on both sides, scrutinising all who passed through. Master Cromwell's security was as tight as I'd thought.

'How are we going to get in?' panted Cat.

I ducked behind a row of tar barrels, pulling Cat down beside me. I thought it best to stay out of sight. The Yeomen guard wouldn't look kindly on two young beggars trying to push their way into a royal occasion.

'The gate's well guarded,' whispered Cat, peering round a barrel. 'We've no chance of sneaking in.'

'We'll see about that.' I took Cat by the sleeve and we crept towards the cart that stood at the end of the line, waiting to pass through the gates. It was draped in velvet with royal pennants hanging down over its sides. Several courtiers were sitting on cushions, muttering crossly about the delay.

'Are you mazed?' hissed Cat. 'Those rich folk would never agree to share their seats and even if hell froze over and they did, we'd be in plain view for everyone to see – especially the guards.'

'We're not going to ride up with them,' I replied. 'We're going to ride underneath.'

'I was right,' said Cat. 'You *are* mazed.'

The guards were pushing the rabble back so that the procession would be able to move again. This was our chance. We crawled beneath the cart and hooked hands and feet round its axles, pulling ourselves as

356

high as we could. The cart jerked into life and off we went. I fought the urge to cough in the dust thrown up by the wheels. Soon my shoulders felt as if they were on fire and the sweat was pouring off my face. But we were heading the way I wanted to go.

'Changing the day of the launch put everything into a rush.' The voice came from above us – one of the women riding in the cart. 'But when the King commands . . .'

'I'm most eager to see the statue,' said one of her companions. 'It is said to be marvellous.'

'If it's finished,' a man's voice added with a chuckle. 'I was told there's been no time to fix it properly to the deck. I hope the paint's dry, at least, or Lady Anne will have something to say. Ah, here we are.'

Craning my neck sideways I saw that at last the cart was trundling towards the gate.

And with that, the cart came to a stop. I could see the shoes of the guards, decorated with the red and white Tudor rose. For one dreadful moment I thought they were going to search the vehicle before letting it through the gates.

Then we jolted violently. We were on the move again.

In my desperation to get to the King, it seemed an age but it must have been only a few minutes before we passed through the gates. Whenever the overhanging pennants of our cart parted a little, I glimpsed workshops and shipyard stores. The cart rumbled to a halt. We saw the fine robes of the passengers as they climbed out and hurried to the dockside. I was desperate to let go but the carter seemed determined to stay where he was. My heart sank. Was he going to be there all day? At last he jumped down too and his footsteps faded.

'I didn't think I could hang on much longer,' groaned Cat, dropping to the ground. She looked at me and grinned. 'Your face is so dusty your eyes are like two currants in a bun!'

'You're not much better yourself!' I retorted.

We scrambled out from under the cart to a terrible sight.

The *Fair Anne* was slowly moving along the channel towards the river, towed by lines of men who heaved on ropes attached to the hull. Harbingers played their loudest fanfare yet and the crowds thronging the dockside cheered loudly. I felt as if the ground had fallen from under me.

The King had no idea that he was at the mercy of a man with murder in his heart.

28

'What are we going to do?' Cat sounded desperate. I swallowed the panic that was threatening to choke me and forced myself to think.

'We have to get on board,' I told her.

'We can't just jump onto a moving ship!' gasped Cat.

'Yes we can. If we don't stop Gilbert before the *Fair Anne* reaches the palace he'll kill the King.' I took her hands. 'Listen, Cat. You don't have to do this. But I do. It's our monarch's life we're talking about.'

'And yours,' said Cat in a small voice. She shook herself. 'I'm ready.'

I grinned at her. 'Follow me!"

Before I could give myself time to think about the folly of the plan, I ran full pelt through the crowd towards the men who were preparing to let go of their towing ropes. Cat at my heels, I leapt for the nearest rope.

'Oi!' shouted the man I'd snatched it from. 'What do you think you're doing?'

'Entertainment for the King,' I shouted back.

'We're the Rough and Tumblers,' added Cat, grabbing another rope. 'Surely you've heard of us.'

The pull of the ship swept us off our feet. I just caught a glimpse of the bemused faces of the men on the dockside before we were swung violently towards the hull. Like me, Cat was gripping her rope for sheer life as she was buffeted against the wooden boards.

'Make for a porthole,' I yelled to her.

It took all my strength to haul myself up the rope. Glancing back, I thought I saw some of the crowd cheering us on. They must have believed our story! And if they didn't, it was too late to stop us now.

At last my fingers were clutching one of the round windows. I eased myself past the cannon that practically blocked the hole – and came face to face with a gunner. He gawped back at me in shock. There were more of them, each manning a cannon, ready to fire a royal salute. Cat appeared further along the deck. I'd warrant their training had never prepared them for urchins popping in through portholes!

Cat did a quick curtsey. 'Seamstress to the King!' she explained as we rushed for an open door. 'Emergency repairs to His Majesty's cloak . . .' She glanced down at her ragged clothes. 'I'm in disguise.'

I had the feeling that we weren't going to get away with it. Behind us a shout rose up.

'Intruders! Get them!'

We hurtled down a walkway, heavy boots pounding behind us.

'Quick!' hissed Cat as we rounded a corner and out of sight. 'In here!'

She bundled me through a narrow door and we stood, panting, in a cupboard. At least, I thought at first it was a cupboard. I could feel a wooden bench pressing into my legs.

'The King's privy,' Cat whispered.

'How did you know it was here?'

'I found it when I was exploring,' she replied. 'No one will dare look in.'

Our pursuers thundered towards us and we both froze.

As soon as the sound of their boots had died away, we crept out and headed in the opposite direction along a dark, deserted passage. Cat led me up a staircase and into a wide room lined with padded seats. The wall paintings showed victorious men waving wooden rackets. Each one looked like the King. I didn't need the net stretched across the middle to tell me we'd reached the royal tennis court.

'We should be safe here for a moment,' said Cat. 'I did the salamanders on these hangings – good, aren't they?'

'No time to examine your needlework,' I said. 'How well do you know this ship – apart from the privy?'

'Pretty well,' replied Cat. 'I pretended to get lost and

managed to explore the best bits. You wouldn't believe the—'

I interrupted her. 'Gilbert will be with the woodcarver, and the carver will be near the King – up on the foredeck.' I pushed away the image of Gilbert with an assassin's knife hidden under his cloak. 'How do I get to it from here?'

'Foredeck?' said Cat puzzled. 'I've never heard of that.'

'It's the high one at the front,' I told her. 'That's where His Majesty will be showing the statue to Lady Anne.'

'Why didn't you say so? But you're wrong. Gilbert won't be there.'

'How do you know that?' I demanded.

'I heard a couple of courtiers talking in the crowd earlier,' answered Cat. 'They said the King had changed his mind about having loads of people around him for the unveiling. One of them said they could understand not having ordinary folk like the carver and the astrologer, but they were proper put out that even those His Majesty usually favoured would have to watch from a lower deck. It's just the King, Lady Anne and the statue up at the front.'

'Are you sure you heard right?' I asked urgently.

'Absolutely sure. And anyway, I saw them when the ship was leaving.'

Terror gripped me like a vice. 'If Bolivar had the ship's plans then he'll be able to show Gilbert the best place to hide and make his attack on the King.' A wave of guilt washed over me. If I was right I had helped the plot by allowing the drawings to fall into the wrong hands.

'Surely the yeomen guard will stop him before he gets near,' protested Cat.

'He wouldn't risk trying to get past them,' I said. 'He'll make some excuse to sneak off. And he'll get away with it. He acts the innocent far too well. He won't be on the rigging or anywhere in view. Think, Cat. What's directly below the foredeck?'

'The King's bedchamber,' she answered.

'Can I get there without being seen?'

Cat's eyes narrowed as she concentrated. 'The next room from here is the Presence Chamber . . . and then that great big banqueting cabin . . . that was where I had to finish those cushions the other day . . . from there is a private stairway up to His Majesty's bedroom.'

'The perfect place! He'll be able to get out of a porthole, up the outside of the ship, over the rail and . . .' I broke off. I couldn't stomach describing the attack on the King. 'If he's not there, then I'll climb up and warn His Majesty.'

'And if Gilbert is there?' asked Cat.

'Then I'll have to stop him.'

'This way!' came a shout.

The gunners were on our trail.

29

'You go, Jack,' hissed Cat. 'I'll distract them.' She slipped out of the door.

'Can't catch me!' I heard her yell.

I belted through the Presence Chamber and banqueting cabin, laid ready for a feast. Ahead rose a narrow stairway, carved with royal lions.

Through the portholes, a flotilla of small boats was visible travelling along beside the *Fair Anne*, the passengers cheering and waving and the rowers heaving at the oars to bring them as close as possible. They had no idea of the terrible drama that was being played out here on board.

I suddenly caught sight of the palace in the distance. There was no time to lose. I hurried up the steps to a heavy oak door that bore the King's crest. I hesitated. Gilbert could be inside. Gilbert who was in this murderous plot up to his neck. Gilbert who had already tried to kill me once. My throat tightened with fear.

I swallowed hard, put my ear to the wood of the door and listened. I couldn't hear anything. I opened it a crack and peered in. The luxurious room followed the shape of the deck above, tapering towards the bows. It seemed empty. I'd beaten Gilbert to it. I hurried inside.

Hot pain shot through the back of my head and I stumbled forwards onto my hands and knees. My arms were pulled up behind me so roughly I cried out in agony.

'Keep quiet!'

It was the voice of Gilbert. The command was low and menacing.

He held me tightly and I tensed in terror, waiting for the knife that would surely be thrust between my ribs. But instead Gilbert dragged me across the carpeted floor and threw me face down on the ground. Holding me with a knee that nearly broke my spine he began to lash my wrists together. I tried to keep them apart but he pulled viciously at the bond. I kicked out and heard an angry curse. Now my ankles were being tied together. I forced myself not to struggle.

'You won't get away with this!' I shouted, hoping to distract him.

'Silence!' He clouted me round the head again.

In spite of the searing pain I concentrated on my feet and inched them apart. It was enough.

He finished the job and stood.

Surely he was going to kill me now. I was helpless, after all. The fear rose up again, almost choking me. Then it came to me. Gilbert couldn't have a weapon. He would have slain me the minute I came into the room. So how was he going to kill the King?

I twisted onto my back. And there was the same brawny man I'd met in the woodcarver's workshop. But now there was no trace of the helpful assistant who'd greeted me with such friendliness. Now the eyes below the bushy brows stared at me with cold, murderous intent. I had a moment of grim satisfaction as his expression turned from menace to shock. But he was quick to recover. Unlike Bolivar he knew I was no ghost.

'What the devil?' he exclaimed. 'How did you escape the mast pond? No matter, you'll die with the King.'

He strode to a large porthole, stared intently through the thick glass and let out another oath. I knew with dread that we must be nearing Greenwich Palace!

Gilbert pulled a tinderbox from his pocket and tried to get a spark. I didn't understand. Was he going to set fire to the *Fair Anne*? The ship would burn, no doubt about that, but not fast enough to stop His Majesty being rescued.

Gilbert turned and reached up to a long thin rope that snaked down from a hole in the ceiling at the narrowest point of the room.

I'd never seen a fuse before – I'd only heard of them being fixed to cannon or kegs of gunpowder. Yet I was certain that's what the villain had in his hand. For a moment I didn't understand. Gilbert couldn't have put a keg of gunpowder on the foredeck for all to see. And there were no cannon there. And then, as if a shaft of sunlight had suddenly pierced through a dense fog, I understood. Gilbert didn't need kegs or cannon. He had the statue. He'd hollowed it out and packed it full of gunpowder. And yesterday he'd been able to come down to this room, no doubt under the pretence of fixing the bottom of the statue to the deck. Instead he'd been setting up the deadly trap.

I rolled onto my side and forced myself into a sitting position.

I could do nothing to free my hands but I'd gained myself some leeway by inching my feet apart when he tied them. I tried to slip one free. It was beginning to work when my shoe caught on the cord.

Gilbert had got a flame going in the tinderbox. Time was running out.

I looked for something to catch the shoe on so that I could force it off. The legs of the bed had ornate carvings. I thrust my feet out to use an angel's wing as a lever. I couldn't reach.

Gilbert was putting a candle to the flame.

Gritting my teeth, I shuffled forwards. Now I felt the carving digging into the back of my foot. I pulled. Suddenly my shoe flipped off and slid away under the bed. Gilbert hadn't heard. He was intent on his task, holding the candle to the fuse.

I wrenched my feet from their bonds just as the fuse began to burn.

'You will excuse me.' Gilbert laughed coldly as he ran towards the porthole. 'But I have to leave. You, however, will shortly meet your end. Unlike drowning it will be over very quickly.'

As he fumbled with the window clasp I clambered to my feet, hands still tied, and launched myself at him, head-butting him hard in the side. He grunted and staggered away from the window. I went after him and jabbed my knee upwards. I hadn't learned such tactics at the abbey, of course, but playing football with the Acton Village urchins had taught me a trick or two. He crumpled up in agony. I looked about, frantically searching for something to cut my bonds. Something sharper than the padded cushions and silk sheets I could see all around. But it was hopeless.

Gilbert was on his feet again. He started towards me, but then seemed to change his mind. He glanced briefly at the burning fuse and his eyes flickered in panic. Before I could stop him, he was flinging open the gold-framed glass of the porthole.

'Brave try,' he gasped, heaving himself through the gap. He leapt and was gone.

Cat suddenly appeared in the open doorway. She dashed to me and began to work at the knot tying my wrists. 'What happened? Where's Gilbert? Did you find him in time?'

'Forget him – and forget my bonds,' I shouted.

'You've got to put out that fuse. The statue's above and it's full of gunpowder.'

Cat's eyes widened with shock as she took in the full horror of what was about to happen. She gasped when she saw the thin rope that was sending out a shower of sparks from the flame. The flame that was climbing relentlessly to the ceiling.

'I'm not tall enough.' She gave a final tug at my bonds and my hands came free.

I pushed past her to extinguish the spluttering flame, but it was too late. As I watched, it disappeared through the hole in the ceiling. I dragged a silk coverlet from the bed, bound one corner round my hands, grabbed the still-smoking fuse and pulled hard. It was firmly fixed. Gilbert had done his job too well. There was no disguising the faint crackle and hiss of the flame above.

'We're not giving up!' I cried, pulling my other shoe on.

I ran to the open porthole and climbed through it. Just over my head, the ends of the rigging were fastened to the ship's side. They made useful handholds and I pulled myself up, legs swinging. I kept my eyes fixed on the foredeck above. It was better than looking down at the churning river.

'I'm right behind you,' came Cat's voice.

The noise was tremendous with trumpets blaring and people cheering above the gusting wind. And all the time, the fuse was burning up towards the statue.

Fear gave me strength. I hauled myself over the rail, Cat close by my side.

King Henry and Lady Anne were standing at the very front of the foredeck, leaning over the rail, waving to the onlookers that lined the shore. They were not a yard from the deadly statue.

'Your Majesty!' I yelled.

But my words were lost in the swell of sound from the lower decks and the flags that flapped madly all around us.

Bolivar's words hammered relentlessly through my mind. The King would meet his fate 'right in front of his palace at Greenwich'. I glanced at the south bank – and saw with horror that we'd already reached it! We were sailing past the turrets and pennants and cheering crowds on the landing stage of the royal palace.

I had to act now. Ropes covered in bunting hung from the yards of the foremast. The lower ends were knotted to the rigging above my head. I scrambled up and untied one, praying to all the saints that it was strong.

I launched myself into the air, swinging across the deck towards the giant statue, aiming for its head with my outstretched feet. I prayed that the force would be enough to send it over the side. I hit it with such a thud that I was thrown to the floor. There was a splintering of wood as the statue fell onto the rail. But it went no further. It just lay there at an odd angle.

At its base, I could now see the flame eating into the interior towards the deadly gunpowder.

The King and Lady Anne had turned at the sound. Lady Anne looked aghast, the King furious. But this was no time for explanations.

'Move away!' I yelled.

The King took an angry step towards me. 'By St George! What do you think you're doing?'

'Move away,' I shouted again. 'You're in terrible danger!'

It was hopeless. I believe that the King saw only an urchin in rags.

'Guards!' he bellowed.

Praying they wouldn't hear his command, I grasped the bottom of the statue's wooden skirt and tried desperately to lift it. It barely moved. Then Cat was by my side, adding her strength to mine.

'It's not working!' I gasped. 'It's going to blow up any minute!'

Fear gave us strength. We forced our shoulders under the statue and heaved. At last it began to tip. It teetered on the edge of the broken rail. With one more shove it tumbled out of sight.

'We've done it!' gasped Cat.

There were a few heartbeats of astonished silence.

And an almighty explosion filled the air.

30

A shudder ran through the *Fair Anne* and she bucked like a wild horse. I grabbed a rope to keep myself from slipping, Cat clinging to me like a limpet. Shouts and screams burst from the lower decks, growing louder with every lurch of the ship.

Guards pounded up the steps, headed by Nicholas Mountford. Cat and I suddenly found ourselves facing a mass of halberd points.

'Is the ship holed?' the King demanded. He'd been thrown back against the rail.

'She is not, Sire,' replied Mountford, trying to stand steadily as the rocking subsided. 'We saw something fall from the deck. It exploded in the water and rocked her. Nothing more. Shall we escort Your Majesty ashore? The royal barge is close by.'

'My lady must be taken to safety,' replied the King. 'I, however, intend to find out what is going on. It seems that these two' – he pointed at Cat and me – 'have some explaining to do.'

We were thrust roughly forwards.

'Go with my trusted yeomen, my love,' said the King, kissing Lady Anne's hand. Two of the guards led her away.

Thomas Cromwell pushed through the wall of yeomen who now stood shoulder to shoulder at the top of the steps.

'I give thanks to God that you are safe, my Liege,' he said. He looked as calm as ever but I could hear the relief in his voice.

'And your thanks – and mine – should also go to . . .' The King looked blankly at the two ragged urchins standing in front of him.

Master Cromwell seemed to see us for the first time. He blinked and stared. 'Jack Briars and Cat Thimblebee.' He allowed himself a small smile as he spoke.

The King peered intently at me. 'Is it really my loyal scribe under all that grime?'

I bowed. 'I am ever at your service, Sire.'

'For which I am truly grateful!' said King Henry. 'And where Jack is, Mistress Thimblebee is never far behind!'

Cat curtseyed so deeply I thought she was going to fall over. The King didn't see her eyes narrow, but I did – and I knew why. She would never want to be thought of as behind me!

'But to business.' The King became brisk. 'Master Cromwell warned me of the plot against me – and the cursed statue seems to be at the heart of it. We thought we had taken all precautions to confound the plotters – even as far as bringing the launch forwards, using my astrologer as a pretext. Yet the villains breached our defences once more. If these two brave souls had not sent the statue overboard, the result would be too terrible to think of. Thomas, what do you know of this latest outrage?'

'Jack was dispatched to investigate,' said Cromwell. 'He will tell Your Majesty what he has discovered. But not here. With your permission, Sire, I think it best that we withdraw from this place. I suspect it is rather too public for what he has to say.'

They swept off, followed by a host of guards.

'You've got to warn the King about Bolivar,' hissed Cat as we scurried after them. 'As soon as he finds out that His Majesty is alive he'll be making his escape. He should be arrested. And Gilbert could be getting away too.'

'I know,' I groaned. 'But I can't give orders to the King.'

∂∬

Cat and I stood before King Henry in his Privy Chamber. His Majesty sat forward in his gold chair, Cromwell next to him. The doors were barred to all others and rows of yeomen guard were stationed outside.

374

'Tell me all, Jack,' ordered the King.

'It was Señor Bolivar behind the plot on your life, my Liege,' I said.

'Bolivar?' King Henry burst out. 'So Emperor Charles *is* behind it as you feared, Thomas! I warrant he wants my daughter on the throne to do his bidding. Well, he will pay for his folly. My fleet is ready down at Portsmouth. This means war . . .'

'No, Sire!' I interrupted.

The King's eyes flashed dangerously at my daring.

'The Emperor knows nothing about the plot. Bolivar had the mad idea that once he told Emperor Charles of the success of his secret enterprise, the Emperor would reward him handsomely.'

'Can you be certain of this?' demanded the King.

'I heard it from his own mouth,' I replied.

Cat nodded vehemently by my side, for all the world as if she'd heard it too.

I quickly relayed the events that had led to the explosion.

Cromwell went to the door and snapped an order for the arrest of Hoggett and his cronies.

'And scour the river,' bellowed the King. 'Gilbert may still be alive. You are to hunt them all down like the vermin they are,' he told Mountford. 'But I want them alive. The woodcarver too.'

I felt sorry for Mister Talboys. I was sure he'd been forced to go along with Gilbert's orders – or die.

'Now I understand why Señor Bolivar claimed he was

375

ill and unable to attend the launch,' said Cromwell as he closed the door. 'I imagine he will be in his chamber still. I was told he spent most of the night in the jakes but refused the doctor this morning. A ruse, obviously.'

'The treacherous Spaniard will be arrested immediately and persuaded to confess,' declared His Majesty. 'It won't take my men at the Tower long to get a confession from the coward.'

'All his herbs and amulets won't help him then,' muttered Cat in my ear.

'A word, my Liege.' Cromwell spoke softly, but there was authority in his voice, and the King listened. 'The accusation and . . . persuasion . . . of one of the Emperor's envoys might be considered unfriendly.'

'Then what is to be done?' The King was growing angry.

Cat's muttered words swam round my head. Bolivar was a highly superstitious man and had been quick to gibber in terror when he thought I was a ghost.

'I have an idea, Your Majesty,' I said.

'I hope it's not as risky as all your others,' Cat hissed.

Luckily the King didn't hear. He and my master looked at me, waiting.

'I believe Bolivar to be a fanatic who is close to madness. If my scheme works, he will give proof of his guilt without need of any accusation.' I hesitated. What I was about to say would very probably sound like treason. If the King misunderstood me, I would face the heaviest of penalties. 'We make sure he thinks he has succeeded. We tell him that Your Gracious Majesty is dead . . .'

'Jack!' Cat looked ashen. 'How can you dare to speak of His Majesty's death?' She threw herself at the King's feet. 'Please don't be hard on him, my Liege. He doesn't know what he's saying.'

'He knows exactly what he is saying,' said the King grimly.

There was a silence that could only have been a few seconds but seemed to stretch away like hours. Finally the King spoke.

'I warrant that Jack is hoping we can trap the miscreant into a confession,' he said eagerly.

Heaven be praised! He'd taken my meaning.

'I doubt the plan will work, Sire,' said Cromwell. 'Although possibly crazed, Bolivar has been very clever so far. If I were he, I would pretend innocence when I heard the news and would stay in my sick bed.'

'With your permission, Your Majesty, there is more to my plan,' I said. 'Mistress Thimblebee was so anxious on my behalf that she didn't let me finish.'

If Cat's looks were daggers I'd have been dead on the spot!

'Once the news has been delivered to him, I suggest that he receives a visitation from the ghost of his royal victim.'

31

We stood silently outside the ambassador's apartments. Guards blocked either end of the passageway and Nicholas Mountford led a group of yeomen to stand directly outside the middle room, the one that Bolivar shared with Donis. The King crept through the door of the servants' chamber and took up his position behind the curtain that separated it from where Bolivar lay in his supposed sickbed. His Majesty had thrown himself into his part. His face was white with chalk and he wore a tattered cloak soaked in pig's blood. My master and I went silently into the ambassador's room and waited behind the curtain on the other side.

Cat was the other actor in our play. Her costume had been much simpler. She was a seamstress again. We heard her come along the passageway and knock on Bolivar's door. She was answered by a bout of coughing.

Then a feeble voice called out. 'I am unwell and can see no one.'

'But I must speak with you, sen-yor,' Cat answered, putting a sob into her voice. 'Something dreadful has happened.'

'Enter.'

'Our Gracious Majesty. He's dead!' wailed Cat as she rushed inside. 'His new ship blew up and sank. I saw it all from the landing stage and I was told to come and spread the terrible tidings.'

'That is tragic indeed,' the Spaniard answered weakly. 'I am too ill to leave my bed but if God grants me a speedy recovery I will go to the chapel and pray for him.'

'As we'll all do, sir.'

'What news of my master, the ambassador?'

'He was on the ship too. And Sen-yor Donis. All lost I fear.' More sobs from Cat. 'There were bodies everywhere – and loads of blood . . .'

'That's enough!' Bolivar cut in quickly. 'Leave me to my woe.'

'Yes, sir.'

A fresh volley of coughing followed her out. It stopped the moment the door shut behind her. Immediately, we heard the creak of a mattress, light, hurried footsteps and odd excited mutterings in Spanish.

'Hardly the actions of a sick man!' murmured Cromwell.

'Bolivar!' It was the King. His voice was scarcely more than a whisper, but the Spaniard's footsteps stopped immediately and we heard an exclamation of alarm.

'Hugo Bolivar!' The King drew out the name in a deep sonorous voice that sounded as if it had come straight from the grave.

Although I knew my monarch was alive, I felt chills run up my spine.

'It is I, Henry, King of England. I am returned to earth to avenge my death!'

I peered round the edge of the curtain. The room was dark and shuttered, lit only by one candle. The Spaniard was standing stock still, as if he couldn't believe what he was hearing.

'Speak, Bolivar. You have committed murder. Murder of an anointed monarch. Your crime will not go unpunished.'

'I don't understand,' squeaked Bolivar, scrabbling wildly for the chain of charms on the table beside him. 'I have committed no murder. I have been ill in my bed.'

I exchanged a worried glance with my master. This was not going to plan. But the King hadn't finished.

'In death I see all. I know how you had me killed with foul gunpowder hidden in the statue of my Lady Anne. Confess now and save your immortal soul or burn for ever in the fires of hell.'

Bolivar gave a wild laugh. 'I don't believe you. This

is a cruel trick played on an innocent man. If you are truly the ghost of King Henry, you will show yourself.'

The King stepped into the room. The shadows from the candle made the eyes in his white face look like sockets in a skull. He slowly pointed an accusing finger at Bolivar. Blood dripped from his cloak. The Spaniard staggered back as if the King had stuck a knife in his chest.

'Mi Dios!' he cried, falling to his knees. 'Don't hurt me, Spirit.'

'I will not if you confess,' snarled King Henry.

'I confess, I confess!' whimpered Bolivar, averting his eyes from the sight of the blood-drenched ghost. 'I planned your death. May God forgive me.'

'You have condemned yourself with your words,' thundered the King. 'You will be punished in this world and the next.'

'Begone, spirit!' wailed Bolivar. In a frenzy of fear he made for the door. His hands were shaking so much that they couldn't grip the latch. 'But wait!' he said suddenly. He was talking to himself now, eyes flashing madly. 'No one of flesh and blood has heard my confession. I am safe. I will be ambassador yet. I will go to the Emperor. This foul spectre cannot follow me across the sea.'

Cromwell stepped into the room. 'You are mistaken, Señor Bolivar.' He flung open the shutters. The light flooded in. 'Here is flesh and blood who heard every word of your confession.'

'As did the living monarch of England,' declared King Henry, throwing off his cloak.

Bolivar's jaw fell open, his face whiter than the King's. 'It was a trick!' he croaked. He grasped the latch again and forced it open. He stumbled out – and found himself encircled by guards. He began to rant and curse in his native tongue as he was dragged away. However much he and the others deserved their punishment, I felt a shudder of horror at what they were about to endure. Then I remembered someone else.

I dared to pull at Cromwell's sleeve. 'If I may beg a favour, sir,' I whispered. 'Hoggett's boy – the mute. He has done nothing wrong.'

'The greater good comes at great sacrifice,' said my master grimly.

'But he is just an innocent soul caught up in this terrible business!' I struggled to keep my voice down. 'And he contributed to that greater good. If he hadn't misdirected Hoggett's men I would not have escaped and saved His Majesty.'

Cromwell stared at me for a long moment. Then he followed the King out of the ambassador's apartments.

'Well done for trying, Jack,' hissed Cat in my ear as we hurried after them.

His Majesty came to a halt at a window and gazed out over the river at the *Fair Anne*. She looked a sorry sight, her bows burnt by the explosion.

'I never want to see that damned ship again!' he declared, thumping the ledge. 'I will have it broken up – and the plans destroyed. See to it, Thomas.'

The plans! I felt a sensation of relief flood over me. I wouldn't have to find them after all. If Bolivar had them, they wouldn't be any good to him where he was going.

We bowed low as King Henry marched off towards his chambers, flanked by yeomen.

'We must still try to find His Majesty's drawings, of course,' said Cromwell as if he'd read my mind. 'Come to my office, Jack, as soon as you are more suitably dressed, and we will work out our next step. The King may say he doesn't want them but a monarch is entitled to change his mind.'

He was right – curse the man!

32

Cat gave me a sympathetic look.

'I'll fetch your livery, Jack,' she said.

I trailed after Cromwell. If Bolivar had masterminded the theft of the plans, then finding them would be like searching for a black cat in a coal store, as Brother Jerome might have said. I climbed the stairs of the gatehouse to my master's office. He'd already gone in and closed the door. I stared at the wood, reluctant to start what I feared would be a hopeless task.

'What are you up to, Jack?' came a familiar weaselly voice.

Oswyn Drage sauntered along the corridor. Mark was scampering in his wake, a worried expression on his face.

'Jack!' he gasped. 'Did you hear the explosion?' He peered at me. 'Why are you in rags? Are you all right? You didn't come back last night.'

'I'm well, thank you, Mark. And my livery is being fetched as we speak.'

'I wouldn't bother if I were you,' said Oswyn. 'It's not as if you're going to have a job here for much longer.'

Weasel-face was always trotting out the same old threat, but this time he sounded strangely confident. I held his gaze. He didn't look away. A nasty smile curled his lips. Had he found out about what I'd just been up to in the service of the King? If that was made public, I would be no more use as a spy.

'I'm sure Jack will explain . . . everything,' Mark put in timidly.

'I'd like to know how he will explain what happened to the important documents he was entrusted with a day or two ago,' Oswyn drawled.

I cringed before him although I was singing inside. Weasel-face had given himself away.

'What important documents?' I pretended to bluster.

'The plans for His Majesty's ship,' said Oswyn.

Mark gasped in horror. Oswyn smirked.

'I've been searching everywhere for them,' I hissed. 'But they've vanished!'

'You obviously can't be trusted,' said Oswyn, 'and the sooner you're away from Court the better.'

'I'm sure I'll come across them,' I said, putting on a beseeching tone. 'Please don't tell His Majesty.'

'I do not need to trouble His Majesty yet. I will speak to Master Cromwell first.'

He probably expected me to grovel at his feet and

beg for mercy. Instead I gave him a beaming smile. 'That is an excellent idea.'

Oswyn looked dumbfounded. 'What do you mean?' he spluttered.

'Only Master Cromwell and I knew that the plans were missing,' I said, enjoying every moment. 'So the one other person who has that information is . . . the thief.'

Oswyn gulped as if he couldn't breathe.

'What are you waiting for?' I asked, stepping aside from the door. 'Master Cromwell is at our disposal.'

'Wait . . .' Oswyn's eyes were bulging with terror. 'I was being hasty . . . It's a shame for you to lose your job over such a silly thing . . . I'm sure the plans will turn up soon. Very soon. Stay there.'

He bolted up the stairs to the scribes' room. Mark gave me a huge grin. 'I don't want to know what went on just then but it was fun – in the end.'

He headed off after Oswyn.

I felt my guilt at losing the plans washing away like water down a drain. The King's drawings had played no part in the attempts on his life.

'Jack!' Cat was waving my livery at me.

I was just sticking my cap on when Cromwell opened the door of his office.

'Are you ready now, Jack?' he asked. 'We have a heavy task ahead.'

'I bring good news, sir,' I said. 'I warrant that the plans will be here in a moment.'

'How so?' said Master Cromwell quizzically.

There were hurried footsteps on the stairs and Weasel-face appeared, carrying a roll of familiar-looking papers. He turned pale at the sight of Cromwell.

'I found these. Under a table. I don't know what they are.' He thrust them into my hands as if they were vipers.

I passed them to Master Cromwell.

Cromwell looked severely at us. 'So they were in your office all the time?'

Oswyn nodded dumbly.

'It seems so, sir,' I answered.

'And how did they get there?'

Weasel-face Drage stared at me with pleading eyes. I was pleased to see that he was sweating. He'd been trying to get rid of me ever since I'd arrived at Court. And he must have thought his moment had come when he knocked me over and stole the King's plans.

This was my chance to turn the tables. One word and I'd be free of him.

'It's a mystery, sir,' I said at last. I knew that if I began to think like Oswyn Drage I would be no better than him.

If I'd expected gratitude I'd have been disappointed. Oswyn raised an eyebrow.

'You're lucky you got away with it this time, Briars,' he muttered as he bowed to Master Cromwell and swept off.

My master waited until he was out of earshot. Then

he smiled at Cat and me. 'This matter is concluded at last, I am glad to say. You have done well, both of you. The King is fortunate to have you here at the palace.'

This was fine praise indeed. I wondered how I'd ever thought that Thomas Cromwell doubted my loyalty. Cat's face split into a huge grin.

'I was thinking about something you said earlier, Jack,' Cromwell went on. 'How innocent souls have been caught up in this sorry business. I know of a Thames wherryman who needs an apprentice and will be kind to a lad who is mute.'

'I'm glad of it, sir,' I said, my smile as broad at Cat's. 'I owe that boy my life.'

'That's all fine and good,' piped up Cat with great daring. 'But something for Jack himself wouldn't come amiss.'

Cromwell threw back his head and laughed. That was Cat Thimblebee down to the very soul. She always had the last word.

About the authors

Jan and Sara were already friends when one day they decided they wanted to write children's stories and it would be more fun to write them together. That was 21 years ago. Since then they've written over 160 stories – including some about ghosts, football, ghosts playing football and naughty gargoylz. Jan lives in Essex with her family and Sara lives in London with hers.

For more information, visit Jan and Sara's website at www.burchettandvogler.co.uk and follow them on Twitter @BurchettVogler.